"Catch Me If I Fall"

M/M Gay Romance

Jerry Cole

Special thanks to the following volunteer readers who helped with proofreading: Bailey H.S., D. Fair, Lea B., Jim Adcock, C Mitchell, Julian White, Craig C. and those who assisted but wished to be anonymous. Thank you so much for your support.

Chapter One

"Oh, darling, give us a smile! Aren't you excited?"

The little girl nodded and promptly burst into tears. Her mom, red-faced with embarrassment, paused the video she was recording on her cell phone and hurried over. "I'm so sorry," she said. "I think she's a bit shy."

"It's not a problem," said Dax, and he got down on one knee and took the little girl's hand in his. "It's a little overwhelming, huh?"

When the girl rubbed her eyes with her free hand, Dax gently reached up and stopped her. "Don't do that," he said. "You'll hurt them. Come on, what's wrong?"

While the girl's anxious mom looked on the scene, crestfallen, Dax was unfazed. He lowered his head and spoke to the girl as though they were the only two people in the room. "Want to whisper what's wrong? Go on, tell me. Nobody else can hear it."

And he moved his head toward the little girl's lips. She hiccoughed, and, with a tiny voice, said, "I'm not sad. I'm just so happy."

Dax grinned and gave her a hug. "Well, I'm happy to meet you, too!" he said. "It's one of the best days of my life!"

The girl looked at him wide-eyed, her tears drying up as quickly as her mouth fell open. "Really?" she whispered.

His face a picture of seriousness, Dax placed his hand over his chest. "I promise," he said. "Hand on heart. Now, let's smile for this picture, okay?"

With his grin a gleaming band of white against his tanned skin, Dax placed an arm over the girl's shoulder and beamed at the cell phone her mother was holding with trembling fingers. She snapped one picture after the other, stopping to apologize as she then switched to video mode. She had her daughter put her arms around Dax's neck, plant a kiss on his cheek, and then finally asked Dax to take a selfie of all three of them, as his arms were the longest.

Patient to a fault, Dax spent five minutes with the family, as was promised when little Abigail had won the coveted prize to meet her hero. It was her mom, of course, who'd commented on the social media post, and her mom's account that had been the lucky winner, picked at random from over half a million comments, but tonight, Dax was apparently making both their dreams come true, no matter how much Abigail's mom attempted to convince everyone that it was all for her daughter.

Finally, the meet and greet came to an end, and with one final hug, Abigail let go of Dax. Her mom gave him a huge hug and stole a kiss on his cheek. He grinned. "Sneaky!" he said. He waved the lucky fans goodbye, and they were politely ushered out of the door.

Once they were gone, he frowned and turned to a huge, bald guy with muscles as wide as his own waist. "What the fuck do I have to do to be rescued?" he demanded. "She could have had a knife on her or something!"

"Sorry, sir," said the bodyguard. "I was watching the situation carefully. Some people just get over-excited, but I didn't see any threat of harm to you or any of us."

"Yeah, well, it wasn't your face being mashed by those dry lips of hers," Dax said. He held out his hand, and his assistant immediately knew what he wanted, and placed into it a closed bottle of water. He opened the cap and took huge gulps. "And her breath smelled like onions. No doubt she and the kid had been for burgers before the show."

"Speaking of burgers," said the assistant, "Grant called. He wants to know if you're interested in doing a commercial next week to help raise funds for starving kids."

"Where?"

"Um, I guess it's back in LA, but I'll have to check."

No, I don't mean that," said Dax. "Where are the starving kids?"

"I have no idea," the girl replied. "Africa?"

Dax considered this for a moment, and then shook his head. "It's not really my kind of thing," he said. "Starving kids don't seem to fit with my music."

The assistant opened her mouth, then thought better of it and closed it again.

A short man with a red beard came into the room, wearing a headset. "Five minutes," he said. "Everyone, please get into your positions."

"Come on," said Dax, taking a final sip of water and checking his hair in the mirror. "Let's go finish this tour and get back home. God, this country's cold. I'm tired of freezing my ass off and my tan's completely gone."

His entourage walked out with him, and after a few minor delays, in which his makeup was touched up, and his hair given a little extra gel, he stepped into a cage, and held onto the bars. Then there was a hiss as steam enveloped him, and Dax was whooshed upwards, where he appeared in the center of an elaborate stage, already inhabited by backup dancers, who fell straight into their routines.

The first song was a powerful number, the third track from Dax's newest album. Entitled *Until You Wake,* the beat was frenzied, the lyrics simple, and the message relatively generic, but the crowd of seventy thousand didn't stop screaming from the second the number began, until long after it had finished. Dax Monroe was there to put on a show, and he hit the ground running, making dreams come true for both young and old.

For the next ninety minutes, he danced, sang, and spoke to the crowd. Sometimes he directed a slow love song to a young girl who caught his eye, winking at her as she screamed his name. Other times, he walked along the platform that jutted out from the huge center stage, his hand grazing against the outstretched, clamoring fingers of frantic fans. He wasn't shy at all either, and he showed this by popping open the silver shirt to reveal his beautiful body, the rippling chest and rock-hard abs sending teenagers into dizzy hysteria.

There were eleven costume changes, carefully choreographed into the numbers he performed so that the dancers took over the stage, giving him time to dash away from view, tear off a sweaty shirt and replace it with another, as he gulped down water and grabbed a towel to mop up the sweat that flew from the ends of his dark hair. It was chaos backstage as everyone knew their cue and fulfilled their roles with minute precision.

Dax Monroe's last show of the tour was, without a doubt, a resounding success. When his final song, *Remembering the Future*, faded out, he looked out into the crowd and saw that there were people crying. It wasn't unusual; many times at his concerts both men and women were known to be overcome with emotion. He bowed deeply as the applause continued, and left the stage, only to return for an encore, in which he completed the night with his first ever hit. Then, with a final wave to the crowd, he was gone.

Chapter Two

Backstage, they had to move fast. The London arena was in the middle of the city, and crowds began to pour out onto the busy streets immediately. Dax was whisked away by his security team before he'd even had a chance to change his last outfit, which was a simple black suit and white shirt, a bow tie securely fastened at his neck. His dressing room had already been cleared, and the entourage seated in the huge estate car. The door was opened, and Dax leapt into the back seat. His bodyguard, Rocky, slammed the door shut, got into the front passenger seat, and they were away.

Dax got his breath back, leaning his head on the back of the headrest. "Thank God that's over," he said. "I'm not sure I could have taken any more nights."

"You were incredible," said his assistant, handing him another cool bottle of water. Dax took it.

"I could really go for a couple of beers," he said. "Anything in the cooler?"

His assistant looked hesitant. "We didn't bring any," she said. "From what you said last time, we thought you were giving it up."

"Is that what I said?"

"Yes."

"I was probably drunk when I said it, Kelly," Dax replied. "Let's stop off and get a few beers. For the whole team. Come on."

He opened the bottle of water, but after a few sips gave it back to Kelly. It just wasn't cutting it. He wanted a real drink. He didn't like to think about it, and he'd certainly never mention it to his assistant, but he remembered telling her that he wasn't going to drink anymore. And he remembered why.

Having a few drinks after a show was a matter of course. He could have anything he wanted, from beer to heroin, although the furthest he ever went was to snort a few lines of coke during costume changes on his Australia tour. Once the press got wind of there being drugs backstage at a Dax Monroe concert, it had to stop. Dax made a public announcement on social media that he despised drugs of any kind, and that he'd found the member of staff responsible for taking it, without his knowledge, and had immediately fired them. To everyone's relief, there were no photographs of him bent over the vanity table, a rolled-up hundred-dollar bill in his hand.

It was a near miss, and once Grant had screamed at him on the phone for nearly an hour, he vowed to both his agent and himself that he wouldn't touch drugs again. It was too easy, Grant said, to destroy everything that had taken so many years to build. *It could all disappear in an instant if any scandal like that was leaked to the papers.*

It hadn't been too tough for him to give up the coke, but the booze was another matter altogether. A few beers became many beers and then shots of vodka, and in his more sober moments he found there was a correlation between the amount he drank, and the number of his staff who walked away from him, many of them saying he'd become someone they didn't want to work for anymore.

But, despite all of this, he was craving a drink. And he'd earned it, after all. Fifty nights in two and a half months all over the UK and Ireland, with barely time for him to take a breath before heading back home and into the studio for another new album. Then, there'd be talk show appearances, radio interviews… he was beginning to get a headache just thinking about it.

He leaned forward and pointed out of the blackened windshield. "Here," he said to Rocky. "Pull over here at this store. Get me a six-pack of something and a bottle of Russia's finest."

He could see that Rocky looked into the mirror above his head, catching Kelly's eye as he did so. Kelly simply shrugged. "Get him what he wants," she said. So, Rocky did. He pulled his huge frame out of the car, as interested onlookers, who had no idea who was in the back seat, marveled at both the vehicle and the giant who'd emerged from it.

While waiting for his bodyguard to return with the liquor, Dax prodded Kelly, who was swiping through the many emails on her phone. "Have you got my cell?" he asked, and Kelly reached into her purse and got it out for him. The battery was fully charged, the way he liked it. He opened the cell and began to search through his social media apps. He had several. Most of them were managed by his team, and were places for them to announce news, upcoming tours, and the occasional personal musing, most of which didn't originate in Dax's own head.

But he had one or two social media sites under a pseudonym, where he connected with family and personal friends. They kept in touch with him while he was on the road; he was especially eager to read any messages from his mom, whom he missed deeply. In the last five years since his career had gone through the roof, Dax had seen Diane no more than a handful of times, and even then, they were flying visits. He begged her to get on his private jet and come out to see him wherever he was, but as a real home bird who shunned the limelight, she wanted nothing to do with the glitz and glamour of his career, settling with being proud from the sidelines and speaking to him on the telephone whenever she could.

There were a few sweet messages, one or two funny posts, and reminders of birthdays for which he sent quick messages. Then he exited the app and subconsciously shifted to the left, so his hip touched the door to his left, and he brought the cell phone closer to his chest. He knew Kelly, seated on the other side of the spacious car's back seat, would never have dreamed of looking at his screen, and she couldn't have seen it anyway, but still he kept the next few moments to himself.

He pressed into an app that could only be opened with his own fingerprint. Once inside, he was lost in another world. He scrolled through page after page of beautiful, hot bodies, some in underwear, some in nothing at all. He could feel himself beginning to get hard. And it wasn't as though the pictures were of people many miles away. They were all, according to the app, within five miles of his current location. Damn, London, he thought to himself. You have some incredible talent here.

It had been difficult for Dax to contain himself throughout the several weeks of his UK tour. But finally, enough was enough. He'd closed his final show, earned millions for both himself and the rest of his team, and he deserved a reward. He was about to look seriously at the app, when the door to the front passenger side opened again and Rocky was back, holding a white plastic bag, bulging with familiar shapes.

Rocky sat down and opened the bag. "All right,

all right," he said. "We've got some regular lager, some stronger lager, and some dark beers. I also have a bottle of vodka and some miniature whiskies."

Kelly rolled her eyes. "Come on, Rocky," she said. "We're not here to party. We have to be on the plane in less than eight hours, for God's sake. Plus we have drinks back at the hotel if we want to get totaled but we all know it's a bad idea."

"I think he's earned it," Rocky said. Dax didn't get involved in the power struggle between his assistant and his bodyguard, who clashed on most decisions made on his behalf. He certainly didn't want to say anything now; instead he reached forward and Rocky placed a large can of beer into his hand. Dax took it and raised it.

"To my incredible team," he said, appeasing his two most faithful employees. "We've smashed the UK, and now I'm finally going home. Here's to a safe journey and a great night."

The others cheered, including the driver, Charles, who'd been silent up until now. Rocky pulled open the ring pull to his dark beer, and even Kelly took a can of lager. They banged the cans together, and took a gulp, Dax taking the deepest. It felt incredible. The icy cold beer slid down his throat with ease, and he settled back into the seat as the car sped through the streets of London toward the hotel, on the other side of the city. He opened the phone app again, and began to browse once more through the beautiful bodies before him, grateful that the car was so dark nobody could see the erection bulging against the seam of his pants.

Chapter Three

Back at the hotel, Charles took the car straight through to the underground car park, at a speed much greater than the one insisted by the hotel. It was necessary, though; plenty of fans were gathered outside, waiting for a glimpse of their beloved pop star hero. Some of them had been uncanny, doing detective work that only just fell short of obsessive stalking. Others had simply been lucky in choosing the right place. There were plenty of other die-hard fans scattered around the city, shivering in the February cold and holding placards, hoping with all their heart that a large car with blacked-out windows would motor into the parking lot of the hotel they were standing outside of, but most were disappointed.

In the parking lot, it had already been arranged for hotel security to stand guard and ensure that Dax was shielded from the screaming fans. Despite the large, bulky guys on hand as he got out of the car, there was no mistaking the screeches of girls and, unsurprisingly, the harsh, bright lights of paparazzi camera flashes. One after another popped in his face as they held their cameras over the hands of the large security guards, pushing past them as hard as they could.

They knew how to work the guards, who weren't allowed to touch their cameras, no matter how much they may have wanted to grab them and toss them onto the floor. The paparazzi clicked hundreds of photographs, not caring that ninety percent would be useless; they'd look over the images later on their computers, sending the best ones to papers who'd pay them handsomely for the best shots of the most famous pop star of the moment.

Leaving his beer in the car, Dax was hurried

through the parking lot to the elevator. His life was in Rocky's hands, and the bulky security guard, untouched by the beer he'd swilled in the car, engaged all his senses, looking around, shielding Dax as much as possible with his huge frame, and checking the elevator before he stepped inside.

Both the screaming fans and the unrelenting photographers called out at Dax for him to turn around, to wave, to smile. They begged him for a few words about his time in the UK, and when he'd be back. Dax couldn't remember a time, particularly in the last five years, that someone didn't want a piece of him. Sometimes, he'd wave and smile, at other times he'd even stop for autographs and selfies. Tonight, though, he shut out the noise and the lights, getting into the elevator as fast as possible.

It shot him and the team up to the penthouse suite. Finally back to safety and quiet, Dax breathed a sigh of relief. Rocky immediately set about checking the room, as Dax collapsed onto the sofa. Kelly made calls to his manager, Grant, and to his agent. She held up a takeout menu. "Are you hungry?" she asked.

"Starving," said Dax. "What's the pizza like in this city?"

He put his hand in the pocket of his pants and brought his cell phone out again. He re-opened the app, and once more began to browse the beautiful bodies in the photographs before him. He wanted a bath, another drink, and some food. But he also wanted sex. And he was going to get it.

"I think I'll head out into the city and grab something to eat," he said.

Kelly wasn't pleased. "It's not safe," she said. "Everyone knows who you are."

"I can get away with it," Dax said. "It's winter. I can put on a hat and have a scarf around my face. I need some fresh air."

There were glances between Kelly and Rocky, along with other members of the entourage who'd been following in another car behind theirs, and who had joined them in the hotel room. They were all of the same mind, but there was very little they could do to stop a thirty-two year old multi-millionaire who was within his rights to make his own decisions.

It was nearly midnight when Dax lay in the huge, claw-footed bath, nearly buried by a mound of suds. One arm was out of the bath, holding his cell phone. The other was under the water, slowly stroking his stiffening cock.

He flicked through more photographs, until one in particular caught his eye. The guy in the picture had messy blond hair and dark-rimmed glasses. His mouth was shaped into a shy smile. He looked to be no more than twenty-five, and Dax wanted to know more. He was seeing the picture because the guy was online, and less than two miles away. He fired over a message. *What are you up to?*

The reply came back within seconds. The guy was sorry, but he didn't reply to messages without photographs. Dax knew this, and he explained. *I'm not one for revealing my face over the internet,* he said, leaving the recipient to draw his own conclusions. But for a taster, he stood up in the bath, and took a picture of himself from the neck down, revealing his beautiful, sculpted body, complete with soapsuds.

The response was immediate. The cute blond, whose name, he said, was Andy, was impressed. He wanted to know where Dax was. Dax was both honest and dishonest in his reply. He gave the name of the hotel, and explained he was in the city on business. By now, the excitement was beginning to build, and his cock was rock hard. He stroked it, trying to stop himself, because he didn't want the night to be over before it had even begun. He snapped a few more pictures of his cock in his hand, and sent them to Andy, who obliged him by sending some return pictures.

Dax couldn't help but lick his lips at the sight of Andy's cock, thick and hard. He saw from the guy's surroundings that Andy was lying on a bed, the duvet a pale blue. The room he was in was dimly lit. He asked Andy where it was. *My apartment,* came the reply. Dax asked if he lived alone, but the answer was no. Andy had two roommates, both of whom were home, one of whom was straight. They never brought people back for sex, as was the agreement between all three of them. Andy asked if he could come to Dax's hotel room, instead.

It was a tempting offer. There was nothing stopping Dax from bringing the guy up to his room, because the others would soon vacate the place at his command. But it was far too risky. There was every chance that he'd be exposed within seconds, and with cell phones able to record far too much, his cover would be blown.

Internet forums, papers and online gossip video channels had been abuzz with talk of Dax Monroe's sexuality for many years. Occasionally, a guy would surface on one of these mediums, bragging about the night he'd been asked back to Dax's dressing room after a concert, where he'd been pushed onto his knees and presented with Dax's big, delicious dick.

He'd either be believed, or shot down. Dax had learned long ago not to peruse these sites on the Internet, because he couldn't deal with the spurious gossip. After all, it was often true.

He remembered reading an online thread about how Dax Monroe had met a guy at the after-party of an awards ceremony, and how the two of them had fucked in an alleyway, surrounded by trashcans. He read the whole thread, including the comments where responders joked that the writer was a fantasist, living in a world of make-believe. Dax's thumbs had itched to reply.

Because the guy spoke the truth. Dax really had fucked a hot man, whose name he'd never asked, behind the huge green trash bins at the back of the most prestigious Los Angeles hotel, where both the award ceremony and the after-party was held. Dax walked away that night with three awards, and the elation of the evening meant a hard, fast fuck, where he'd fired his seed into the waiter's ass within thirty seconds of entry.

Dax hadn't been all that selfish, though: he'd sucked the guy's dick for the next ten minutes, until he knew the guy was about to blow, and he'd removed his cock from his mouth just in time, so that the guy fired onto the wall behind them. The last thing he needed was to go back inside with cum on his tuxedo.

There were times when the gossip was so ridiculously untrue that it made him laugh, but there were others when he realized he'd gone too far. Images he'd taken while naked in another hotel room had included not only his cock but a very expensive watch on his wrist, one that he'd been snapped purchasing only days before, the images of which had appeared in a number of gossip columns. Other selfies he'd sent to prospective hook-ups had included a little too much of his face, and these too had made their way onto social media sites.

Gay guys were convinced he was one of them, but the women who adored him insisted that any rumors about him being other than a red-blooded straight guy were nothing but spurious lies. They insisted the pictures of his cock had been digitally altered to include his face, something that was easily done these days. As for the expensive watch, weren't there plenty of other people who wore them, both real and fake?

But Dax Monroe's image was vital to his success, and he'd worked hard at remaining as squeaky-clean as possible. Once the rumor mill turned a little too fast when fueled by stories of gay hook-ups, a meeting with his manager had confirmed that the mill had to be halted immediately. As was the case with the cocaine scandal, the subject of Dax Monroe's sexuality quickly took a more palatable turn. He was snapped, none too accidentally, with one hot model after another, and even a famous actress or two.

These were, of course, all manufactured by his team. The appearance of too many photographs and stories had resulted in Dax being very honest with those closest to him, but he'd steadfastly promised to remain single. In the meantime, there were several "meetings" set up with famous beauties, in hotels and bars, where they'd meet for nothing more than a casual drink, only for one of the team to put in a call to a couple of photographers who'd soon be on their way.

There was no doubt that most, if not all, of the huge tabloids knew the truth. For every photograph that made it out into the open, there were five or even ten more quickly shut down with legal injunctions or cash payments made to the owner of such photographs. Dax Monroe had on his payroll a large number of very experienced lawyers whose entire business was keeping his image the cleanest it could possibly be.

The tabloids themselves knew that they could sell just as many papers of Dax with the hottest model of the moment than as they could with a scandal involving the hot pop star with another man. Especially, of course, if the one story that exposed him meant the annihilation of his career, which would then result in fewer stories altogether. For now, keeping Dax on the straight and narrow benefitted everyone, not least the fans who were fed the image they wanted.

But Dax Monroe was human. And he wanted sex. For now, he was willing to engage in a little risk in order to hook up with his latest target: a hot twenty-four-year-old named Andy, who was only two miles away, and was already describing the things he wanted to do to him. Dax put his plan into action.

Chapter Four

He pulled on a t-shirt, and over that a thick sweater. He put a woolen scarf around his throat, and shades over his eyes. Completing the ensemble was an ugly woolen hat, one that had served him well many times. Once dressed, he went out into the lounge area of the large penthouse hotel room. Kelly looked at him and although she tried to smile, instead her face fell. "Are you really going out?" she asked.

"Yeah," Dax said. He took his wallet from the side table.

"You know," Kelly said, walking over to him and lowering her voice, "we can party here if you like. Get a few people to come over? Get some drinks? We fly back to the States tomorrow so I think it's a good idea if we all stay together..."

She stopped speaking once she saw that Dax wasn't about to change his mind. Instead, he drew a pair of expensive sunglasses from the top pocket of his jacket. "All right," she said. "Call us as soon as you need a ride home. And stay safe."

As Dax left with a smile, he felt the tiniest pang of guilt. He knew Kelly worried, and he knew she had good reason. She'd been the best assistant he could have asked for, and she was the one who prompted him to be honest with the rest of the team about his life. Since coming out to the small entourage, reminding them, of course, that they were bound by confidentiality, Dax *had* felt a lot better. They didn't think he was a freak, didn't tease him about it, and a few said they'd known for a long time. That night, Dax could have asked for hot male escorts to be sent up to the room and nobody would have batted an eyelid.

But he didn't want to pay for sex. He'd done it

before, and it left him feeling empty and angry with himself. He wanted a human connection that wasn't reliant on a couple of hundred dollars, or in this case pounds, changing hands. He knew that Kelly organized for the men who came and went to get extra cash to keep them quiet, but he also knew that eventually, when one of them wanted a little more cash, they'd go to the newspaper anyway and try to sell the story of how they spent the night with Dax Monroe.

It was a hamster wheel Dax wasn't sure he'd ever be able to step off. Even in the hotel lobby as he pressed the button and waited for the elevator, as he pushed aside the sexual excitement that had begun to grow since seeing Andy's photograph he felt hollow. Exhausted. And it wasn't simply from the hundreds of nights spent on the road, either. There was something more inside that was troubling him.

But he pushed this aside, too, as the ding of the elevator snapped him back to reality. The doors opened and a large, jolly-looking concierge in a black suit tipped his hat. "Good evening, sir," he said. "May I help you with anything?"

"No, thank you," said Dax. "I'm just heading out for a walk. Get a little fresh air."

"Of course," said the concierge. He seemed to hesitate, and Dax picked up on the awkwardness hanging in the air.

"Is everything okay?" he asked.

The concierge laughed. "Of course, sir, of course," he said. "Only, and I shouldn't say this, but my daughter is the biggest fan of yours. My wife took her to see your show tonight, and I know she'd be so thrilled if..."

"Do you want a picture?" Dax asked.

The man's mouth fell open. "Would you mind?"

Although there was nothing in the world he'd like more than to tell the guy to fuck off and leave him alone, Dax grinned. "Hey, get your cell out and let's take a video!" he said. The concierge fumbled for the phone in his pocket. "What's your daughter's name?"

"Emily."

Dax smiled as the concierge started the video. "Hey, Emily!" he said into the phone. "I'm with your dad, here in the hotel, and he told us that you came to see my show tonight! Wow, I'm so thrilled. Thank you for being a fan. See ya!"

He blew a kiss into the phone and thankfully the concierge stopped the video, just in time for the elevator to reach the ground floor. He shook Dax's hand vigorously. "I can't tell you how grateful I am," he said. "I know they hate it if we talk to the celebrities here and I always manage to keep my cool around most of them but when I saw you, I couldn't help myself."

"Don't worry about it," said Dax. He managed to break away from the man's firm, pumping handshake, and reached into his pocket for a tip. He only had high value notes, and in the low light of the elevator he couldn't tell which note was which. As he passed over a red-colored bill to the concierge, the man was even more grateful, and shook his hand once more. Finally, Dax was free from his grasp, and he walked quickly through the hotel. He pulled the woolen hat lower down over his forehead, and once clear of the doors, put on the sunglasses he'd momentarily taken off to record the video for "Emily," who may not even have existed. The world was full of crazy fans.

There was certainly no sun in the sky at one o'clock on a cold Sunday morning in London, but Dax felt better to have the sunglasses on. He tugged up the collar of his jacket and put his hands in his pocket, trying to look as incognito as possible. He looked around for photographers and was sure he spied one or two talking together, having a cigarette, so he turned the other way quickly and walked over to a cab rank. He leaped into the car.

The driver seemed nonplussed by his latest customer. "Where to, fella?" he asked. It was then that Dax realized he wasn't sure where he was going.

"Hang on a second, please," he said. "Let me just check." He fired off a text to Andy, who replied within seconds, much to his relief. They were to meet at a hotel called Monroe's. Dax's blood ran cold. How could Andy have known who he was?

But as he suggested the name, the cab driver nodded and pulled the taxi out of the lane and into the road. Dax quickly searched online for the hotel. It was two miles from his own, and the name appeared to be nothing more than a coincidence. He couldn't see much about the place, but his eye certainly caught the single red star out of a possible five. Dax winced. He wasn't heading to the plushest place in London, that was for sure.

He could have stopped the driver at that very moment. Asked the man to pull over and hand him a wad of cash for his trouble. He could have put in a call to Kelly and the whole team would have been there in a flash to pick him up and take him back to the beautiful hotel he was staying in. They could order gourmet food and party until dawn.

But he didn't want that. He wanted something,

anything that resembled a life before the fame, and before the money. Before his life was micro-managed and controlled down to the tiniest detail. He wanted to remember what it felt like to get into a cab and have it take him to meet a new person, a date. So, he sat back in the cab, and thankfully the driver didn't bother to make small talk.

It wasn't a long drive along the river, and Dax dared to take down his shades to watch the scenery around him. London was one of the most beautiful cities he'd ever visited, the history seeping through every inch of the place. He saw bridge after bridge crossing the Thames, and he caught sight of the iconic Houses of Parliament, lit up by footlights. Next to them, of course, stood Big Ben, chiming without fail. Much like New York, London was a city that never slept, and Dax saw hundreds of folk milling around, many of them taking photographs.

Others were diving in and out of bars, wearing very little. Dax had endless respect for the British women who were able to walk around in freezing cold temperatures wearing little more than a tiny dress and eye-watering high heels. Dax shivered at the sight of them, even though the cab in which he was sitting was quite warm.

His phone beeped, and a text from Andy had come through on the app. "First floor," it read. "I'm in room 102. Just come in." Dax's heart began to beat a little faster, and he wondered what was awaiting him on the other side of the hotel door. Still the driver moved through the city, no doubt taking twice as long to reach the destination thanks to the endless one-way streets causing havoc with GPS systems.

Finally, the cab pulled up in front of a red building on a tiny street. There was no doubt they were at Monroe's: its namesake blew a kiss to them from a fiberglass mount against the wall. Dax asked for the fare.

"Eighteen-fifty," said the cabbie, and Dax pulled out two twenties. It meant nothing for him to hand over double the fare. Simply sitting in the cab for the ride had probably earned him at least a couple of thousand dollars. He barely had to move to make money, these days. But for the cabbie, it was a gesture for which he was grateful. He thanked Dax and wished him a good night, and the young man jumped out of the cab and onto the sidewalk.

The street was so narrow and the buildings so old that Dax wondered what part of London he was in. The city had a character unlike anything he'd seen back home in the US, and part of him wanted to walk around and explore. He knew that if he pulled out his phone he could find out the name of the street, and no doubt along with that would be some information about famous people of history who'd walked there.

But, he wasn't there to learn about London. He was there for sex, and if he stayed out much longer there was every chance that he might be spotted. He suddenly felt very vulnerable without his team, and once again he doubted himself for being in a city he didn't know, on a street he couldn't even see the name of. He was about to meet a stranger, who could endanger not just his career but his very life.

Dax opened the door to the hotel, and walked quietly up the stairs, relieved that nobody batted an eyelid.

Chapter Five

He tapped on the door, and saw that it was slightly ajar, kept open by a sock. He let himself into the room and closed the door again. He took off his shades and saw the blond guy sitting on the double bed ahead of him, barely five feet away. The room was smaller than the bathroom he'd just left at his own hotel, and the wallpaper was peeling from the ceiling down the walls. The place smelled of damp, and he wrinkled his nose.

Andy was, thankfully, even cuter than his online pictures had suggested. When Dax took off his shades and hat, he was so shocked he lay on the bed, not moving, his mouth open, as was the reaction of practically everyone Dax met.

First, Dax had to take all necessary precautions. "Where's your cell phone?" he asked.

Struck dumb, Andy held up the phone. Dax pointed to the bedside table. "Turn it off and put it in the drawer," he said.

Andy stood up from the bed. He couldn't stop staring. "Don't tell me it's really you," he said.

"Yep," said Dax. "I don't mean to be a dick but I can't have you taking any photographs of me while I'm here. Is the phone off?"

Andy was about to place it in the drawer when he held it up and pressed the home button, the black screen proving that the phone was indeed switched off. "I won't tell anyone," he said, his voice trembling. Dax could see he was shaking with nerves, and he took off his jacket.

"I've got my team in a car outside," he lied. He saw that Andy was still stuck to the spot, and he smiled. "Relax. You're hot."

"I don't think anyone would ever believe I've got Dax Monroe alone in a hotel room," he breathed. "Fuck me, I'm shaking."

"Hopefully not too much," Dax said. "I've seen what you've got under those jeans and I'd really like to get to know it a little better, if that's okay." He hoped that the guy's nerves weren't about to ruin his performance. Dax had already been through enough that evening, and to leave here without the very thing he came for would be too frustrating for him to comprehend.

To set the ball rolling, he lifted up the thick woolen sweater to reveal the slim t-shirt underneath. He stopped undressing there, and walked over to Andy. He didn't have far to go; the tiny box of a hotel room was easily crossed in just a few steps. He reached out and stroked down Andy's arms, fair and muscular, and moved in for a kiss. He could feel Andy's nervous breath on his lips, but after a few moments, their lips against each other, Andy relaxed, and with relief Dax felt their bodies press together.

The light of the room was far too bright, and Dax turned it off, keeping on only the single bulb over the bed. It was tacky, and not particularly arousing, but he didn't like to fuck in the dark. He had a body of which he was proud, one for which he'd worked hard. And he loved other men's bodies, too. He could feel Andy's muscles underneath his t-shirt, and he wanted to see more of it.

Andy smelled of shampoo and cologne, as though he'd only just stepped out of the shower. Dax liked this; when he had sex with someone he didn't know, their being clean was the most important thing for him. It meant that he didn't hesitate to get on his knees and pull at the button of Andy's jeans.

Looking down at him, breathing heavily, Andy still stood with his mouth open. Dax knew he couldn't believe it was happening, and was sure the guy wouldn't get another opportunity like this one. Knowing he'd surprised him, and that the hotel was indeed only a coincidence, meant Dax relaxed. He felt better to know Andy's cell phone was safely turned off and tucked away in the drawer, so there was little chance that incriminating footage could be taken.

Dax was already hard, and he slid his hand up Andy's t-shirt, groaning as he felt the man's toned body under his fingers. He lifted the shirt up and pressed his nose against the soft blond hair that ran from Andy's bellybutton. He smelled sweet, like fruity soap. But underneath that smell was the scent of man. And Dax had missed that smell a lot. Once the button of his fly was open, Andy began to stroke Dax's dark hair, and Dax liked the feeling of another man's fingers in his locks.

He began to stroke the soft bulge underneath the white cotton of Andy's underwear, and as he did so, he smiled to himself as he felt the bulge harden. He pulled down the waistband of the underwear and his mouth automatically watered at the sight of Andy's shaven cock. It was thick and veiny, curled like a python in his underwear, and Dax knew he had to free the beast from its cage. He pulled the underwear down further, and Andy's semi-hard dick popped out of the boxers, hanging down, twitching as it began to rise.

Dax didn't wait for it to get any harder before he grabbed the base of the shaft and opened his mouth. He took the tip of Andy's cock between his lips and tasted that first delicious tang of another man. It was like the first cigarette in a morning, the first cool glass of water after a long walk, the first sight of home after being away for months. And Dax relished the way Andy immediately became hard in his mouth, so that he had to move his head up, as Andy's cock sprang up against his stomach.

It took everything Dax had to stop putting his own hand into his jeans and stroking his cock, but he wanted Andy's lips around it. For now, he was content to be on his knees, his hands on Andy's muscular ass, moving his head back and forth as he opened the back of his throat and took as much of the other man as he could. He felt Andy press inside him, poking the tip of his cock against the back of Dax's throat, so that Dax felt he wanted to gag.

He closed his eyes and moved rhythmically, and Andy fell forward, placing his hands on the bed, his jeans in a bundle at his feet. "Fuck," he said, moving up and down, fucking Dax's mouth. "That's so fucking hot."

It turned Dax on to see how horny this other man was for him, and he wanted more. His own cock was aching in his jeans and although he was sad to release Andy from his mouth, he got up from his knees and held Andy's arm. "Suck my dick," he commanded him. Andy didn't need asking twice. With his own cock on an invisible string that twitched up and down, he got onto his own knees. His blond hair was floppy and soft, still a little damp from the shower, and Dax took pleasure from combing his own fingers through it slowly.

He opened the fly to his own jeans, took out his cock, and ran it over Andy's cheek, teasing both of them. Andy moved his mouth around, trying to catch it, but Dax smiled as he pulled away just in time. "Ever had a star in your mouth?" he asked. Andy gulped and shook his head. Not that Dax needed to ask the question; the guy's eyes still had the look of those of a frightened rabbit caught between headlights.

"Put it in your mouth," Dax whispered. "Take that dick and give me a good, old-fashioned English suck."

Without hesitating, Andy obliged. He held onto the shaft, his lips open wide. His hazel eyes closed and he gave a groan that Dax could feel reverberate from the back of Andy's mouth and right through the rest of his body, making him shiver. It was like slipping into the hottest of baths on the coldest of days, and Dax tipped back his head and gazed up at the grimy hotel ceiling.

For some reason, being in such a dive only made things even sexier. While he liked the way Andy had shown up to the date clean, he felt the whole situation was a little dirty, dangerous and far from the obsessively clean and tidy format his life was lived in day-to-day. He held the back of Andy's head, pushing his cock into the guy's mouth, feeling the hot wetness of his throat engulfing the tip.

Both men were uncut, and when Dax's foreskin was pulled back by Andy's gentle but eager fingers, he flinched at the sensitivity. Andy's tongue grazed against the head, which was red and glistened with precum. He opened his mouth and Dax watched as he licked at the head, poking his tongue against the slit, licking up the clear pearls of sweetness and swallowing them down.

Dax wanted to be someplace even hotter, and

darker, and tighter. He nodded toward Andy's wallet, which was sitting on the nightstand. "Have you got a rubber?" he asked.

"Yeah, yeah," Andy said, getting to his feet. They didn't need to have a conversation over who was going to be the one wearing it; the app on which Dax had found his date had clearly stated that the guy was versatile, and Dax was a die-hard top.

Andy grabbed his wallet and took out a condom. He left it on the nightstand as Dax pushed him onto the bed, kicking off his jeans. Andy pushed his own jeans off the end of his feet so both men were wearing only their t-shirts. Andy was face-down on the bed, his slim ass cheeks tight together. Dax would have liked his ass to have been rounder, fuller, but there was no mistaking that the rest of the guy's body was perfect. He bent over him, kissing his shoulders, licking down his back, coming to rest at the top of his ass.

As much as he loved to suck another man's cock, he loved eating out his asshole even more. He knelt on the bed, parted Andy's cheeks, and his tongue searched for the tight rosebud of the man's ass. His crack was filled with fine, fair hair, but Dax didn't mind that, either. The hair caught the manly scent and held it there, and he ran his tongue up and down, flicking it against the clenched skin of Andy's asshole.

It made Andy groan with pleasure, as he clenched the bed sheets with his fists and stretched out his toes as far as he could. Dax buried his head between the guy's ass cheeks, eating the tight hole, poking his tongue in. He grinned as he felt his sphincter relax a little, and he poked his tongue inside as far as it would go. Then he brought his head away and spat at it, getting it wet, and ready for him. In all this time his hard cock hadn't softened at all, and now he pressed the tip against Andy's ass, a foreshadow of what was to come.

"Yeah, give me that dick," Andy said, reaching around and stroking Dax. Dax liked the gritty, cockney tone in his voice. He sounded like an east-end gangster from the dramas he liked to watch when he had an evening to himself.

There was no lube in the room, and Dax spat on the guy's asshole again, rubbing the saliva around it. Then he picked up the condom and carefully tore open the packet. He hated to use them. For Dax, the sensation of sliding bareback into another guy's ass was unbeatable, but there was no way he could risk being so careless. He rolled the condom over his dick, snapping the end against the bottom of the shaft. The reservoir stuck out on the end of the tip, ready to do its job.

With the slippery feel of the condom and the saliva around Andy's asshole together aiding entry, Dax pressed the end of his cock against Andy's flesh, only this time there was less teasing and more intent. Andy turned his head to the side on the bed, his eyes tightly shut, bracing himself for what was to come.

Dax knew that up his ass was an organ guaranteed to give him unbelievable pleasure, but he'd never envied those who liked to bottom. Like many tops, he'd attempted to take a cock up his ass a few times, but each time had brought a rapid halt to the proceedings. It simply hurt too much, and it wasn't worth enduring the pain for the joy on the other side. He liked his asshole to be fondled, stroked, licked and gently played with, but he was firmly on the giving end when it came to penetration.

Andy got up onto his knees, crouching so they touched his chest. He presented himself, ankles wide apart, and as the tip of Dax's cock popped inside, he gave a gasp. Dax paused, not wanting to move too fast, but Andy was the one who moved backward, and both men groaned as Dax slid inside Andy with one glorious movement.

Dax could feel the tight muscles of the asshole clamp around his cock, not wanting him to move any further, but he pushed slightly, and felt Andy's bowels open up to him. Andy moaned as Dax pushed against his prostate, and after a few short, slow movements of his hips, Dax fell into a rhythm, and Andy joined in with enthusiasm.

The old, rickety bed had no doubt seen plenty of action in its time, and as the two men fucked hard and fast on it, it rocked with loud creaking noises. Dax gripped Andy's slim hips, his fingers sliding into the groove below his stomach that came from hard work at the gym. Andy sat up a little, arching his back, turning his neck to find Dax's lips with his own. Dax cupped his chin and plunged his tongue into the man's mouth, sucking at it as he fucked him, hard, from behind.

Andy grinned and took the cock like a champ, holding onto Dax's head and grinding his knees into the duvet. "That's it," he said. "Give me that big fucking cock, you sexy fucking superstar. Jesus, that's so beautiful you're going to make me blow all over this bed."

It spurred Dax on further, and he pushed Andy down onto the bed, moving on top of him, pistoning in and out with increasing speed. Andy was looser now, relaxed, and Dax was inside him as far as he could possibly go, his balls slapping against the man's ass.

Then he felt Andy clench around his cock, and he grinned as Andy cried out into the bed and soaked the sheets with cum, firing his seed up the bed so it hit his chin, and Dax kept on massaging his prostate with his cock until Andy begged for mercy.

The extra stimulation of Andy's muscles around his cock brought Dax to the edge of climax. Andy groaned, knowing he was close. "I want your seed inside me," he begged. "I don't give a shit about the condom. Take it off and give me that Dax Monroe cum!"

Dax pulled out and whipped off the condom, but instead of going back inside Andy's ass, he grabbed the man by the hair, turned his face around, and slapped his cock against the man's cheek. "Open your mouth," he instructed him. "Take my seed down your throat."

Andy was only too happy to oblige, and he moved to the side, rolling over and taking Dax's cock, pumping it a few times before Dax felt the heat rise to the point of no return, and he watched as climaxed in Andy's face, most of his cum firing into the man's mouth. Andy took every drop he could, swallowing it down in gulps, licking his lips and then holding Dax's cock between then, until Dax couldn't cope with anyone touching him anymore and he withdrew, panting heavily.

"Damn, I needed that," he said. "You wouldn't have a clue how hard it is to get a good fuck when you're on the road."

Andy lay on his back, casually stroking his cock, which Dax could see was beginning to get hard again. "Well, I've got the room all night, mate," he said, winking. "How about you stay here a bit longer and we do that all over again?"

The millionaire pop star was back. Dax flashed Andy a large smile. "I wish I could," he said. "But I've got a flight to catch in a few hours and my guys are going to be wondering where I am."

Before Andy moved, Dax pulled his clothes on quickly. He donned the shades and hat, and left the room without looking back.

Chapter Six

His heart sank when he walked down the stairs and caught sight of men in thick winter jackets, standing outside the hotel. They were the kind of jackets designed for the cold, so the wearer could stand around for hours at a time, waiting to catch a glimpse of the thing they came out to see. And not just to see. To photograph.

Before they caught sight of him, Dax turned around and ran back up the stairs, taking them two at a time. He banged on the door of the room he'd just left, pounding his fist against the wood until Andy opened the door a crack, peering outside. Dax pushed the door open and rushed into the room, closing the door quickly, and bolting it with a chain, as though someone was coming to get him.

Panting, he searched for his phone in his pocket. He was about to dial Kelly's number when he had another idea. He looked up at Andy. "Have you got a car here?"

"What?"

"A car, dammit!" Dax shouted, not caring how rude he sounded. "A fucking car. I need to get out of here. They're outside."

"Who's outside?"

"Fucking paparazzi." He looked over to the nightstand, where Andy's phone was switched on. Andy followed his gaze to the nightstand, and in horror looked back at Dax.

"It's not me," he said. "I haven't called anyone. I swear."

Dax knew it. There was no way that even if Andy had known a paper or photographer to call, that they'd have arrived at the hotel so quickly. The paparazzi were the kind of scum who operated at lightning speeds, but even they weren't that fast. It had to have been the cab driver from earlier. After such a good tip, he'd probably received ten times that amount for information about the world's most famous heartthrob being dropped off at a well-known gay hookup site. Just one look at the hotel, and Dax had known what the place was used for. That's why nobody had cared to question him when he slipped in through the lobby. Hell, there might even have been a guy on the desk who saw him and phoned the press straight away.

Whoever was to blame for the betrayal, Dax had to think fast. He called Kelly and told her the situation. She tried to calm him down. "Has your friend got a car of his own?" she asked. Dax put the question to Andy again, who was quickly dressing.

"Yeah, but it's parked in the car park down the street," he said. "If we leave we'll have to outrun them."

Dax wasn't sure, but he thought he caught a glimpse of excitement in the young man's eyes. He gritted his teeth and rubbed his eyes. He wanted a drink. Now the sexual desire had subsided, all he was left with was an exhausted headache, and a huge amount of anxiety. He had to get out. The tour of London had been such a glorious success, capping off the rest of the tour around the whole of Europe, and here he was, fucking everything up with only hours to spare before he got on the plane back home.

He could have kicked himself and he paced around the room, answering Kelly's questions. No, he couldn't see how many were outside. Yes, he was sure they weren't simply standing outside having a cigarette. For starters, people were allowed to smoke in the hotel, flouting British law. There was no need for anyone to be outside, and Dax had bumped into so many photographers in his career that he knew exactly what he was seeing.

Despite that, Kelly made him go to the window. "Just take a look outside and see if you can see anything," she said. "What's the place called? Monroe's? I've got Rocky and the guys looking at it now. Stay right where you are, and we'll come get you. I need you to see if there's a quiet place at the back where we can pick you up."

At the window, Dax pulled the curtain aside and peered down into the street. His hunch had been right. He saw a guy with a large camera and obnoxiously huge flash hurrying across the street to join the melee. They all knew he was inside, and he was trapped. Dax pulled the curtain back over the window and sat on the bed with his head in his hands. Andy tied his sneakers and grabbed his jacket. "I thought you said your people were outside?" he asked.

"I lied," Dax murmured into his palms. "It was just so that you wouldn't murder me."

"Oh." Andy slipped his phone into his pocket. "Look, I can go out the back of the hotel and get the car. Behind the place there's an alley where they put all the bins."

Bins in an alleyway. Dax could only laugh with bitter irony at the memory of the last time he was very nearly exposed, only the alley of the last place was behind a much, much nicer hotel than this one. Still, it was the only hope he had of getting out of this without being exposed. He thought carefully. "Yes," he said, finally. "Go get the car. Go out the back entrance and whatever you do, don't talk to a fucking soul. Not even if someone comes up to you and asks for a light for their cigarette. Do you understand?"

"Yeah," said Andy. "I'll go out the kitchen door at the back. I'll go and get the car. You won't be able to see me from the window, though. Just come down in about five minutes and I'll bring the car to the end of the alley. It's an old thing. Noisy engine."

"Perfect," Dax muttered. Nothing like a banged up old vehicle to herald his presence when all he wanted to do was disappear into the shadows. It was a terrible plan, but it was the only one they had. If he called Rocky over to the hotel in the huge, expensive vehicle, they may as well have stuck a flag on top, advertising that Dax was indeed holed up inside the grimy hotel.

Andy left the room, and Dax closed the door after him, taking a second to sweep the hall. So far, there was nobody outside waiting for him. He was a little surprised; usually the paparazzi didn't have the good grace to respect boundaries. If they were outside, it was because the hotel didn't want any trouble inside.

He couldn't wait for a whole five minutes. He called Kelly, told her of the plan, and left the hotel room. He took the back stairs and slipped to the ground floor, where there was a strong smell of mold and cooking oil. There was a fire door ahead of him, and he prayed it wasn't connected to an alarm when he pushed it, and found that it opened into the alley. Breathing a sigh of relief, he ducked his head out and looked for the car. There was no sign. He prayed that Andy hadn't simply walked, or driven off, into the night, leaving him stranded.

After a few minutes, although it felt like a lifetime, there came the sound of an engine. Dax was about to leap into the alleyway and run to the end when he saw two men pass by the entrance to the alleyway. He was sure he'd been spotted, but they were simply two men on a night out, walking along the street, with no idea that an international star was only a few meters away.

The engine belonged to the car Andy described, and Dax saw the flash of lights beckoning him. He wasted no time in running down the alleyway, barely noticing the rat that scurried way and hid under a bin. He opened the car door, and as he jumped into the passenger seat, he looked up and caught the eye of a paparazzo standing near the front of the building. *Fuck,* Dax thought. He sat in the car and didn't bother doing up his seatbelt. "Go!" he cried to Andy. "They've seen me! Let's get out of here!"

Andy pressed the accelerator down to the floor, but it had much less effect than Dax was hoping. The wheels gripped the road with a screech, and they lurched forward, then the car stalled. "Sorry," Andy muttered. "Brought the clutch up too soon."

By now the photographers were running down the side of the hotel, toward the battered old car. They'd already begun to take photographs and Dax held up his hands to shield his face from their lenses, and his own eyes from the invasive glare of their camera flashes. Andy drove forward, but they ran in front of the car, and he slammed his feet onto the brakes. "What the hell are you stopping for?" Dax cried. "Get us the fuck out of here!"

This time, Andy didn't stop. He tore down the narrow street, taking a sharp left to head down another street, before ending up on a main road. He joined the traffic and slowed down. "I think we lost them," he said, looking in the rear-view mirror.

"Don't be too sure," said Dax, through gritted teeth. "They're fucking parasites. Oh, shit."

As though on cue, there was a roar of a large van, and it pulled up beside them, as the passenger leaned over the driver and snapped furiously. Andy edged forward but the lights were red. "Just go," Dax shouted. "I'll pay the fine."

Once again they began to tear through the streets of London, along the river and past the Houses of Parliament. This time, Dax was in no condition to look dreamily at the iconic buildings. Instead, he was slouched in his seat, trying to cover his face. The photographer's car had been joined by another, then another, and Dax now had three cars trailing him, all with engines much more powerful than Andy's old motor, and all being driven by much more accomplished drivers.

Still, Andy did his best to weave in and out of the traffic, and he headed toward the highway that would take them out of the city. Dax was on the phone to Kelly, yelling at her to send help immediately, repeating the names of streets to her as Andy called them out.

Dax looked in the mirror and saw the headlights of one of the unrelenting vehicles behind him, and he was about to scream at Andy to go even faster, when suddenly there was a loud bang, and he was sure he'd been shot. Then, he was moving, out of his seat and through the windshield, and broken glass was raining down on him. He came to a halt on the hood of the car, and then there were flashes in his eyes, but he couldn't tell if they were from cameras, or from the burning pain that seared in his head. And then, despite trying to force himself to stay awake, he was dragged down into blackness, and all was quiet.

Chapter Seven

The only thing Dax Monroe could remember of the night after his final show in London was a strange dream. In it, he lay on the hood of a car, and there was confetti thrown around him in slow motion, only it wasn't like regular confetti; instead it was made of shards of glass. He tried to move his arm and ask that people stop showering him with the glass confetti, but they didn't seem to hear him, and his arm was a dead weight by his side.

He didn't recall any pain, save for the strange flashes in his eyes that burned like white-hot needles at the back of his retinas. There was a song he recognized that played over and over in his head, but the song wasn't a song, it was a siren. Maybe from a police car, maybe from an ambulance. He knew what it was, but it didn't sound like the sirens he knew from back home. He was freezing cold, and shivered, wanting to reach for a blanket or duvet, but once again his arm was too heavy to reach down the bed and cover himself.

He woke up when in the dream he felt a needle prick his arm. Then he fell back into the dream again, and this time there were voices, and more flashes, and something that felt very much like pain, but it became impossible for him to wake up and stop the dream. The cold was so bad he wanted to cry but when he opened his mouth he could only manage a garbled whisper. Finally, he begged for help, and another needle pricked his arm, and he disappeared into an even darker blackness than before.

The next time Dax opened his eyes, the first thing he noticed was that he was no longer cold. In fact, he was very warm, and it felt good. His eyes were sticky with sleep, and he was sure he had such a bad hangover that he must have drunk more than he ever had. He tried to lift his arm to reach for his cell phone but as it was in the dream, the arm wouldn't move. He swallowed, his throat dry as a bone. *Shit,* he thought to himself. *I've really overdone it this time.*

There was a strange, repetitive beeping in the room, which didn't feel like a bedroom. Instead, as he connected the beeping noise to the sharp tang of disinfectant, he realized with horror that he wasn't at home at all, nor in a hotel. He was in a hospital. He forced himself to open his eyes fully, and as he did so, the glare of the light forced him to close them once more. He tried again, blinking a few times, and then he heard a voice. "He's awake!"

It was Kelly. At least, it sounded like Kelly, but Kelly with a cold. Her voice was thick, and Dax was beginning to be so confused he wanted to get up and ask everyone what was going on. But he couldn't move. It wasn't just his arm that was rigid but his legs, his back, his neck. Everything was stiff and numb. The only part of him that could move were his eyes and his lips, and frantically he began to blink, and try to speak.

Kelly's face came into view, as she stood over his bed. "Don't try and move," she said. He could see her eyes were red, as though she'd been crying. Now she smiled down at him, and he could see her smile clearly. He implored her with his eyes to tell him what had happened, and why he was there, and she understood.

"It's the first time I've seen your eyes in three days," she said. "Do you remember the crash?"

The crash. That's what it was. It wasn't confetti but real glass from the windshield. He'd been in a car that was going far too fast, but it was an old car, and there was a guy driving it, but he didn't know where he was going. Dax frowned. "Andy," he croaked.

"That's right," said Kelly. "You were in the car with your friend Andy, and you were trying to get away from the press, and one of the cars clipped yours and sent you flying into a wall. You went through the windshield. So for now, you're staying where you are until you've healed."

"What did I break?" his voice was a whisper, and no matter how hard he tried, he couldn't clear the frog that seemed stuck in his vocal chords. He began to panic. If he couldn't talk, he couldn't sing. And if he couldn't sing...

"Your right arm's been fractured in three places," said Kelly, her voice low. Dax began to hear movement and low voices coming from elsewhere in the room, but he was flat on his back, unable to turn his neck to see who was speaking. He had so many questions. If it was just his arm, then why couldn't he move his neck? What happened after the crash, and why had it taken him three days to wake up when he only had a busted arm? If his arm was busted, why did that mean he couldn't speak?

He needed to pee, and there was a burning sensation in the tip of his cock. He didn't want to tell Kelly about it, but he was helpless to do anything else. "It's okay," she said. "You've got a catheter in, so go ahead and let go." There was an attempt at warm humor in her voice, but it didn't make him feel any better. He closed his eyes.

Then he opened them again and looked at Kelly. "Why can't I feel anything?" he asked in horror. "Oh fuck, am I paralyzed?"

Kelly placed a hand on his arm. "It's just the morphine," she assured him. "Can't you feel my fingers on you?"

With relief, Dax realized he could clearly feel her stroke his arm. He breathed out. "Yeah, yeah," he said. "My head's just so fucked and I don't know what's going on."

"It's okay," Kelly said. "We're all here. Even your mom. She's just stepped out to get some food but she's been here since the day after the crash. We flew her out here straight away."

"Am I going to die?" his voice was becoming clearer. He needed a drink of water, but there were more pressing things to sort than even hydration.

"Of course not!" Kelly said, brightly. Dax was sure he picked up the anxiety in her voice. He knew she was trying too hard to sound breezy, the way she did when a photograph of him looking worse for wear coming out of a club was splashed on the front page of a gossip rag. *You don't look too bad at all! Your cheekbones are still killer! Of course you're not going to die!*

He was desperate to stay awake to see his mom, who Kelly said would be back in just a few minutes. He was sure he'd burst into tears as soon as he saw her, but for now he couldn't keep his eyes open. He had the niggling sense there was deep pain somewhere inside his body, but he couldn't tell where it was, and he was sure that if he didn't let sleep take him now, then the pain would know he was awake, and would come for him with a vengeance. So he closed his eyes again, and disappeared once more into the blackness, because for now it was the only place he could feel safe.

Chapter Eight

The next few hours followed the same routine: Dax would wake for several minutes, and absorb as much information as he could in the form of the most pressing questions. Once these were answered, he'd fall back asleep again, thanks to a cocktail of painkillers and other drugs that had been pumped into his system since the second the ambulance arrived on scene. Each time he went back to sleep he had a little more knowledge of the accident, and what had followed, but while he knew that his family and team were keeping plenty from him, he didn't have the energy to press them further.

He had no knowledge of days, or time, or whether it was even light or dark outside. He requested the curtains remain closed. He was unsure why this was, but when he slipped into unconsciousness he was plagued by nightmares where photographers climbed up the walls of the hospital or flew drones up to the windows and snapped picture after picture of him lying prone on the bed, unable even to shield his face.

When he felt the soft, familiar hand of his mom stroke his face, he wept, thick hot tears emerging from his eyelids and disappearing immediately down the sides of his temples to the pillow beneath him. He recalled the time he fell off a climbing frame at the park when he was ten years old and broke his left wrist, and how his mom had done exactly the same: lovingly caress his cheek while he wept from pain and frustration.

There were times he tried to talk to her, but she would only lean down, press her nose against his, and tell him not to worry. Everything would be fine, she assured him. He needed to sleep as much as he could, and get well, and everything would work itself out. He tried to ask about the rest of the family, and how long she was staying, and her answers were the same every time: loving, but vague.

It was only as he drifted back into oblivion that Dax understood how much he'd missed his mom while he'd been on the road. His brain decided that rather than concentrating on the strange, dull ache that occupied his body, it would throw up memories of the past, and of his childhood. He thought a lot about the Christmases he woke up so excited he'd bound down the stairs before he even went to the bathroom. He was shown memories of summers with his friends, riding their bikes around the park, climbing trees and playing softball.

The slideshow of his life played like a movie on repeat inside his head. In each of the memories he felt safe, and nostalgic. He knew he could call out for his mom and she'd be there, the way she was now, beside his bed. Only now, she looked older, and the worry in her eyes had bled out to the lines around her face, on her forehead, so it looked like she was frowning even when she smiled down at him.

After a particularly long nap he opened his eyes and felt more awake than he had in a long time. He stared up at the ceiling, waiting for someone to come over to him, because he couldn't alert them. Nobody came for a few moments, so he opened his mouth and called out weakly. Then his mom's face was there, as it had been constantly, and she looked tired once more. "Mom, why don't you go get some sleep?" he asked. "I want to talk to the doctors, so go get some rest."

She looked behind her, and then into his vision came Kelly, and then Rocky. "Hey, guys," Dax said to them, attempting a weak smile. "Guess I should have listened to you, huh?"

They were kind, and shook their heads, and smiled. Dax was sure that if he closed his eyes again, he'd end up falling back to sleep again. The dull ache was there, and it was getting louder, but he wanted to ride it out, to sense where on his body the pain was coming from. He couldn't tell if he was hungry, but he was definitely thirsty. He mentioned this to his mom. "How am I alive if I haven't drunk anything?" he asked.

"You're on a drip, right here." She tapped a plastic bag over his head, which Dax could just about make out, if he rolled his eyes as far back in his head as he could before it gave him a headache. "You haven't been able to drink anything yet but you're still well-hydrated. Nice, clear pee."

She grinned at him, and he felt embarrassed, like a kid being shown up in front of his friends. As a nurse, his mom had always looked out for his physical health. For now, if he had clear pee, and that made her happy, then he'd take it. He didn't like the dark shadows under her eyes, especially as he knew he was the cause of them.

"Mom," he repeated. "I want to talk to the doctors. Can you go get someone?"

"Honey, just rest," she said. "The doctors are taking amazing care of you. There's nothing to worry about. You're due to have your meds soon, so—"

"No!" It was the first time he'd made a noise over a croaky whisper since he first woke up in the hospital, but he desperately needed to be heard. He didn't know why, but he started to cry again. "Please, Mom. I want to talk to someone who can tell me what's going on. I know it's more than a broken arm. I can take it. I just want the truth."

Diane Monroe looked at her son and swallowed. She pursed her lips together and looked at Kelly. "I'll go get the doctor," she said. "He's right. It's not fair to keep talking about him like he's not here."

She left the room, and Kelly smiled down at Dax. "I really like your mom," she said. "You look a lot like her."

"I forgot the two of you hadn't met before," Dax replied. "Yeah, people say we look alike. I've got my mom's eyes and my dad's nose. Or that's what I've heard, anyway."

His father. Dax hadn't thought about him since waking up. "Has he been called?" he asked.

Kelly nodded. "He's been talking with your mom several times a day," she said. "Your mom calls and tells him how you're doing. He wants to come over and see you, but your mom seems to think it wouldn't be a good idea."

Dax managed a small smile, although moving his cracked lips made him wince. "She's probably right," he said. "It's a long story I'll tell you about sometime." He paused, and looked up at her. He wanted to ask her about that night, and about what the press were saying, but he had to push the worry away for the moment. It was more important that he learn what was really going on with his injuries, and how long it would be before he could sit up, at least, and take stock of what to do next.

The door opened, and then his mom came back into sight, in the small window of vision he had above his bed. He'd started to become used to seeing everyone with their hair dangling down over him. "The doctor's here," his mom said. "Her name's Doctor Pravenda."

A pretty woman with clear brown skin and glasses perched on the edge of her nose was the next face above Dax. He narrowed his eyes. "I think I've seen you before," he said.

"That's right," said the woman, smiling. Her voice had a clipped British accent, tinged with a soft Indian lilt. "It's good to know you're memory's doing well. My team and I have been looking after you for the last few days, and I must say it's been a real pleasure, although I wish we were meeting under different circumstances."

"Me too," Dax said. "It's nice to meet you."

"So how can I help?" the doctor asked. "I believe your mother said you'd like to have a chat with me."

"I just want the truth, Doc," said Dax. "Just you and me. No bullshit. Okay?"

"No bullshit," repeated the doctor, and she smiled warmly. "That sounds like a good idea."

She looked up at whoever it was who was still in the room. "You've heard the man," she said, with an authoritative, but not cruel, air. "He wants everyone out, please."

Dax heard the shuffling of feet, and he tried to work out how many there were, but he lost count. But the door clicked, and he knew he was alone with the doctor. "I know it's bad," he said, looking up at the ceiling, trying not to cry. "Just tell me. I haven't felt my legs since I woke up, and I know I'm in pain, but it's like my head can't tell where the pain's coming from."

Doctor Pravenda nodded. "You've had both a terrible accident, and a very lucky escape," she said. She crossed her arms and leaned on the railing that ran down either side of the hospital bed. "When your car hit the wall, you went right out through the window, and it was only the wall that stopped you from going any further. If it hadn't been there, there's a good chance we'd have had to fish you out from the Thames."

"It's because I wasn't wearing a seatbelt, right? It was all my stupid fault. The whole night."

"I wouldn't beat yourself up about it too much, Mr. Monroe," the doctor said. "There was no airbag on the passenger side of the car, so there was every chance that with the impact, you might have been jerked back by the belt and could actually have caused even more damage. We'll never know. But, you ended up outside of the car. Now, the preliminary x-rays showed extensive damage to your right arm, and you've had a three-hour operation to insert pins inside to keep everything together while it heals. You've got a few cuts on your face and hands but you're still as beautiful as you are on the posters in my daughter's bedroom."

Dax appreciated her mix of candor and humor, and he stayed silent, waiting for the next news. He knew there was more to come, and he was right.

"We've taken you for several scans," said Doctor Pravenda, "and it's been very hard to tell exactly what damage you've sustained to your neck and back, because of the inflammation. When we have someone in your situation, we have to balance the drugs very carefully. We have to give you strong painkillers, along with anti-inflammatory drugs, but we can't give you too much of either, so we've been relying on the passage of time for much of the swelling to go down, so we can get a proper picture.

"The main thing I can tell you is that you have incurred some rather extensive damage to your back. You're scheduled to be taken for another scan later today. Now that you're awake and can tell us where you have the most pain, or where you have little or no feeling, it'll help us to determine what sort of injury you have, and what the next options are."

Hanging onto every word, Dax didn't take his eyes from the doctor's face. He waited for her to stop speaking, and she asked if he had any questions. He only had one. "Am I going to be flat on my back for the rest of my life?" he asked. His voice cracked, and his eyes welled up with tears.

"Not if I have anything to do with it, Mr. Monroe," said Doctor Pravenda. "How could I ever break the news to my daughter that I'd failed her hero?"

Chapter Nine

Despite the doctor's optimism, Dax went through a roller coaster of emotions over the next few days. He was, without doubt, in the best hospital in London, if not the whole of the UK, and there was no denying that money would be no object. Dax knew the team he had on hand twenty-four hours a day were all doing their best, and that the only thing that was going to determine the extent of his recovery was time. Nothing more than time.

And he had plenty of it, for now. He lay supine on the bed twenty four hours a day, with no time to get up and even go to the bathroom. He had scan after scan, and went under anesthetic for the surgeon to correct a further small issue with his right arm. He was poked and prodded, wheeled down for scans and wheeled back up again, and throughout it all his team were at his side. He knew the press must have been going wild, and one week after the accident he dared to ask what had happened.

Kelly wasn't keen to talk about anything to do with newspapers, or websites, or gossip magazines. Dax could hear her phone ringing every few minutes, during the times she wasn't speaking on it to somebody back in the States, and she would leave his bedside to take the call. She was tired, and harassed, and even though she was staying in a suite next to his hospital room, she spent very little time in it.

She was only fifty-five, but she might as well have been thirty-five from the way she looked. Her blonde hair, usually iron-straight and beautifully shiny, was pulled back into a ponytail. Her roots were greasy and in need of touching up. She'd pulled off all her false nails, probably with nerves, and she was wearing the same jacket and shirt she'd had on for the past three days. She'd attempted to freshen up with a touch of makeup, but it was rushed, leaving mascara underneath her eyes and a pimple on her forehead. Dax asked that she put her phone on silent for a few moments, and she dutifully agreed without question.

"Come on," Dax said, as she stood over him with a straw hanging out of a cup of water. "I need to know everything that's going on. While my mom's not here."

"I don't think it's a good idea," Kelly said. "What I *can* tell you is that right now there are about two hundred teenagers outside with banners and gifts for you."

"That's nice," said Dax. "It's a shame I can't exactly get to the window and give them a wave."

"You will," said Kelly, brightly. "Very soon."

"I need to know the rest," Dax said, pressing her again. "Look, you're my assistant. We can't keep working together and you can't get me through this if you're not honest with me. You need to promise me right now that you'll be honest with me whenever I ask."

He paused, closed his eyes, and chose his next words very carefully. "What's happened to me isn't something that's going to just go away if we give it money. It's going to be fucking hard work. I need you on my side, and I can't walk away and have you fix it anymore." He managed a weak laugh. "I literally can't walk away and leave it with you. I need to know everything, from now on."

It was the first time he'd ever spoken to Kelly so personally. Despite her having been by his side over the past few years, they knew very little about each other. Dax had no idea what day her birthday was, or whether she had a boyfriend. He'd simply never cared to ask. Instead, she'd only had one job: keep him happy, whatever the cost. And for Dax, the cost wasn't important. He'd never cared if whatever it was he wanted cost him ten thousand dollars, or cost his assistant a night off. He strongly believed that if there was something about the job she didn't like, she was free to leave. If she talked about him, he'd sue her for everything she had. If she walked away, there'd be plenty of other people to take her place.

But as he lay utterly helpless in a hospital in a country he desperately wanted to leave, he knew he needed to swallow his pride. He wasn't a superstar any more, or at least not for the foreseeable future. He was a thirty-two year old cripple who wore white socks up to his knees to prevent blood clots, and who had to pee through a tube into a bag that a nurse came to empty several times a day.

Though he was completely unable to move his right arm, he had moderate movement in his left. He reached up to his left and gently grazed the arm of Kelly's jacket. "Give it to me," he said. "I don't care if it's all over. All I care about is getting out of here."

Kelly rubbed her eyes and took a deep breath. "I daren't turn the television on," she said. "I think things have calmed down for now but this was the biggest thing to hit the showbiz world in a long time. Because you were running from the paparazzi, they were right on hand as soon as the car hit the wall. The bastards called the ambulance with one hand and took pictures with the other. As for that scumbag you'd been with that night... Jesus."

"Andy?" Dax raised his eyebrows. He'd barely given the guy a second thought, and realizing that gave him a pang of guilt. "What happened?"

"He wasn't badly hurt. I think he was wearing his seatbelt. There wasn't an airbag on your side of the car, but there was on his."

"The doctor said that," Dax replied. "I remember it was a shitty old thing. I'm surprised it was even still running."

"Well, it isn't anymore," said Kelly. "Don't worry. We're going through his insurance. He'll pay up."

"I don't care about that," said Dax. "Just tell me what he did."

"He gave interviews to anyone who asked," Kelly spat. "Told everyone he'd been with you at the hotel. Told them you'd fucked like rabbits and you were the best fuck he'd ever had. Said that he'd tried to save your life by driving you back to the hotel. Maybe that part's true, I don't know. But all it took was for one or two papers to go with the story he gave them and it was out. Along with you sprawled on the hood of the car, you've been outed, and nearly killed, all in one night."

"Outed?"

Kelly gave a wry smile. "We've not made an official comment about anything just yet. The only thing we've released is a short statement to one news network about how you had an accident and were currently receiving the best care and you were doing well and were out of danger. Sure, they want more, but we're not giving it to them."

Dax breathed in heavily, and then stopped as his chest hurt. He winced and looked up at the ceiling. "What a way to destroy it all," he said. "I'm surprised my mom's still speaking to me, let alone standing by my bedside every minute."

"Don't underestimate moms," Kelly said. "I don't think anything about your private life has been a shock to her. She knows you better than you think and she hasn't bothered to watch any news or read anything on her phone. All she cares about is you getting better. That's all anyone cares about. I promise."

But Dax knew that wasn't the case. In his experience, nobody in the media wanted happy endings and good news. The best thing that could have happened for their ratings was literally for him to be in a car with his gay lover, and for that car to crash in one of the biggest cities in the world. And right at the end of his tour, too. It was perfect timing. All the scandal, but none of the fans had to be reimbursed for any of their tickets.

His head hurt. His arm hurt. His chest hurt. He closed his eyes and breathed in and out through his nose. "I know I said I wanted them to lower the morphine but right now I just want to sleep," he said. "Can you be a doll and go get the nurse to give me a shot?"

But Kelly didn't move. "You know something, Dax?" she said. "You'll come out of this. I know you will. I can see it in your eyes. You've done nothing to be ashamed of. Right now, it seems like things couldn't be any worse but I promise we'll get you through this. It's just gossip. You know what it's like."

"Kelly?" Dax said, not looking at her. "Please go get the nurse."

And she did.

Chapter Ten

The next scan Dax received showed that there was no permanent damage to his neck. He was bruised and sore, but the swelling quickly went down. For the first few days after the accident, when he was unconscious, doctors were frustrated by the lack of healing deep inside. It meant they couldn't read the scans underneath all the inflammation. However, once awake, Dax was determined to do everything he could to heal quickly. He began to eat and drink, although sparingly, given that he was unable to get himself off the bed and go to the bathroom. All the money in the world couldn't make up for the embarrassment of someone else having to deal with that side of things.

He lay on his back and concentrated on what he could feel, often refusing pain medication despite the healing nerves causing agony to flood through him with even the slightest movement. His left arm was the only limb to come through the accident relatively unscathed, and he used it one morning to take a mirror from his mom and look at his face.

The stitches in his forehead and cheek explained the itchy, stinging pain he felt every time he frowned, or cried, or even smiled. They were only small cuts, neatly sewn up, and would leave only the tiniest trace of a scar once fully healed. The nurses explained he'd be given a special gel made from cortisone that would also aid in the fading of the scars.

His face was the least of his worries. His right arm was pinned together under the cast, and he ached to scratch it. He sweated with frustration when he couldn't move to alleviate the itch, and at one point the agony of both his body and his predicament welled up inside him that he took in a deep breath and bellowed toward the ceiling in a fit of rage. His mom appeared at his bedside immediately, and stroked his face. He batted her away with his left arm. "Leave me alone," he said. "I can't fucking move. I can't fucking go to the bathroom on my own. I can't even fucking scratch my own damn arm goddammit!"

There was a cup of water on a tray over him and he knocked it away in anger. His mom said nothing, then left the room. She returned with Doctor Pravenda. Like a chastened child, Dax was silent, his lips together in a pout. "Good morning," said the doctor cheerfully. "I was just on my way to see you. Your scan from yesterday seems to show a marked improvement in the swelling, and we have a better idea of how to go forward. How about we have a chat?"

"Yes, please," said Dax. "I heard yesterday that my neck is fine."

Doctor Pravenda nodded. "That's right. The good news is that when you were first attended to by the paramedics, you were breathing on your own, and you were trying to move. This is an excellent sign. It meant that we didn't have to breathe manually for you, or do what we call a *jaw thrust,* where we push your jaw forward and insert a breathing tube. It also meant that because you were breathing on your own, we were less worried about something called *ischemia.* Do you know what that is?"

"No," Dax replied. He noticed that as he spoke, he also shook his head, as though to re-emphasize the point. It was something many people did every day, but took for granted. But as he moved his neck, he noticed that he wasn't in any pain. He mentioned this to Doctor Pravenda.

"That's good," she said. "It confirms what we

know from your scans. I think the reason you're going to heal more quickly than others is because you've not had any trouble breathing. As I was saying, ischemia is when the blood vessels die from a lack of oxygen. It's very common in patients with spinal cord injury, because their diaphragm no longer has nerves, and it basically forgets to do its job. But your breathing is excellent, and we haven't had to give you much help with that at all, apart from some extra oxygen in the ambulance to keep you stable before we knew exactly how to proceed."

Dax liked her voice, its softness mixed with clarity. He trusted the doctor, and hung onto every word. She seemed positive, and he believed that she could cure him. "What's next?" he asked.

"The best news we've had in the last week is that you haven't severed your spinal cord. When you have so much inflammation it's difficult to know what's bruising, and what's permanent damage. Now, we have two specialists looking at every scan over and over again but comparing them to those we took last week there's already a marked improvement."

"Really?" Dax was overwhelmed. He let out a deep breath in a long, low whistle. "I'll walk again?"

Doctor Pravenda smiled. "Didn't I say we wouldn't let that happen?" she asked.

"Yeah, but it's going to take more than optimism," Dax said, soberly.

"You've already taken the decision to lower your pain medication," the doctor went on, "which I think shows a real determination and a desire to get well. But you don't have to be a hero all the time. Take the medication. I believe that you will walk again. I believe that you can recover from your injury, but it won't be pain free."

She reached under the bed and pulled out a white board, and a pen. "We use these to help our patients understand their injuries," she said. She drew a crude picture of a man standing from the side, his spine curving naturally from the shoulders to the hips. "The back is made up of five parts. The cervical, thoracic, lumbar, sacrum and coccyx. Altogether, they make up the thirty-three bones of your spine. You've broken three of the twelve pieces of the spine in the lumbar region. Here."

She drew a circle around the segments of the spine. Behind them ran a thin line. "This is your spinal cord," she said. "It runs down these vertebrae. Now, when you went through the windscreen, there was every chance you could have done so much damage that the broken vertebrae would have sliced through the spine and severed it completely. We knew this hadn't happened because the rest of your vital signs were good, and as I said earlier, you were breathing on your own. So the broken pieces of your spine are simply that. Broken. Broken bones heal. Broken spinal cords do not. Thankfully, only your bones are broken."

"Well, I've got to say that's a relief," Dax said. "I mean, I can't even tell you how much. One thing confuses me though. If I'm only bruised, then why can't I feel anything? You could have cut both my legs off and I wouldn't know."

"I can assure you that we haven't done that," Doctor Pravenda said. "But the numbness is the body's way of dealing with the shock to your spine. Just like us, your brain didn't know what damage your spine has, so it shut off everything in the lower half of your body. If it hadn't switched it off, you'd be in agony. Now, as the nerves heal and begin to transmit sensations once again, this is when you'll begin to feel a whole range of strange things down there."

"Like what?"

"You'll feel pins and needles, prickling, and maybe you'll feel your toes one day and then you won't feel them again until the following day. Sometimes it may be like an icy hand moving up your legs, and other times it might be like a red hot poker in your ass."

She paused. "The hardest bit comes when the recovery really starts, Mr. Monroe. I'd like you to keep taking your pain medication when it's prescribed, so that you can get all the rest you can and save your strength for when you're going to need it the most."

"Aren't those pills really addictive, though?"

Dr. Pravenda was quiet for a moment, and then she gave a small nod. "They can be," she said. "You're right. But we have you on a very managed plan, with the best doctors, and I believe that if you feel you can cope without medication for now, then that's great. But what I suggest is that you don't battle the pain without a little help. There's no shame in it."

"I hear you, Doc," Dax said. "But for now, I think I'm happy taking the lower dose."

She seemed satisfied with this, and Dax relaxed when he knew both he and his doctor were being honest with each other. If he were able to, he would have reached up and kissed her when she gave him the best news he'd had all day; better, even, than hearing he would indeed walk again. "How about we remove this collar?" she asked.

"Are you serious?"

"Yes." Doctor Pravenda smiled her friendly

smile. "We have enough evidence to show that your neck is only bruised, but isn't in any danger of further injury. Let's get this off."

She fetched a spare pillow and gently tucked it under his head, moving his neck forward enough so that Dax was able to see something other than the ceiling for the first time since his accident. The pillow was so soft and luxurious he was sure his head had never felt anything more wonderful. And then, with a ripping of hook-and-loop fastening and a clicking of plastic, his neck was free, the warm air touching his skin.

With his good arm, Dax reached up and stroked his neck, gently prodding it. "Let me do that," said the Doctor, and her cool fingers pressed him along either side of his spine, watching his reactions and listening for any cries or grunts of pain. Satisfied, she raised the pillow a little more, and held onto the brace. "You don't need this," she said. "I'm happy we have other things to begin to work on, and you should be in a little less discomfort, now."

"Thank you," Dax said, genuinely grateful. "I feel better just getting that off."

"Great," said the doctor. "Keep talking to us, keep communicating with us, and tell us if you're in pain. I don't have to tell you that you're in the best hospital money can buy, so don't be shy, okay?"

And she winked at him, and with a pat on the arm, she left the room.

When his mom and Kelly came back in again, Dax looked at them sheepishly. He felt guilty for his earlier outburst, but it seemed all was forgotten. Their faces were bright with the joy of seeing him sitting up for the first time since the accident, and his mom was so thrilled to hear that he would walk again that she burst into tears, which made Kelly begin to cry, too, and before long, all three of them were weeping.

Dax brushed the tears from his face with his good hand and set his jaw in determination. "I'm going to get through this," he said. "I'm going to pick up where I left off and it's going to be nothing more than a rest period for me. The time I'm going to use to get well is the time I should have had as a vacation anyway. As soon as I'm well enough to fly, let's get the plane back to the States and I can get the right therapists and this time next year, I'll be back for another sell-out tour, right?"

He looked at Kelly, and noticed the smile on her face seemed more forced than it had been earlier. "What?" he asked.

"Nothing," she said, but her voice gave her away.

"Tell me," said Dax. "I need to hear it. I know there's something you've been keeping from me."

When his mom didn't leave the room, Dax knew she already knew what it was everyone seemed to know. Everyone but him. He frowned, and listened as Kelly began to speak.

Chapter Eleven

As they'd all feared, the news of Dax's accident was overshadowed by the media frenzy surrounding who he'd been with before the crash. Paparazzi photographs adorned the front pages of newspapers all over the world, and tabloids on the internet posted picture after picture of the crash, and the hotel he'd been in before the crash, and then pictures of Andy. Dax had insisted that Kelly give him his phone, and after days without checking his messages, he spent hours trawling through his inboxes.

His family were all concerned for his health, but he didn't have time to appreciate their messages of goodwill and hopes for a speedy recovery, because his world was swiftly collapsing all around him. Once he managed to get Kelly to begin to speak, Dax convinced her to tell him absolutely everything.

He'd been in the hospital for ten days, and in that time he'd been dropped by three of his sponsors. One of them was a soft drinks company, another was an underwear designer, and the third a famous brand of razors for men. Kelly was sure they'd be able to convince them to stick with Dax, and that they'd reverse the decision, but Dax knew the score.

Since being plucked from obscurity at the age of eighteen at a talent show, Dax Monroe had been marketed as a hot, wholesome hero for young girls. His stunning good looks, dark eyes and boy-next-door charm had meant that he was perfect for plastering on posters that adorned walls of teenage girls all over the world. He was pictured with a string of beautiful women, and one in particular, who'd been strangely absent since the accident.

When he was younger, Dax had been the face of

a line of teenage boys' clothing, and as he got older, he progressed to more adult clothes. He was relieved when he no longer had to be seen wearing low-rider jeans and open shirts and could finally dress the way he wanted to when he went out. He was twenty-six before Grant would let him be seen out in bars, especially if he was going to have more than a couple of drinks. Everything about his life was micro-managed.

In the conservative USA, which had seemingly become even more so since the election of President Dean Murphy, companies seemed more and more determined to maintain "wholesome" values; this meant advertisements where a hot guy could only be seen with a hot wife, in a world where homosexuality simply didn't exist. After all, the country had spoken up with a voice that apparently said this was what they wanted, and companies had to placate them if they wanted to sell their products.

It simply wouldn't do for Dax to be the face of these companies any longer, when his private life was so scandalous. As he lay in his bed, Dax's dream of returning to the UK for a world tour in the future began to slip away from him, and it had nothing to do with whether he was able to walk or not.

Grant called several times a day, wanting updates from Kelly. Dax could practically hear him tearing his hair out, sitting in his office with his head in his hands, reading the latest scandal surrounding his once most-profitable client. With every day that passed that Dax didn't appear to deny the rumors of his homosexuality, cash drained from Grant's fingers, and he couldn't claw it back, no matter how hard he tried.

"We need to leave," Kelly said. "That's the main

thing. Get back to the States, and be with people you know. We can't do anything to help when we're stuck in a hospital."

"Go, then," said Dax. "Leave me here. Go get yourself a new heartthrob. A new hero. It's not me anymore, is it?"

As the next few days passed, he sank deeper and deeper into a depression that it seemed nobody was able to shift him from. Doctor Pravenda spoke to him many times, assuring him that his low mood was completely normal. After all, his body and brain had suffered a tremendous shock, and while they could fix the body, the brain was a much more sensitive organ, its own injuries invisible.

She put him on a course of anti-depressants, and Dax was simply too low even to care what they were. Each day, when his pills were delivered, he knocked them back, with a sip of water. He didn't want to eat, and he refused to see anybody but Doctor Pravenda from his care team. The black hole he was descending into terrified him, but he was unable to stop himself from falling into it.

Kelly and his mom tried to remove his cell phone, but he refused to give it to them. He became addicted to scrolling through page after page of tabloid gossip. He created a username and logged into a forum so that he could follow, in real time, the discussions about his sex life. He was surprised to see how many men came forward and declared that they, too, had spent a night of passion with Dax Monroe, at his house in California, at his New York apartment, at his condo in Hawaii. None of these were true. Dax had never once invited a man back to his place. What was the phrase his father used to use? *Don't shit on your own doorstep.*

But there were a few who emerged from the shadows with more plausible stories. One man said he filled Dax's tour bus with gasoline on his tour of France and later that night had given Dax a blow-job in his luxurious kitchenette area while Kelly and the rest of the guys were out at dinner, and Rocky waited outside the bus patiently, his head turned the other way as it always was. When he read this account, Dax knew the man was telling the truth. He never got his name, not thinking for a second that he'd read about the account on a forum. The man was mocked and shouted down for being dishonest, and Dax even felt a little sorry for him, his thumbs itching to type that Pier959 was telling the truth. Not that it would have made any difference, though.

One or two of the messages on the forums were strangely touching, though. There were those who swore they'd always known Dax was gay, and now that he was out, then he'd be welcomed into the community. There were others, though, who were more vitriolic in their replies. He had no right to be part of a proud community, they argued, when he'd lived the life of a privileged straight guy and had denied the many rumors over the years in order to further his career.

Many an hour was spent numbly torturing himself on the internet, and this did nothing to help Dax's mood. He became too lethargic to speak to Kelly, and even to his mom, despite her sitting at his bedside for hours on end. He wanted to tell her that while he understood a mother's love transcended any of the spurious bullshit that glared at him from the screen of his phone, he just wanted to be left alone.

Diane Monroe hadn't broached the subject with her son. Dax knew from her face that she'd seen plenty of magazine and newspaper covers when she'd gone downstairs to the hospital shop, and of course, she had her own cell phone with access to the internet. But while Dax felt there was something she wanted to say to him, she only managed to open her mouth and close it again, never quite knowing how to begin. And Dax didn't know, either, so the two of them remained in awkward silence with each other, relieved when there was a reason for the silence to be broken, such as the delivery of a meal, or even the emptying of Dax's catheter bag.

He knew Doctor Pravenda was becoming a little frustrated with his lack of progress. He refused to engage with any of the physical therapists who came to massage his legs and begin gentle exercises that would prevent his muscles from wasting away until he was able to stand up and begin to walk again. One morning, when she breezed into his room with the same cheerful demeanor she always had, she pulled back the blanket on the bed and tapped his thigh with her pen. "This won't do," she said.

Dax shrugged and stared blankly ahead of him. Doctor Pravenda tapped his forehead with the same pen. "This won't do, either," she said. "When we talked about you getting well, Mr. Monroe, you were excited. I was excited. And now you've lost the spark. But you need to get that back before you start your exercises, or you won't walk again, even if you're healed."

He knew she was right, and yet he didn't want to hear her speak to him. He brushed her hand away gently, and a single tear rolled down his cheek. "They all hate me," he said, hoarsely. "What's the point in walking again when I don't have a life to walk back to?"

Doctor Pravenda's face softened and she leaned over his bed and patted his hand. "From what I've seen," she said, "the press have a short memory. Outside this hospital there are plenty of people who've been out here many times, holding banners saying that they hope you get well. Men, women and children. Don't think you have nothing left, Mr. Monroe. Because many people love you, but until you love yourself first, then nothing will move forward. All right?"

"Love myself," said Dax. He closed his eyes. "I don't even know myself."

Chapter Twelve

It was a mild day at the beginning of March when Dax woke up to a smell he recognized from a long time ago. At first, he couldn't place it, but as he saw his mom standing over him with a smile on her face, holding a plate, he couldn't help but grin. "That looks like peanut butter and jelly toast," he said.

"That's right," Diane replied. "You wouldn't believe this but I went out for a walk this morning in the city, and they have a store there full of everything you could ever want from back home. It's a little expensive, sure, but I found Mason's crunch peanut butter and I even found Mrs. Cooper's grape jelly. How about it?"

"I won't say no," Dax said. "Would you mind getting me a fresh glass of water?"

While his mom was at the sink, Dax pulled the plate toward him on the tray that went over the bed, and he picked up a toasted sandwich. It was exactly as his mom used to make it: two slices of toast pressed tightly together, inside which was a mix of his favorite peanut butter and sweet purple jelly. Along with fresh butter, coated not only on the middle but the outside of the toast, it made for a perfect combination that took Dax back to being ten years old again. He closed his eyes and didn't care that the toast was a little cold from his mom bringing it from the kitchen downstairs. It was heavenly.

He knew that she'd been trying to get him in a better mood but so far her attempts had failed. The sandwich, while delicious, wasn't going to bring him out of his depression, but it certainly wasn't a terrible way to start the day. He polished off both sandwiches and looked regretfully at his empty plate. "I can make you another if you like," Diane said. "There's plenty of stuff left in the kitchen."

"I'd better not," Dax said. "That's the most sugar I've had at once in weeks. I don't want to throw up. But it was great, Mom. Thank you."

He gave her hand a squeeze as she took his plate. He could see the bags under her eyes, knew that she wasn't going through an easy time, either. She'd left behind her own home and family to come and care for him, and even though he insisted on sending her home first-class, she wouldn't leave. It made him want to get better faster, or at least well enough that he could leave the hospital.

The arrangements to fly him home were coming together. It made sense for him to be treated in a hospital in New York, for several reasons. He had an apartment there, and his manager, Grant, lived a few blocks away from it, so his business affairs could be handled effectively. His apartment, Kelly said, could easily be remodeled so he could get himself around in a chair, and later, handrails would better aid him in his walking. Dax didn't like to think about wheeling himself around the apartment, but said nothing.

New York made even more sense when he thought about how his mom could keep an eye on him. From her home in Connecticut, it wasn't a long drive into the city, even if she refused the car he offered her and insisted she drive her old sedan herself. He'd be near the rest of his family, who could come and visit him. He'd even be close to his dad, even if he still wasn't quite ready to talk with him yet.

It meant being away from the sunshine and glamour of California, but the more Dax thought about it, the more he was relieved. There had always been something about Los Angeles that had seemed unreal to him, disingenuous. While he'd built up a circle of friends, he noticed that many of them had been strangely silent since his accident, even though they'd long known about his sexuality.

He'd be going back to New York as a gay man, a shamed pop star who was no longer marketable to the teenage girls who'd supplemented his fortune. While there would always be progressive families who didn't care about his sexuality when it came to his music, he knew there would be mothers and fathers all over the world, ripping down his poster from their daughter's walls, and insisting that they find a new idol.

While this particularly depressing thought played on his mind, Dax heard the door open and turned his neck. He was pleasantly surprised by what he saw. In walked Doctor Pravenda, and behind her came a tall, slim man with curly red hair and the greenest eyes Dax had ever seen. He was breathtakingly beautiful. He didn't dare show it, though, and wanted to kick himself for being laid up in bed with a tube coming out from under the sheets, depositing his urine into a plastic bag.

The man stood at the foot of his bed and smiled at him with a friendly grin. Dax gave a small nod of his head, and looked to Doctor Pravenda for an introduction. It wasn't the first time he'd seen a new specialist, another doctor, a nurse he didn't yet know. But none of the team had so far been anywhere near as hot as this guy. Dax found himself scanning over the man's body. He was wearing a white t-shirt and blue training pants, and his arms were full of freckles. There were freckles over his face, too, which was bright and friendly. His arms were behind his back, so Dax couldn't see if the guy was wearing a wedding ring.

"Mr. Monroe, this is Cameron Wilson," said Doctor Pravenda. "He's your new physical therapist."

Cameron Wilson waved with his right hand, and his left was still behind his back. "Hi there," he said. He had a strange accent, one that Dax couldn't place with only the two short words of introduction.

"Hey," Dax replied. If the situation was different; if Dax had been in a bar, or even a store, or anywhere else than a hospital in which he'd lain on his back for weeks, he'd have flashed the guy his hottest smile and tried to gauge the reaction. Dax had become a master at working out the gay guys from the straight ones. With the two words Cameron Wilson had spoken, nothing was given away.

He looked at the doctor. "I have a physical therapist," he said, and he knew he sounded a little rude.

Doctor Pravenda raised an eyebrow skeptically. "Yes, but I'd like you to actually engage with Cameron," she said. "He's come from a hospital on the other side of London, and we've specifically requested him because he's an expert in back injury, and has as much determination as I do to have you walking again."

There were very few people Dax would let speak to him so sharply. Yet another of the endless perks of fame for Dax was that if there was someone he didn't like, didn't get a good vibe from, or who spoke to him in any manner he didn't care for, he could dismiss them without a thought and was never forced to suffer interaction with them again. On the other hand, there were certain people who never minced their words, who gave it to him straight, and who he always listened to. One of these people was, of course, his mother, and another was Rocky, his bodyguard. To his mom, he'd always be a little boy who needed keeping in line and feeding. To Rocky, he was a precious vessel who must be protected at all costs, and it made sense for Dax to follow every command from the man who'd been charged with his very life.

But, during his time in the hospital, he'd become more and more used to being chastened by Doctor Pravenda. He appreciated that she didn't sugar-coat anything, never lied to him or gave him false hope, and always insisted he understand everything she explained to him. At the same time, she often berated him for his rudeness, was quick to offer a sarcastic quip on the days he felt particularly cranky, and simply had no time for anyone who wasn't there to look after Dax's health.

It meant that Dax listened to her. He'd come to trust that she knew what was best for him, and he knew what she meant when she talked about engaging with the therapist. Three of them had come and gone, unable to touch a patient who refused to give consent and barked at them to fuck off when they attempted to explain how important it was for him to do his exercises. If she'd called for a guy from across the city, it was clear she meant business.

Dax was silent. He allowed Doctor Pravenda to explain that Cameron Wilson was going to begin a whole new regime of exercises, and that these were going to be tailored directly to his care plan and his needs. Dax listened, ensuring he kept his eyes on the doctor at all times, no matter how much they wanted to stray over to the therapist's face. "So, I'm going to leave you two together for your first session," Doctor Pravenda said. "If he leaves this room in the next thirty minutes, I'm going to cut off your internet."

She gave a devilish smile and Dax couldn't help but grin. She left the room, and Diane went, too, and Dax was alone with the beautiful stranger.

Chapter Thirteen

"Is Dax your real name?"

The lilt in his voice was much easier to place this time. He was either Scottish or Irish, Dax thought. He tried to remember on which of his tour dates he'd heard that voice the most. Was it in Edinburgh or Dublin?

"It's Darren," said Dax. "But I always hated it, and when I got discovered at eighteen and they wanted to change it, then I was only too happy to let them. I've been Dax for so long it's how I know myself."

"Right," said Cameron. "So, I'll call you Dax, and you call me Cameron. Okay?"

"Sure," said Dax. "I've told Doctor Pravenda to call me Dax so many times I've lost count, but she won't."

"Consummate professional, that one," said Cameron, and he grinned. Dax's mouth was dry, and he reached for a glass of water, but his fingers trembled, and he knocked over the glass, soaking his bed sheets.

He blushed as Cameron grabbed some paper towels from the dispenser and mopped up the water from his chest. "Sorry," he said. "Sometimes my fingers shake, and I don't know why."

"I read that in your notes," Cameron replied, tossing the paper towels into the trash. "It's one of the things we're going to work on fixing. Sometimes spinal injuries manifest themselves in strange ways, and you might find one day you have feeling down one leg, and the next it's gone. One day your fingers shake, and the day after that, they're right as rain."

"Right," said Dax. "No two days seem to be the same at the moment."

"Let's start with your hands." Cameron came beside him and asked him to stretch out his good arm. Dax did so, and as he held it out, he wasn't sure if the tremor in his fingers was from the injury or from nerves. Close-up, Cameron Wilson was even more beautiful. He had a light red stubble over his cheeks, and Dax was certain that underneath that t-shirt, he sported red hair over his chest. Maybe more freckles, like the ones that ran down his arms.

"What about the other hand?" Cameron asked. "Can you flex those fingers?"

"They've told me to move them," Dax said, "but it hurts."

"I know. It will." Cameron brushed his fingers over Dax's, as they stuck out of the plaster cast. "Can you feel me touching you?"

"Yes," Dax said. He could most certainly feel Cameron touching his fingers.

"They're curled up pretty tightly. Can you straighten them out for me?"

Dax tried, but it was too painful. Weeks of keeping his fingers tensed into a fist, from both his injury and the tension that hadn't left him since he got the news that his career was in ruins, had left them sore and seemingly immovable. Cameron took his hand gently and went through a series of tests. He tapped here and there, testing the feeling in Dax's hand, careful to stay away from the area of the break in his arm.

Although the last thing he wanted to do was cause himself pain, Dax knew it was going to be necessary in order to get his body working again. While he was desperate to get back to full fitness, just the thought of the weeks and months of therapy made him exhausted. Cameron tried to get him to move between making a fist and flexing his fingers, but after a few movements, Dax sullenly pulled his arm away. "It's too fucking painful," he said, gruffly.

"I know," Cameron said. He moved away from his arm and went down to his legs. "Let's make a start on these. This is where we have to do the most work."

He took out the patient notes at the bottom of Dax's bed and read through them. Dax watched as he did so. He felt ashamed and pathetic to be in the presence of such a hot guy and be so disabled, and so weak. Cameron was silent as he read. Then he placed the clipboard back into the slot and looked up. He smiled. "Now, let's get to the real work," he said, and before Dax could stop him, he tugged the blanket away.

Dax was shocked. He felt the breeze of the blanket leaving his body, and Cameron tossed it onto the floor. He moved the extendable tray that moved across in front of Dax's chest, clearing it out of the way completely, so that Dax lay on the bed, nothing covering him but the hospital gown he'd worn since his accident. He felt very exposed, with Cameron looking at him intently from his face down to his toes, examining every inch.

He frowned. "What are you doing?" he asked. "I'm not sure I'm comfortable. I'd like my blanket back."

"No more blankets," said Cameron. "Not when we have a session. It's not cold in here, and it's important your limbs remain uncovered at all times."

"Why?" Dax asked, rudely. He didn't care how good looking this guy was. Nobody ever told him whether he could or couldn't have something. He was Dax Monroe. Millionaire superstar. Worshipped by everyone.

But Cameron Wilson seemed to have absolutely no interest in Dax's prestige and he hadn't given any interest since entering the room that he even knew who Dax was. He continued to stare at Dax's body, and he appeared to be chewing on the inside of his lip, before he took out the patient notes once again and consulted them. Finally, he took a deep breath and smiled. "I think you need another x-ray," he said. "Either that, or a scan. I think we're missing something. It appears that your left leg is a little shorter than your right. That wouldn't happen simply as a result of lumbar fractures. I think you've got a small fracture in your pelvis."

"You can tell all that by looking at me lying down?" Dax was doubtful.

"Want to make a bet?"

"I'm sorry?"

"Ten pounds says you've got a fracture in your pelvis."

"I've had so many x-rays I've lost count," said Dax. "And I've had as many scans as I have x-rays. If I had another fracture, they'd have found it by now."

"Does that mean you'll take the bet?"

Dax sighed. "Sure. If it humors you."

"It does," said Cameron. He took out his cell phone, found what he was looking for and held it to his ear. Within seconds, he was put through to the radiology department, and just ten minutes later, Dax was lying once again under an x-ray machine. Cameron stood behind the screen with the radiologist, and they were talking to each other as Cameron pointed to his own hip, indicating where he wanted the clearest picture possible.

Back in his room, Doctor Pravenda joined them, and she and the physical therapist stood looking at a tablet in front of them on a stand. They zoomed in and out at the black and white shot of Dax's pelvis, until Cameron's finger suddenly flew up and pointed at something. "There," he said. "That's it."

"That?" Doctor Pravenda narrowed her eyes and zoomed in even closer, and then she raised an eyebrow. "It looks like a tiny fracture, but it's healed."

"I don't think it's from Dax's latest injury," Cameron said. "I think it's an old one. It's been there a while but I think it's what's causing the leg shortening. We're talking millimeters, but it makes all the difference."

"How old do you think it might be?" the doctor asked, and Dax watched them, becoming more and more irritated that they appeared to be talking about him as though he weren't even in the room.

"I fell off my bike when I was thirteen," he said in a low voice. Doctor Pravenda and Cameron turned to him. Cameron came over to the bed.

"Did you hit your pelvis?"

"All I know is that the pain was so bad, I didn't even register it as pain," Dax said. "It was like someone had kicked me so hard up the ass I couldn't breathe. I limped home and didn't even care that I'd left my bike on the street. My friend brought it home for me. I just needed to lie down. It hurt for days but nobody ever said anything about going to the hospital.

I just got out of sports for a few weeks."

"Sounds like that's it," Cameron said. He held out his hand to Dax. Confused, Dax shook it and Cameron laughed. "No, you don't get away with it that easily, Mister."

"I don't know what you're talking about," Dax said.

"Ten pounds," said Cameron. "Cough it up."

"The injury's nearly twenty years old," Dax protested. "It's nothing to do with my injury now. It's healed, and it doesn't count."

Cameron folded his arms. "I don't believe we ever established that the injury had to be from the car accident," he said. "I said there'd be a fracture there. I was right. I won the bet."

Dax looked at Doctor Pravenda. "Is this how you treat your staff here?" he asked. "Making money from my injuries?"

Doctor Pravenda held up her hands. "I'm staying out of this," she said. But she looked at Cameron. "Maybe you let him off the bet this time, Mister Wilson?"

Cameron shrugged. "I guess I can let this one go," he said, and Dax was bewildered. He couldn't tell if the guy was being serious. He certainly looked like he was, but he knew that British people were known for their dry sense of humor. Maybe this was simply an example of it. Either way, he was uncomfortable. He wanted to speak to Doctor Pravenda alone, but Cameron was too quick for him. He thanked the doctor for coming in, and asked that she leave them alone. To Dax's amazement, the doctor left immediately with little more than a wave and a smile.

Then, they were all alone once more.

Dax wanted to tell his new physical therapist to get out and never come back, but before he could, Cameron lifted his notes once more and wrote something down on them with a pen he brought from his pocket. As he did so, he talked to Dax. "For us to work together, I have to know the exact state of your body," he explained. "While an injury from twenty years ago might not seem important, everything that affects your posture, your spine alignment, the positioning of your back... it all makes a difference to how you'll recover. It'll impact the time of recovery, the exercises you do, and the optimum physical shape you can get back to."

Taking in every word, Dax said nothing. He felt a little chastened. Maybe the guy knew what he was talking about, after all. He just had a strange way of going about his work. He decided to take a deep breath and try to trust him.

As though reading his mind, Cameron smiled, and the smile seemed warm, and genuine. "I know what I'm doing," he said. "Trust me."

In the meantime, he left Dax with his number. It was a strange-looking thing, a mix of numbers in odd places. He was used to the standard cell-phone number arrangement of the USA. But this was different. Zeroes, and sevens. He punched the number into his cell and saved it under *Physical Terrorist.*

Chapter Fourteen

The next few days passed in a slow haze of hellish pain. Dax no longer saw Cameron Wilson as a hot guy he could fantasize over in times of quiet solitude, but as a someone he loathed; a torturer, a devil. Every day, he turned up at ten o'clock on the dot, and he put Dax through a grueling regime of exercises and movements that often left Dax sobbing, and begging for mercy.

But after a few days, Dax found that the mobility in the fingers of his right hand had returned almost to normal. He was able to make a fist and flex his fingers with ease, and they no longer hurt. Although his arm was still in a cast, it was out of the sling, and he could move it up and down, even above his head, although the weight of the bulky plaster meant that he couldn't hold it up for long.

The most important change had come in that he could now sit up in bed and had even begun to transfer his weight from the bed to a wheelchair. The relief at being able to take himself to the bathroom and finally rid himself of the catheter was priceless, and the first time he sat up on his own on the toilet, Dax wept. He couldn't believe he'd enjoy peeing while sitting down so much, but it was the first time he'd been able to attend to his own bodily functions without people helping him, for weeks.

By the first of April, he was moving from the bed to the chair with surprising ease, and while he was still in a great deal of pain, he was able to use his left arm to push the wheels to move the chair to the bathroom and back. Kelly offered to push him, but he was determined to do it himself.

His manager, Grant, had taken a room in a hotel

in the city, and became a regular fixture at the hospital. At the end of March, Diane Monroe returned to the States, and Dax promised to follow her soon. Grant was keen on the idea, too, and for what seemed like the hundredth time, he came into the room one morning, as Cameron had Dax's leg bent at the knee while Dax lay on his side, gritting his teeth against the pain.

"I've got a plane booked for tomorrow evening," he said, with no regard for the therapy session being conducted. Cameron ignored Grant, as he always did, and Dax tried to concentrate on his exercise, giving the smallest nod to Grant.

His manager had been a presence since the very beginning of Dax's career. Since he was signed to the TerrorCorp Records label at eighteen, he'd been beholden to almost everything Grant Beaumont requested. And since the accident, Grant had lost more money than he dared to think about as a result of Dax's disappearance from public life and the silence from the singer's camp while rumors continued to circulate about his sexuality.

While the tabloids had taken Dax Monroe off their front pages, they still dedicated several column inches every day to his progress, or lack of it. In some of them, Dax was paralyzed for life and only able to breathe with the help of a ventilator. In others, he was already dead, and that's why his mom had returned to the USA but had steadfastly refused to give any interviews. In still others, he was alive and well and back in the States, living as a hermit in New York because he feared for his life.

Grant was keen to get him back under his control, that was for sure. He butted heads with Doctor Pravenda and Cameron daily when he first arrived, and they shooed him out of the room to talk to Dax alone. It didn't matter that Grant had owned Dax for fifteen years. In the hospital, he had no power, they said. But on the first of April, when Grant showed himself into the room and interrupted the session, he knew he could get away with it, as Doctor Pravenda was away at a seminar.

"Did you hear me?" he asked Dax, who moved his leg up once more to his chest with gritted teeth, before moving it back down and looking at Cameron.

"Can you give us a second?" he asked. Cameron was clearly unhappy about the interruption to the session, but with a small nod of his head, he stepped back. Dax looked at Grant. "What? You've booked a flight? Okay, great. You don't need to tell me. I'm hardly going anywhere."

"But you are," said Grant. "It's not just a flight for me. It's for us. You, me, Kelly and whoever else is still here in this fucking freezing place. It's all settled. I've managed to pull some strings, and we're taking a private jet to New York tomorrow evening."

Dax frowned. "I don't feel ready to quit in the middle of my therapy," he said. He looked at Cameron, who remained silent. He could see a twitching in his jaw, as though the therapist was grinding his teeth, but still he said nothing.

"Therapy's therapy. Jesus, it's not like the therapists in the UK could possibly be better than anyone back in the States." He looked up at Cameron. "No offense."

Cameron didn't react.

Dax stared down at the floor. He'd spent so many days and weeks flat on his back, that finally as he was beginning to make progress and was moving with more confidence, he didn't want to break his stride. "I don't feel ready to go back yet," he said to Grant. "Cancel the plane."

Grant made a sound that seemed to be a combination of a laugh and groan. "Are you fucking kidding me?" he asked. "We're talking a half a million dollar arrangement I just made. The flight's booked, the hospital in New York's getting your room ready and the press have been alerted."

"I'm not fucking kidding you," Dax said, and with gritted teeth he pushed himself up into a sitting position. Cameron was behind him quickly, supporting his back without speaking. "If I tell you I'm not ready to go back, then that's that. Cancel the plane. Cancel the hospital. I'll leave when I'm ready."

But Grant Beaumont wasn't a man about to back down. He looked at Cameron. "Get out of here," he said. Cameron didn't move, but Dax gave him a reluctant nod, so the physical therapist slowly walked around the bed, picked up his jacket, and left the room.

Dax sighed and shook his head. "You can't just tell me when I'm ready to leave, Grant," he said.

"Oh, I fucking can," Grant spat. "Do you know how many days I've spent in this God-forsaken place, ignoring other clients so I can be with you? Getting rid of reporter after reporter who wants the first interview with Dax Monroe after coming out of the hospital? Do you realize how much your value sinks every day you're not out there, getting better and denying the fucking fag rumors?"

This stung like a slap across the face, so much that Dax winced. He looked up at Grant. "No, I don't know how much my value sinks," he said. "Tell me,

Grant. What am I worth to you now?"

"A lot less than you were six weeks ago," Grant said. "Before your addiction to cock ruined both of our lives."

Taking a deep breath, Dax felt every muscle in his body tense. The pain that never really went away now pounded away at his body with louder screams than ever, and he rubbed his eyes. "So, what happens when we go back?" he asked, softly. "I learn to walk again and pick up where we left before?"

"Pfft," Grant said, rudely. "If we're fucking lucky. We need to do a shit-ton of damage control, and none of it is getting done while we're sitting on our asses in England. We need to get you back to being photographed. Get Alicia back in the picture. Hell, get Cara back in the picture. I don't care if she costs us ten grand a day in coke and vodka. Anything to get you seen with a pair of tits again. Resurrect this fucking shitty career of yours."

His face was red, and Dax could see a white line on his neck, where the vein underneath the surface was straining so hard he was sure it was about to burst. He knew Grant was right, despite the somewhat unsavory way he was serving the truth. He needed to go back. A therapist was a therapist, right? He'd find someone else in New York, someone just as good as Cameron Wilson, someone who would be able to pick up where Cameron left off.

But Dax didn't want to leave. He didn't want to go back to cameras flashing in his face. He didn't want to return to a life of hanging out of the backs of cabs with women in heels and fur. He didn't want to croon to thousands of screaming girls and pretend to be bashful when red-carpet reporters insisted he tell them when he and Alicia were finally going to settle down and get married.

He had no choice. He was signed to a label, and he had responsibilities that had been put off for long enough. If he were ever going to have a chance at a career again, he was going to do exactly as Grant ordered. With regret that he was unlikely to speak to Doctor Pravenda again, he managed a small nod. "All right," he said. "I get it. We'll go home."

Grant exhaled with relief. "Good job," he said, patting Dax's knee awkwardly, knowing that a hearty clap on the back probably wouldn't be too well received. "I'll go get Kelly and get everything moving. I might send her back tonight to get a head start. Maybe I'll call my security guys in LA and get them to come over and give us a hand. I wonder if it's too short notice..."

Muttering under his breath, the red-faced, fifty year old left the room, and Dax moved slowly back against the pillows on the bed. Seconds later, Cameron came in, and he took one look at Dax's defeated face and shook his head. "Don't tell me you've agreed," he said. "Please, for the love of God, don't tell me that."

Chapter Fifteen

"I didn't have a choice."

Dax watched as Cameron gripped the end of the bed and put his head down. He watched as the soft, floppy curls of Cameron's red hair fell forward and dangled over the sheets. He knew that Cameron was trying not to get mad. "I'm sorry," he said. "I know it feels like I don't appreciate the work you've put in for me."

The therapist lifted his head. "What are you talking about?" he asked. "I couldn't give a shit what you thought of me."

Dax had known from the very beginning of his treatment with Cameron that the no-nonsense Scot wasn't the type to mince words. Perhaps it stemmed from his ancestors, the ones who pounded the freezing cold moors in the highlands of Scotland, wearing little more than scratchy woolen kilts with no underwear underneath. Perhaps it came from the generations of whisky-drinkers and haggis eaters who had descended from Vikings who came from the North. Whatever the reason, Dax had known since the beginning that Cameron Wilson was the kind of no-nonsense person who'd be allowed to say what they thought in his presence.

There were very few people Dax allowed to talk to him with direct, brutal honesty, no matter how much he may not have wanted to hear what it was they had to say. The first was, of course, his mother, but Diane Monroe had a soft tongue by nature, and wasn't the type of woman to ever want to hurt her son's feelings, so her honesty was always tempered with sweetness, and reassurances that she wanted the best for him at all times.

Then there was Grant. Dax simultaneously hated and respected the man but however he felt about him, he had little choice but to shut up and listen when Grant talked. As his manager, he controlled the bookings, the money, the deals, the press. He'd done a good job up to now, that much was indisputable. He'd made Dax a multi-millionaire and had him touring the world, playing at the biggest venues to sell-out crowds. While he hated the way the red-faced man sneered at him, and spoke with such venom with regard to his sexuality, he couldn't imagine that anyone else could have brought him greater career success.

Kelly, his assistant, was good at delivering the truth, but like his mom, she wrapped everything up in rolls of optimism and pleasantries. She may have reminded him that he needed to get painful shots for his Malaysia tour, but she always said 'please' and 'thank you' when getting him in the car to go to the doctor. He knew how much she hated the way he drank so heavily after shows, but she never once would have dared to stop him. Grant, of course, would have grabbed the bar and thrown it out of the window if he'd have been present.

When it came to Doctor Pravenda, Dax had nothing but the highest regard and like for his primary caregiver. She was gentle but firm, honest but never hurtful. Whatever she asked him to do, he'd do it. She was the one who'd pried the flask of vodka Kelly had procured for him out of his hands and clearly instructed him that while he was in her care, he wasn't to have a single drop of alcohol, and Dax had simply nodded, and remained sober since.

And then, finally, there was Cameron. Although Dax wanted to lash out and punch him in the face because of the rigorous exercises he was putting the star through, the kind that left him in sheer agony, weeping in his wheelchair, he knew that Cameron wanted nothing more than for him to be healed. He knew that his sharp instructions and brutal honesty, while hurtful in more ways than one, were for his own good, and there was little doubt that since Cameron's arrival, his recovery had increased by leaps and bounds.

It meant that when Cameron uttered that he "couldn't give a shit" about what Dax thought of him, Dax was confused. Over the weeks they'd worked together, Dax had come to rely on Cameron of literally being the one to hold him up. He had to trust a man who held his body in his hands so that he wouldn't fall down. And now, it seemed, Cameron hadn't cared about any of it.

Dax put this to the therapist, but this seemed to frustrate Cameron further. "You don't get it, do you?" Cameron asked, and Dax noticed that when he became angry, his accent became stronger. "I'm not here for me. What you think of me is irrelevant to me. My job is to get you healthy, and the one thing you haven't grasped yet is that it's just as much about your mental well-being as it is your physical health."

He walked to Dax's side, and looked down at him. "When I first saw you, you were flat on your back, kind of like you are now," he said. "Everyone was telling you you'd walk again, but you believed that they were only saying that to make you feel better. You had all these hours to think about how much you'd fucked up your life, and you were happy to believe it."

Dax said nothing. He looked at Cameron as the redheaded man stood with his arms folded. "It's not that you'd given up the fight. You hadn't even begun it. And then when we started working together, I saw something change in you, and believe me, I was thrilled to see it. You want to walk. You want to run. You want to show everyone that you can do exactly the kind of thing that they didn't really believe you *could* do. And I'm not just talking about being able to walk again. I'm talking about being able to live the kind of life that *you* want. The life that isn't governed by album sales or numbers of asses in seats at your concerts."

He paused, and Dax frowned. "What's your point?"

"My point is, that you were on your way to becoming the person you'd always wanted to be," Cameron said, his voice softer now. "You were fighting, and it wasn't just for your legs. It was for your life. And then, just as I thought that fire was getting even hotter, in comes Mr. Beetroot-face to piss all over your bonfire and send you right back to the beginning."

"He's my manager," Dax said. "What am I supposed to do?"

"You're getting over an injury that you may never have recovered from," Cameron said. "You're starting to walk again after suffering the kind of knock that would put even the strongest man flat on his back for the rest of his miserable life. And now you're throwing it all away again because your manager's told you to."

"No, I'm not," Dax protested, and in his anger, he leaned on his elbows and grabbed the rail above his head, pulling himself into a sitting position. "I'm not going back to the States to lie down and be paralyzed all over again. I'm going to continue my therapy, and I'm going to walk—"

"Straight into a club with a hot woman again," Cameron countered, shaking his head. "Straight into the little box they've made for you. Straight into the fake excuse for an existence you call a life."

"And your answer's what?" Dax demanded, holding out his hands in frustration. "You seem to have all the solutions, God dammit. What's the answer? Tell me!"

Cameron placed a hand on his chest, calming him down, and spoke in a low voice. "This is the answer," he said. "This fire in your heart. Getting mad. Getting so mad you're practically standing up to tell me to go fuck myself. Look at you."

And he was right. He still held onto the rail, but Dax had swung his feet around, and his legs were dangling off the bed, his toes grazing the floor. He was so angry he'd barely noticed that he'd tried to stand up to argue with Cameron. He relaxed his grip on the rail, and swallowed, breathing heavily.

"Stop giving up," Cameron said.

"You make it sound so easy," Dax sighed.

"I'll tell you what'll happen if you get on that plane tonight," Cameron went on. "You'll get back to America, and you'll be in a hospital with some of the best doctors in the world. You'll be eating the best food, and you'll have better TV shows to watch too, I'll bet. But you'll also have the media tearing you apart. You'll have Grant the puppet-master pulling the strings and you'll have to dance. You'll be giving interviews where you'll lie through your teeth about how much you love whichever woman you've been put with that week, because Grant's going to be standing behind you, moving your mouth for you, writing the script. You won't live. You'll exist. And without the fire I've just seen, you might walk, but you'll never run."

It was a speech Dax wasn't sure would ever end, but the more Cameron spoke, the more he made sense. Dax knew he was right. He knew that within weeks, he'd be back in his apartment, on pain medication washed down with alcohol, not wanting to do his exercises; wanting only to hide from the world, and from himself.

He looked up at Cameron. "Please tell me there's a point to this," he said. "Tell me this is going somewhere."

Cameron grinned. "I've got a great offer for you," he said. "And you've got one chance to take it."

Chapter Sixteen

When Cameron outlined the plan, Dax wasn't sure he could believe his ears. But it seemed the therapist wasn't joking at all.

"I suggest that you let the plane fly tonight," he said. "Let it go as arranged, and on that plane, there'll be Grant, your assistant, and everyone else attached to your career. Only, you won't be on it."

"And where do you suggest I go?" Dax asked.

"With me," said Cameron, shortly. "I have a place up in Scotland. In Invergordon. It's twenty-three miles north of Inverness."

Dax was confused. "Why on earth would I want to go up there?" he asked. "I don't get it."

"Because it'll mean a total break from the world. The whole world. Your physical heath is good enough that you don't need to be linked up to any machines. You're eating and drinking, going to the bathroom, all by yourself. The only thing we need to fix is your strength. And like I was just saying, you can't fix what's down there until you've fixed what's up here."

He tapped his head. Dax's head was abuzz with possibilities. *A total break from the world.* He hadn't realized until now that was exactly what he wanted. It was simultaneously thrilling and terrifying, but a slow smile began to creep on his face, then it disappeared again. "I can't," he said, looking down. "It sounds great, but there's no way I can go anywhere else but on that plane to New York tonight."

Cameron perched on the edge of his bed and looked at Dax with his piercing green eyes. Dax tried hard to ignore how beautiful the man was, and how he'd suddenly become even more beautiful because of the way he seemed so genuinely interested in Dax's welfare. Perhaps it was the way he entrusted his entire body weight to the man who promised not to let him fall when he was doing his exercises, or perhaps it was simply the way he spoke to Dax with more honesty than he was used to. Whatever the reason, Dax knew only that he trusted him.

"This isn't just about your injury," Cameron said. "It's about choosing what you really want from life. And you can't evaluate things when your head is crazy with everyone wanting a piece of you. I'm talking about silence. Quiet. Green hills and no traffic. Nobody wanting your autograph, or asking you to pose for a picture. Just healthy exercise. Concentration on getting well, and healing your head as well as your back."

"But how will I move around?" Dax asked. "I mean, even if I thought about it as a possibility, which it isn't, then how would I even live up there on my own?"

With that, Cameron gave a nervous smile and ran a hand through his hair. "Well, I wasn't planning on you being on your own," he said. "I'm talking about taking you up there and staying with you. Giving you one-on-one exclusive therapy. I can take a break from work here, and we can call Doctor Pravenda and see what she says, but I can't see how she'd think it was a bad idea."

"Doesn't this cross some kind of patient and therapist boundary?" Dax asked, only half-teasingly.

"I guess it might," Cameron admitted, "but you're being discharged tonight, aren't you? Once you leave this place you're no longer under the hospital and you're not in the care of any of its employees.

That's the official line. And we can go down an official line, with solicitors, and courts, and all that kind of thing, or you can simply say you're taking some time off with a friend, and we leave it at that."

He grinned again. "It's a little like bending the rules, but don't you like doing that?"

Dax took a deep breath. It all seemed too good to be true, but the more he thought about it, the more it made perfect sense. "I'm not saying yes," he said, slowly, "but let's call Doctor Pravenda and ask her what she thinks."

From her seminar in Cardiff, the doctor Dax had trusted to take care of him for the past two months was silent for a few moments. Cameron stayed perched on the end of Dax's bed, holding the cell phone out in front of him with the doctor on speaker. "I can't believe this is happening while I'm hundreds of miles away," Doctor Pravenda said. "Why couldn't they have had this conversation in a few days' time, when I'm back at work?"

"I think you've just answered your own question, Manju," Cameron replied, and it was the first time that Dax had heard her first name being used. "They've seized the opportunity because they knew that you'd be able to talk Dax out of it. I don't think the title of "physiotherapist" holds the same weight that "doctor" does."

With one hand holding the phone, Cameron punctuated the air with quotation marks with the other. Doctor Pravenda was agonizingly silent for several moments, but Dax knew from the faint noise in the background that she was still there. "I don't know that Mister Monroe has a choice in the matter, really," she said, finally. "It's certainly unorthodox, and we haven't even begun to discuss how it's going to affect the rest of your patients here, Mister Wilson, but I made a promise that we'd have our young singer walking again and I don't believe that we'd be giving him the best care that we can by releasing him to the wolves."

To hear the doctor refer to his team as wolves made Dax realize that to those on the outside looking in, it was clear that he was being held captive by a situation that he needed emancipating from, and there were two people who desperately wanted to be the ones to free him.

"He'll have to sign discharge papers," Doctor Pravenda continued, but now the two men in London could almost hear the cogs of her brain turning as the plan was beginning to take shape. "He'll have to have the correct transport, with all the medication he needs, and the understanding that if anything changes, or if there are any issues with his health, then he'll immediately be brought back to the hospital."

She took a deep breath, and exhaled slowly, so it sounded like a loud gust of wind down the phone's speaker. "It's a hell of a risk," she said. "It's one of the strangest decisions of my career, but I certainly understand where you're coming from, and I'm not sure that it's a chance Mister Monroe is ever going to get again without a great deal of difficulty."

Cameron looked at Dax with a *see what I mean?* expression on his face, and Dax shrugged in acquiescence. "I think if we get the paperwork sorted and you can push things with the hospital's legal team, then we can get this done tonight," Cameron said. "We need to move fast, and we need to keep it from his team until the last second."

"Do it," Doctor Pravenda said. "I'm going with my gut, and I'll speak to the legal team now. They'll come and visit you, Mister Monroe, so if at any point you're not happy with the plan, tell them. You're under no obligation whatsoever."

"I know," said Dax. "I'm not sure it's the best idea, and to tell you the truth, Ma'am, I'm pretty fucking terrified, but I think Cameron's right. I think I need to get away, and I can't do it without his help."

They ended the call, and after that, there was a flurry of activity. Unfortunately, they weren't able to keep the plan from Grant for longer than five minutes, because Dax hit on a snag they knew they'd never get away with. "He'll have called every available member of the press," he said. "Both here and in America. They'll be expecting Dax Monroe to get on the plane in London, and they'll be expecting Dax Monroe to get off the plane in New York."

"Right," said Cameron, rubbing his chin. "While Doctor Pravenda deals with the legal team, we need to deal with *your* team. What usually happens when you want the press to think you're someplace you're not? Do you ever use a body double?"

"Yes," Dax replied. "There have been plenty of times I've gone out in the back of a delivery truck to get ice-cream when my double lies by the pool so that the paparazzi we know are on the roof of the house half a mile away still see Dax Monroe in his house, getting a good tan."

"Well, it's either that, or we stick pillows on the bed and put a wig on a balloon," Cameron laughed. "I think we need to face the music and talk to Kelly. She'll tell Grant, but from what I've seen of the girl, she really likes you."

While this was true, Dax's long-suffering assistant was horrified by the idea. She threw up all manner of scenarios that may occur on the trip up to Scotland. They could crash the car. They could get stuck in snow and freeze to death. Dax could get an infection and it'd be too late before they got to a hospital. The press could find out where they were anyway and still make his life a misery. There could be a crazed stalker who discovered his idol's location and set out on a trip of their own to Invergordon and without any kind of protection and no bodyguard, then how could he expect to survive?

Cameron answered each of Kelly's questions calmly. There was only about as much chance of the car crashing as there was the plane or the helicopter from the airport to New York crashing, and as for the snow, it was the beginning of April, and there was every chance all the snow near Invergordon would have thawed enough for them to travel up there safely. And yes, Cameron admitted, there was always the risk of the press discovering where they were, but wasn't that always the case?

"There are only a handful of people who'll know where Dax is," Cameron reminded her. "If the press find out, then the leak must have come from inside, which further reinforces the need for Dax to be away from people he can't trust."

Kelly glowered. "I think that's pretty damn rude of you, Mister Wilson," she said. "Dax *can* trust me. And he knows it. I'd never do anything to risk his welfare, and if the press ever finds out where he is, it's never come from me. Never."

"I'm sorry if you think I'm accusing you," Cameron said, calmly. "I can see that you care for Dax. But Dax doesn't care enough for himself to be able to make the decisions he needs to be happy."

"And what makes you so sure that you know what's best for him?" Kelly asked. "Sure, Grant's a pain in the ass. He's a control freak. But it looks to me that you're trying to control Dax, too, at least from where I'm standing."

From his bed, Dax reached out and touched Kelly's arm. "It's my decision," he said, softly. "I trust you, Kelly, I really do. And I wish you were coming with me. But Cameron's right. If I go back to New York, this is never going to end. I'm never going to make another decision for myself. Every step I've taken for the last fifteen years has been watched by someone. Decided by someone. I haven't even been able to go to the grocery store without hundreds of cameras flashing in my face. I can't take it anymore. I need solitude, and time to recover. It's drastic, but it's necessary."

"I need to know exactly where you're going," Kelly said, and Dax was sure he caught the flash of a tear in her eye. I need to know the address of this house, and Rocky needs to come with you and stay as a bodyguard, at the very least."

"No," said Dax, firmly. "If you know, and Rocky knows, then it'll only be a matter of time before Grant knows, and everyone else will find out, too. Then I might as well be in New York. I'll call you in a couple of weeks, to let you know I'm safe. But anything other than that won't work."

"I need to go get Grant," said Kelly. "I can't do anything unless he gives me the go-ahead on the body double."

When his manager appeared minutes later, Dax had never seen his face so red.

Chapter Seventeen

"Not a fucking chance."

The four words Dax had been expecting to hear ever since he knew Grant was going to have to be informed of their plan. For one glorious second, he thought about how funny it would be if they didn't let Grant in on the secret at all and got a lookalike to make the journey instead, only for him to find out at the other end, by which time it would be too late. But Dax knew that they would never get away with it, because his hawk-eyed manager would insist on practically holding his hand the whole journey, never once letting him out of his sight.

He also knew that Kelly wasn't going to keep her job very long if Grant knew she was in on the conspiracy, and so it was no surprise to him that once she left the room, she was going to return with a fully-informed Grant Beaumont.

Grant didn't care what it was that Dax wanted. He made that clear by saying exactly that when Dax protested. "It's not up to you," he spat. "I'm your manager. You're my asset, and we have an agreement that you are legally obliged to uphold."

This much was true, unfortunately. And Dax knew that Grant had a very firm hold on him thanks to the contract he'd signed not just when he was eighteen, but every time Grant felt the need for it to be renewed, usually at times when Dax's popularity reached new heights, and his bank account swelled even further.

But Dax knew that he'd been offered a lifeline with Cameron's plan, and he wasn't going to refuse it. If he had the use of his legs, and was in full health, he would probably have meekly followed Grant onto the plane, beholden to the career choice he made before he was even legally allowed to drink alcohol. However, he wanted recovery more than money. He wanted health more than fame. He wanted happiness more than notoriety.

"I'm leaving with Cameron," he said. "I've been thinking about it more and more since the idea was put to me, and I've decided that it's the best thing for me."

"You don't get to decide the best thing for you," Grant sneered. "That's my job."

"It *was* your job," Dax said. "But now, your job is to protect my interests, not exploit me. And it's in your interest to have me fully recovered, or we can part ways right now and you'll never get another cent from me."

"Are you firing me?" Grant asked, his brow knitted into what Dax was sure must be a permanent frown.

As much as he wanted to give him the boot, Dax knew that he still needed his experienced, although abhorrent, manager to take care of things in the USA. He knew that Grant was far too comfortable in the luxurious life Dax Monroe's career afforded him to walk away too, and caught together in the stalemate, manager and client stared at each other. Finally, Grant was the first to break.

"I'll give you two weeks," he said, "to get this shit out of your head and realize you're better off with people who know you. The people who've spent their whole careers making you a superstar."

"Does this mean you'll co-operate with what I want?" Dax asked, sensing that for the first time, he was about to score a victory against the man who'd owned him for the past fifteen years.

"I'll lie for you for two weeks," Grant said. "Like I've lied for you for fifteen years every time a reporter or bitch of a news anchor asked me if you're a faggot. After that, you're on your own. And believe me, I'm not going to go down without a fight."

With that he stormed out of the room, and Dax breathed heavily. He looked at Cameron. "Tell me I've made the right decision."

"You know whether you've made the right decision by how it feels," Cameron replied. "Trust your gut. If you want to leave with Grant, it's fine. I get that you have a lot you have to consider and you've got the kind of life and career I know nothing about. But you've always got your gut. Trust it. Ask yourself what's the one thing you want right now, more than anything?"

Dax answered without question. "Peace."

Cameron raised his eyebrows. "You know, even then, I thought you were going to say that the one thing you wanted was to walk again."

"Believe it or not, I can't walk if I don't have the peace to do it," Dax replied. "That's why I want to leave with you. I need to get away."

"Then that's what we'll do," Cameron replied, and the broad grin on his face made him look so beautiful that Dax had to pick up his phone and pretend he had an important text to answer so as to avoid looking at the man like a tiny puppy looks at its rescuer.

He never would have admitted it to him, but Dax was concerned about being on his own with Cameron more than he was about leaving his career behind. The more time they spent together, the more Dax trusted his therapist, but until now, it had been safe and harmless for Dax to look at the guy and imagine what it would be like to kiss him. After all, Cameron left Dax once their appointment was over, and he went home to his life in London, or to another patient, and probably didn't give Dax a second thought.

It was going to be different when the two of them were living alone in the Highlands. Dax had never visited Scotland for any length of time, arriving there only to play one or two shows in Glasgow, or Edinburgh, and then leaving the next day, not even taking the time to get a coffee or check out the local cuisine. He'd certainly never ventured to the north, where they were going now, but from shows he'd watched, and books he read as a kid, he'd always imagined the Highlands to be wild, desolate, lonely places.

He certainly knew he'd be able to get peace there, but he also knew that it meant a lot of time alone with a gorgeous man. Dax knew it wasn't anything he could do anything about, though. There was nothing he ever got from Cameron that might have given him a clue that his therapist liked guys; Cameron Wilson had only ever been the epitome of professionalism and politeness, save for the moments of brutal honesty he fired at Dax to encourage him to push himself in his recovery.

As the team of lawyers and doctors came together to draw up all the necessary paperwork, Dax continued with his daily exercises in the therapy room. After all, Cameron said, there was nothing more they could do until they got the go-ahead to leave, and there was no need for them to take a break from the work they'd been doing. Dax therefore found himself once more on his back, on a thick mat on the floor, and Cameron kneeling over him, looking at his legs.

"Okay, so the same as we did yesterday," he said. "Lift your left leg slowly, so that your knee bends, and your foot's flat on the floor."

"That can't be easy to say," Dax joked weakly. "Foot flat on the floor?"

Cameron laughed. "Yeah, it's a bit of a tongue-twister, that one. But stop trying to delay the inevitable. Foot flat on the floor, please."

Dax bent his knee, dragging his foot toward his butt slowly. His legs were still weak, the muscles having gone far too long without the sort of everyday use he'd taken for granted since he took his first steps at ten months old. His back ached, but then these days his back always ached, and he closed his eyes and gritted his teeth, trying to think of something to take his mind off the pain while he brought his foot to the right position.

"How can you just drop everything and take me up to Scotland?" he asked, his eyes closed. "Aren't you leaving people behind?"

"I used to be a personal trainer for high-ranking members of the British navy," Cameron said, gently pushing Dax's leg to encourage more movement. "When they'd had an injury, they needed to get back to full fitness before they were able to go back to the sea. So I was often asked to go all over the country at short notice. I'm used to it."

"I bet that was an interesting job," Dax said, wincing.

"It was," Cameron said. "But I wanted to settle

down in a more permanent place, and even though I had the house back home, I'd never be able to support myself in the middle of nowhere so I came down to London and met my friend Lydia, and we live together just outside the city. I'm a freelance physiotherapist, so I work for myself. I'm contracted by the hospital, but I'm not under any real obligation to stay. I have a colleague who might be free to pick up my clients here, and Lydia's a therapist too, even she might be interested."

"Can she afford to keep the place without you there?"

Cameron grinned down at Dax. "With the salary you'll be paying me for private therapy, sure," he said.

"Right," said Dax. "I'll talk to Kelly and she'll take all your details. Remind me when we leave here."

"I know you're good for it," Cameron said. "Now, stop talking and move your right leg."

He was tired, emotionally exhausted as much as anything else, and the last thing he wanted was to do an hour's worth of exercises, but Dax's mind was a little more at ease. Cameron had re-established their professional relationship, and Dax wanted to kick himself for not suggesting they talk about the financial terms of the agreement before that moment. He didn't want anyone to presume he'd receive the therapy for free, but everything was happening so quickly that he'd forgotten to do a pretty vital thing in this arrangement: officially engage Cameron for his services.

For the next hour, he stretched his back carefully, trying to lift his hips a little off the floor. "It's to strengthen your pelvic tilt," Cameron explained. "You'd be amazed how quickly your body forgets what it's supposed to do when there are parts that haven't been used for a while."

Later, as he sat in his chair underneath the hot jets of the shower in his room, Dax thought about other body parts that hadn't been used for a while, and he looked down at his cock. He'd tried jerking off a few times since his accident, but he never seemed to have any time to himself without someone coming in to either feed him, give him water, check his blood pressure or turn him over in the bed in order to prevent bed sores. Being under the constant watch of a whole team of people was the perfect way to stop anyone from touching themselves.

Now on his own, knowing that nobody would interrupt him even though the door had to be left unlocked in case he fell, he began to stroke his cock slowly, closing his eyes and lifting his face toward the jets as the hot water fell onto his face. He imagined that Cameron and he were together in front of a log fire, naked on a rug, and he wasn't in any pain, and he could move freely, and he was stroking the red headed man's chest, kissing his lips, moving his hand lower and lower until he felt the firm thickness of Cameron's aroused cock in his fist.

Dax was so horny it was only seconds before he came, weeks' worth of frustration released with a silent cry, his lips forming the right shape but no noise escaping as he forced himself to be quiet, otherwise they'd think he'd fallen out of his chair and come running. With overwhelming relief, he realized that he hadn't lost the power to get an erection or bring himself to orgasm, and it made him cry under the steady stream of water from above.

Chapter Eighteen

Dax had never thought of himself as a paranoid man. If he had any worries, he usually relayed them either to Kelly, or to Grant, and whatever was causing him a problem was dealt with so swiftly it didn't have time to fester. If he was photographed talking to a hot guy, tongues would wag, but soon enough, Grant would maneuver matters to show Dax with Alicia once more, having dinner, seemingly oblivious to the fact that they were being photographed.

In reality, though, Dax knew exactly where all the photographers were at all times on those contrived dates with Alicia, because Grant knew where they'd be, because Grant was the one to tip them off in the first place. Dax knew that sitting in a certain spot and stroking Alicia's hand in a certain way was bound to drive the fans wild, and as much as Alicia hated it, she agreed every so often to encourage rumors that she was pregnant.

Alicia Willis was a twenty-five year old actress, model, and closet lesbian. She hated being on the end of Dax's arm as much as Dax hated it, but she was all too familiar with her own struggle to fit into the mold that Hollywood had insisted she fit. She was beautiful, with long auburn hair and porcelain skin, and had been in the industry since being discovered at a London fashion show at sixteen.

Dax liked her, and she seemed to like Dax, but they had so little in common that the superstar singer often wondered why it was that Grant had put the two of them together in the first place. He surely could have found someone else just as willing to stay quiet, but at least with the kind of personality that Dax could click with. But no; Grant insisted that was the way it should be, so when Dax was on stage in New York to a sell-out crowd, Alicia was there, snapped by photographers leaving the venue with a smile on her face, gushing about how proud she was of her boyfriend, when in reality she'd spent the entire concert filing her nails and getting drunk in the executive lounge.

Grant produced a huge diamond ring and insisted that she wear it on her wedding finger the week after rumors were rife that Dax had given an undercover journalist a blowjob in a hotel room a year earlier. The rumor was true, of course, and Grant came close to murdering Dax for his lack of concentration, his reckless behavior. Alicia wore the ring for the next two weeks, only smiling coyly at journalists who asked her whether it was true she was about to become Mrs. Monroe, until the fever died down and Grant allowed her to take it off and return it to his safe.

After two months in the hospital, Alicia hadn't visited once, and Grant began to spread whispers that she was cheating on Dax with a tennis player. Alicia didn't care; her own career was taking off at breathtaking speed and she no longer wanted to be told what to do by Grant Beaumont. She no longer needed the cash he paid her to keep up the facade, and she was much less concerned about being outed for her sexuality than Dax was. Her fan base, after all, was not millions of screaming young girls who one day wanted to be married to their hero.

While he wanted to leave that night for Scotland at the same time the plane left for New York, this proved to be impossible. There were simply too many things to organize, and so when Grant and Kelly came into his room to say goodbye, Dax was still in his pajamas, watching television. Kelly was crying, and she held onto him for a tight hug. He smiled and wiped away her tears. "When I come back to the States, you're still going to be my assistant," he said. "Nothing changes. I just need to get well."

Grant managed a brief handshake and a gruff "take care" before the two left the room and made their way to the airport along with an entourage they'd managed to recruit. In the mix was a tall, handsome thirty-year-old named Billy O'Halloran, a care worker and part-time Dax Monroe impersonator. He was a little stunned, but more than happy, to take a private jet to New York and lie on a gurney on landing, to be whisked into a helicopter and from there, taken to the hospital. He agreed to stay in a hotel until the fervor died down, before being offered a return flight back to London, only this one wasn't on a private jet. In fact, he wasn't even offered a first-class seat.

Along with Billy there was a company of actors in doctor's scrubs and suits, all employed to construct the most realistic facade. While the transition from the plane to the helicopter would last for all of a couple of minutes, it was plenty of time for photographers with eagle-eyed lenses to capture the moment and scrutinize every detail. And if Grant Beaumont was good at anything, it was the minutest of details.

The day after they left, Dax sat and watched the entertainment news from his bed, the surreal moment when a young man who looked very much like him touched down on a private runway just outside of JFK airport, and was wheeled swiftly along the tarmac to a helicopter, where he was transferred within thirty seconds, and was in the air again after another twenty. Photographers and cameras did a good job of catching every single movement, but Grant had done an even better job of fooling every single one of them.

The helicopter was destined for the rooftop of the prestigious, private New York hospital, a place where no cameras would be allowed. In reality, however, it landed atop another building, a hotel, safely ensconced in the pocket of no other than Grant Beaumont. Nobody but those in the very tight circle that operated strictly on a "need to know" basis had any idea that Dax Monroe hadn't returned to his homeland and wasn't, at that very moment, in a New York hospital bed, surrounded by doctors.

For the time being, he was a free man.

He was still given hospital security outside his room, although Rocky had been on the plane to New York, too; it would have made no sense for the biggest pop star to be transported all the way across the Atlantic without his trusty security guard and the rest of the team, and although there was no reason for him to think he was in any danger, Dax suddenly felt very alone, and very exposed.

That evening, he called his mom. She knew of the plan and was in full support of it from the beginning. "I'm just so glad you don't have to deal with Grant anymore," she said. "I've never liked him. I guess I've always felt a little guilty about allowing you to sign with him in the first place."

"I don't think it would have made any difference if I'd signed with anyone else, Mom," Dax replied. "From what I know, and the people I've met over the years, it's all pretty much the same. It's a facade. Look at tonight. None of it was real."

"And how do you feel now?"

"A little scared," Dax said. "If I'm honest. I just want to get out of here now. The longer I stay here, the more chance I have of my cover being blown because I can't be in two places at once. Now Grant's not here to control everything and there's every chance something could slip out."

"I'm sorry you have to leave that lovely doctor you had," said Diane. "I really trusted her."

"Me too. But I trust Cameron. I know he wants the best for me."

"Don't go doing anything silly," his mom said, meaningfully. "He's a handsome boy, that therapist. Just concentrate on yourself for now, okay?"

Dax swallowed. He'd never once had a conversation about his sexuality with his mom, and now it seemed that such a conversation was never going to be necessary. Like Kelly had already assured him more than once, mothers have a sixth sense about these things, and there was every chance that Diane Monroe knew her son was gay even before he did.

Two days after the fake Dax Monroe left the hospital, the real Dax Monroe was finally discharged. He signed all the necessary papers, spoke to several lawyers and doctors, and was finally ready to be released into Cameron's care. He was escorted in the elevator to the very top of the hospital, where his own private helicopter was waiting. Without the protection of his security team, it was deemed too risky for the long drive right up the backbone of the UK, from London to Edinburgh. Instead, it was both safer and more convenient for them to fly the four hundred miles in a little under three hours.

There were two pilots, a nurse, a doctor, and Cameron in the helicopter with Dax. He was placed from the wheelchair into a specially designed chair that could recline a fully one hundred and eighty degrees should he be uncomfortable on the flight. His luggage consisted of one case of clothes and a laptop, along with his wallet and cell phone. He hadn't traveled with anything less than twelve cases and a whole number of gadgets for the past ten years, but shrugging off all the weight of unnecessary items also made him feel so much lighter.

He felt strange, sitting in the chair in loose pants and a thick coat with a helmet on his head, his entire body strapped securely to the seat and his feet off the floor. Cameron put on his own helmet and strapped himself in, and as the roar of the propellers on top of the craft began, Cameron placed his mouth to the microphone in front of his face. "Are you all right?" he shouted.

"Yes!" Dax replied. "Let's do it!"

And once they had the go-ahead, the helicopter lifted off the roof and into the air, before flying over the London skyline. London was one of Dax's favorite cities, but he was glad to see the back of it after the most difficult two months of his life.

Just getting from his bed into the chair and then into the helicopter amid a flurry of specialists left Dax exhausted, and the co-pilot spoke through the microphone and explained how to turn it off so that he could get some rest. With his body so safely strapped into the chair, he was unable to see out over the city on the gray afternoon in April, and once he could no longer hear the conversations going on around him, he closed his eyes and fell asleep to the rhythmic bobbing of the powerful craft.

There was a car waiting for them in Edinburgh, and once the helicopter touched down three hours later in Scotland, it was only a short walk to the vehicle, with Dax now in his wheelchair. The huge four-wheel drive had a reclining front seat just for him, and Cameron and the team loaded up everything they needed for the drive up to Invergordon. It was a little after four in the afternoon, and Cameron was keen to get out of the city as soon as possible to avoid the traffic of rush-hour.

Once the doctor, nurse and patient were satisfied all was well, Cameron closed the passenger door and leaped into the driver's seat. "Wave," he said, and Dax raised a hand and grinned as Cameron put the large vehicle into gear, and drove away on the tarmac. Once the helicopter was refueled, everyone would make their way back to London, all of them sworn to secrecy about the strange journey they had to undertake.

It was getting dark already, as Dax was alone with Cameron for the first time, completely at the mercy of a man he barely knew anything about.

Chapter Nineteen

"Sorry to have to tell you it's a bit of a long ride," Cameron said, as they pulled out of the airfield. "Living out in the sticks has its advantages, but it does mean that things like airports and even supermarkets aren't exactly on your doorstep."

"It's okay," Dax replied. "It's been nice just to get out of the hospital again."

"I told Doctor Pravenda that I wasn't happy with you staying so long in that place."

"But what was the alternative?"

"Getting out to a hotel or renting out a beautiful apartment overlooking the Thames." Cameron placed his arms on the steering wheel and gestured with his hands. "Some of the old buildings are so beautiful inside. I was in a place once that had survived the Great Fire of London."

"When was that?"

"In sixteen sixty-six."

Dax gave a low whistle. "I don't know anything about American history that goes back that far."

"Britain's got an incredible history," Cameron replied. "And Scotland's had its own fair share of glory years, but a lot of the time was fighting off the English from the south and the Vikings from the north."

"It sounds like a medieval saga," Dax remarked. Cameron grinned.

"I guess it was a little bit like that, back in the day," he said. "My grandfather used to tell me stories about the clans who had the land hundreds of years ago, before our own ancestors settled there and farmed the place. I don't know whether he made most of it up but it was still interesting."

"How did you come to inherit the house?" Dax asked.

"My parents moved to Edinburgh when I was little, because they thought there'd be more opportunity for me in the city rather than being in the countryside. I used to go and stay with my grandparents every summer and I loved it. I'd help my grandfather on the farm and in the evenings, I'd go meet some of my friends in the village and we'd be out until the wee hours. Then after my grandmother died, my grandfather couldn't keep the place on his own and he went into a home, and I figured my parents would get the house when he passed but five years ago we went to the will reading and found out he'd left everything to me."

"That's amazing," Dax said. "You must have been really close."

"Aye."

Dax smiled to himself as he heard Cameron's Scottish brogue becoming more pronounced now that he was back in his home country. While Cameron kept his eyes on the road, concentrating on the traffic as the large car roared down the highway, Dax stole a glance at his handsome face. He'd always had a weakness for a strong jaw and nice eyes, and Cameron possessed both in abundance.

He tried to imagine that they weren't going to stay in a house for therapy and recovery, but that they were a couple, on their way to a vacation house, maybe even their honeymoon. For a few moments he lost himself in the fantasy, but it wasn't long before the ache in his back and the numbness in his fingers brought him back to reality.

Cameron watched him flex his hand. "You doing okay?"

"Yeah, it's just more pins and needles," Dax replied. "It's not painful, exactly. More annoying than anything else."

"You've spent a lot of time sitting and we haven't been able to do any exercise today," Cameron said. "If you want, I can pull over and do a few stretches with you?"

"No, no," said Dax hurriedly. The dark skies and cold wind outside the car was enough to keep him content simply being inside the vehicle. "We'll pick it up tomorrow."

"Wait a second," Cameron said, keeping his eyes on the road and with one hand, setting the chair into more of a reclining position. "I've made the strap a little less tight. Try doing a couple of the exercises I showed you, just lifting your pelvis up a little off the chair, if you can. Try and clench your ass muscles together."

"Excuse me?"

"You know, do a couple of clenches," Cameron repeated. "Don't tell me you've never done them before. Your butt looks like it's done plenty of clenches in your time."

And Dax blushed. He didn't know what to say, and felt like a nervous kid who'd just been paid a compliment from the person they had a crush on. He wondered about whether Cameron had really noticed his ass. He would have had plenty of chance too, after all; there was little of Dax's anatomy that hadn't been seen by practically everyone since he started on the road to recovery.

But Cameron was professional, and respectful, and he certainly wasn't making a pass at Dax. That would have been too much to hope for, and yet hearing the words made him forget the discomfort for a little while.

Once out of the city and over an inlet of sea on the Forth Road Bridge, the urban sprawl of Edinburgh was left behind and Dax began to see some of the most beautiful countryside he could ever have imagined. The sky cleared a little in the later hours of the spring afternoon, and the sun began to peek through the clouds just as they climbed up into the barren hills.

"Where are we?" Dax asked, mesmerized by the lush green all around them, punctuated with brown bushes of bracken. It almost seemed a shame that the landscape was marred in the very center by an ugly gray road splitting it in two.

The pride in Cameron's face was undeniable, and he beamed at Dax. "I hoped you'd like it," he said. "It's funny, when you're a kid you don't want to look out of the window because it's boring. You want to read a book or play on your phone instead. But now I want to grab hold of that kid from twenty years ago and make him take in every inch of the beauty of this place."

"We've got some incredible scenery back home," Dax said, "and I've seen a lot of it. But this is something else. It's so... bleak, but beautiful at the same time."

He blushed at the words; they'd sounded so right in his head, but once he uttered them, he felt foolish. But Cameron raised his hands from the steering wheel with enthusiasm.

"That's exactly it!" he cried. "That's it in a nutshell. Beautiful but bleak. You're right."

He seemed to radiate with pleasure, at being home again, and at Dax's positive reaction to his homeland. Cameron began to whistle, and Dax asked him what it was. "Something my grandfather used to sing to me when I was a kid," he said. Dax was amazed to hear him begin to sing.

"Corrie doon, Corrie doon, Corrie Doon, my darling,

Corrie doon the day.

Corrie doon, Corrie doon, Corrie Doon, my darling,

Corrie doon the day.

Lie doon, my dear, and in your ear,

To help you close your eye,

I'll sing a song, a slumber song,

A miner's lullaby."

He paused, looked at Dax, and laughed, moving his hand dismissively. "Ah, it always sounded so much better when my seanair used to sing it. That's the word we use for grandfather around here. *Seanair.*"

"It's beautiful," Dax said. "The song, I mean. Really. I didn't understand a word you were saying, but the melody's really good. And you have a great voice."

"Well, it's nothing like yours," Cameron replied

modestly. "But I've been known to belt out a ballad once or twice when I've been in the shower. You know, bottle of shampoo in one hand."

Dax didn't want to dwell too long on the thought of Cameron in the shower, so he changed the subject. "What's the song about?" he asked.

"It's an old folk song about a miner singing to his daughter," Cameron explained. "He tells her to "*corrie doon,*" which is basically like saying, "snuggle under the covers and go to sleep." He's trying to get her to fall asleep because he has to go and work down in the mines and he's telling her that he goes to work so that she can sleep easily at night with heat in the lamp and light from the fire."

He looked at Dax. "It's a pretty sad song, really, when you think about it," he said. "I just like the melody. And I guess it's a pretty realistic description of what life was like a hundred, two hundred years ago. Plenty of men had to leave their kids and go down in the mines, and sometimes they'd never come back. I guess we take it for granted, the kind of life that we have today."

Dax blew out a puff of air from his cheeks. "Ain't that the truth," he said, quietly, but Cameron shook his head.

"I wasn't making a comment about your life or anything," he said. "I've seen how hard you work, and I know I don't have the first clue about how difficult it is for you. Believe me. If anything I was talking about myself. You know, growing up in the city, going to a good school to get a good education, and ending up in a job where I get to meet famous people like yourself, although in pretty unfortunate situations."

He ran his hands loving over the leather of the

steering wheel. "I get to drive this beauty. Boy, will I be sorry when I have to give this back."

"It's not yours?" Dax asked.

"Nope. It's rented just for a couple of days. I've got to take it back to Inverness by the weekend and get my old thing out of the shop. It's costing about five hundred pounds a day to drive this thing."

"So, don't give it back," Dax said. "I like it too. Tell them you want to keep it and I'll pay for it."

Cameron seemed to consider the offer, but shook his head. "Nah, we don't need it," he said. "We won't be spending much time in the car. We'll be taking long walks in the forest and up and down the hills before long, don't you worry."

And Dax realized that Cameron's plan sounded much better than anything else he could think of. "Both of us?" he asked.

"In time, yes," Cameron replied. "No doctors, no tests, no manager telling you to think about your career. Nothing to distract you. Not even television, or the internet—"

"Wait, what?" Dax interrupted, his mouth open in shock. "You never told me that I wouldn't have internet at this place!"

"Oh I'm sorry," Cameron teased. "Didn't I mention that?"

"No! What am I supposed to do if there's a power cut and we're stranded in the middle of nowhere but I have to let people know I'm okay?"

Och, yer in ma wee country now, ma friend," Cameron drawled in a dramatic Scottish accent. "Yer've got naw idea aboot life up here in the

Highlands!" And he gave a maniacal laugh, and Dax had no choice but to laugh at the comical accent, too, although something at the back of his mind was beginning to feel the real fear of being cut off from the outside world.

Chapter Twenty

There was little chance that Dax was to get anything other than peace and quiet; that much was obvious as Cameron took the car off-road and headed up a dirt track, thirty minutes after they'd passed through the picturesque town of Inverness. By now it was dark, and the only light came from the car itself, the bright headlights showing them the way.

In the fields around the dirt track, Dax could just make out tiny white blobs he realized were sheep. Apart from them, he could see nothing at all. Everywhere around him was pitch black. It reminded him of the time the tour bus had broken down in the desert in Arizona on the way to Phoenix for a show, only while they waited for the radiator to be filled with water, they sat outside the bus in the sweltering heat of the night, hearing crickets chirp and listening out for the ominous *take-taka-taka* of rattlesnakes.

Here, there was no sweltering heat. Only a wild wind that whipped around the car, causing a whistling sound as it forced its way through the minutest of gaps. Cameron's hands gripped the wheel firmly, as the car bumped up and down over potholes in a road that hadn't been maintained in many years. "Not much longer," Cameron said. "It's funny but sometimes I forget how long this road is. I look out for little landmarks, like a wooden fence to the left, and a little bit further up there's a tree that hangs over the road. There."

He pointed ahead of them, and Dax could make out the branches hanging so low over the road that they brushed against the roof of the car. "I'll have to cut them back," Cameron mused. "I've not been up here in over a year."

And there, in the distance, Dax saw their destination. A small whitewashed building, modest and unassuming, set back at the end of the road, a driveway leading up to the door. Cameron pulled up in front of the house and turned off the engine, yanking up the handbrake. All was still and for a second they sat in silence, until the therapist gave a nervous grin. "I really hope you like it," he said. "It's not going be anything like the luxury you usually stay in."

"I'm ready," Dax said. "What I really need is a pee, to be honest."

"Stay right there and I'll get the house open and I'll wheel you in." Cameron leaped down from the car, the headlights still on for a few minutes. Dax watched as he strode up to the front door and dug a set of keys out of the pocket of his jeans. He opened the door, switched on a light in the hallway, and came back to the car. He opened the trunk first, and took out the wheelchair, opening it up and setting it in front of the passenger door, which he then opened.

"Just a second," he said, reaching over Dax and unbuckling his seat belt. "Now, put your hands on my shoulders, and we're going to shuffle your butt to the edge of the seat and swing your legs to the left, like we do every day to get you off the bed."

Dax did so carefully, not wanting to fall out of the high car onto the hard stony ground. The wheelchair seemed to be far below him thanks to the height of the car, but Cameron stood beside him, watching every movement carefully. "Okay," he said, "put your arms around my neck, and on three, I'm going to hold your weight and put you into the chair. Okay?"

"Okay," Dax breathed.

"Great. One... two... three."

Dax allowed his weight to fall against Cameron, knowing that the man wouldn't let him fall onto the ground. For the first few times since they'd made this maneuver from the bed to the chair in the days since Dax was able to move out of the bed, he was scared he was too heavy and would sink to the ground in a helpless pile. But Cameron knew exactly what he was doing, and now, as he always had, he steadied himself with his feet and used Dax's own weight to move him from the car to the chair in a single movement.

"See? Easy peasy," Cameron said. He fetched a blanket from the back seat and tucked it around Dax's legs, and put his own heavy thick coat around the singer's shoulders. "Now I'll get you to the bathroom and come back for everything else."

There was no need to lock the car, of course, as there was nobody around, Dax was sure, for miles and miles, save for sheep. The path to the house wasn't exactly wheelchair friendly, and Cameron apologized for the bumpy ride into the house. There was a small step, and he took the chair backward over it, and then they were inside the house.

He was as good as his word, wheeling Dax immediately to the bathroom. It was freezing. With Cameron now getting the luggage out of the car, Dax moved the chair next to the toilet and put down the seat. With fingers numb from the cold he undid the cord of his pants, tugged them down, and transferred his weight onto the toilet, where he released his bladder with a small groan of sheer relief. Then he pulled the heavy wooden handle attached to a chain, which was fastened to the cistern above the toilet. It flushed with a mighty roar, making Dax jump a little.

Now back in the chair, he washed his hands in freezing cold water with a nub of a bar of soap, and dried his hands on a scratchy blue towel he was sure had hung there for more years than he'd been on the planet. By the time he came out of the bathroom, Cameron had brought everything inside, and the door was closed to the cold Scottish night.

There was a musty smell in the house, reminding Dax of the time his grandmother's basement flooded after a burst pipe. For years, he'd been scared to go down into the basement because of the dead rats he saw floating in the water when he was six years old, and now the memory came back to him in a clear, terrifying image. He wrinkled his nose as he pushed himself along the narrow hallway, where there was a light in another room.

He was in the lounge, and Cameron, to his relief, was stacking logs into the fireplace. He looked around over his shoulder as Dax entered. "Hey, everything okay in there?" he asked.

"Sure," Dax said. "I thought that toilet was going to beam me up to another planet for a second, though."

Cameron laughed. "Yeah, that thing's a beast. It's been in there for about a hundred years, I'd say. You're lucky. When my great-grandparents were young, they had to go outside to use the lavatory."

Dax shivered at the thought, and his teeth were chattering. Cameron saw it. "I'm really sorry," he said. "It's freezing. Come over here and keep warm. I'm just lighting the fire now. We've got a great heat pump that works like a dream once the fire's lit, and in a couple of hours you'll wish you were cool again, it gets that warm.

Wheeling himself closer to the fire, Dax looked around the dimly lit room. It was sparsely furnished, yet cozy, with a brown leather sofa and two huge matching chairs. There was a television in one corner, and a desk with a computer and lamp. There were paintings on the wall, tasteful modern art that seemed a little out of place in the old country farmhouse. Along the ceiling ran thick, black wooden beams, and along the back wall ran several shelves full of books and jigsaws, board games and magazines.

Cameron had certainly been right about one thing: Dax had never before been in a place like this. It was as though he'd been sent back two hundred years to live as a farmer in the nineteenth century. There was no heat, no internet, and there didn't even seem to be a working telephone. And yet, strangely, he wasn't scared.

The fire was laid with crushed-up newspaper and above that were stacked carefully-arranged logs. Among these, Cameron shook a small can of coal, and the black dust flew up and made him cough. "We've got enough for tonight," he said. "Tomorrow I'll go into the village for more coal and gas for cooking."

There was a box of matches above his head on the mantelpiece, and he struck a match against the side of the box and it sparked immediately. Holding the flame to the edges of newspaper, he carefully ignited three different areas of the arranged fire, then stepped back. "It'll catch," he said. "The wood around here burns really well."

"Do you chop it yourself?" Dax asked. "My grandfather used to do that when we went on vacation to the cabin."

"Erm, not exactly," Cameron admitted. "There's

an ax out back, but Ged brings me wood whenever I ask for it. He's the farmer who rents the fields from me."

"You own all the land with the sheep?"

"Sure, it came with the house in the will."

"Didn't you ever want to be a farmer?" Dax could imagine Cameron walking over the fields in wellingtons and an oilskin coat, perhaps whistling through his fingers at the sheep with his trusty dog by his side.

"Not a chance," Cameron said. "I have no desire to get up at five every morning of my life and never have the chance to take a holiday."

"Why did you keep the house?" Dax asked.

Cameron took a moment to answer. "I thought about getting rid of it," he said. "I know Ged would have bought it off me if he could, but I knew he wanted to turn it into a holiday place and I didn't want that. You know, a different family coming every weekend and destroying the place. I don't really know why I've held onto it. I've always imagined I'd do it up and live here, but I like living in the city, too. Then my ex wanted to keep it and even after we split up I didn't want to let the place go."

It was the first time Cameron had mentioned an ex, and Dax's heart skipped a beat at hearing him mention it. He resisted asking whether the ex was a man or a woman. The more he looked at Cameron, the more he was convinced he was straight. It was only wishful thinking that had made him wonder if he might have preferred guys. Dax had never really been the kind of man to have a finely-tuned gaydar, but he wished he'd spent a little more time honing his skills so that he wouldn't spend so much time wondering now.

His therapist had been right about the fire. It caught quickly, the cool air coming down the chimney being enough to circulate the oxygen it needed, and within a few moments it was roaring. The wood began to crackle as the flames licked the edges of the logs, and the dry kindling spat and sparked with bright orange flickers of light. One or two flew out onto a rug at their feet, and Dax could see tiny black holes where they'd smoldered in the wool before dying out.

"You don't have to stay in that chair," Cameron said. He fixed the large leather sofa so that there was a stack of cushions at one end, and he helped lift Dax out of the chair and onto the sofa, carefully lifting his legs and turning him slowly until his back rested against the pillows. Then he covered Dax's legs with a thick blanket.

"Tea?"

"To drink?"

"Of course!" Cameron laughed. "We don't have fresh milk but I have some cans of cream in the cupboard we can use until I get milk tomorrow."

"Sounds good," Dax said. "I hate to say anything but I'm a little hungry, too, and I need to take my pills."

"I'm on it," Cameron said, walking to the kitchen. "There's a loaf of bread in the freezer and I'll put it in the toaster. No butter, I'm afraid, but I've got a jar of honey. Will that do?"

Dax tried not to think too much about how much he wanted a steak sandwich or a plate of fresh, delicious sushi. He hadn't eaten honey on toast for more than ten years, and the idea of it without fresh milk certainly wasn't too appealing.

But he was warm from the fire, comfortable from the sofa, and all around him was nothing but quiet. His cell phone hadn't rung, he wasn't itching to check the internet, and for now, he was simply happy to just *be.*

Chapter Twenty-One

His eyes were heavy, and the crackling fire in the hearth had a rhythm to it that lulled him into sleep. But his back was beginning to ache, too, and when he began to shift his weight on the sofa and grimace, Cameron caught the expression on his face. "You need to move," he said, putting his mug down on the coffee table. "You can't sleep on there. It's not supportive enough for your back."

Dax sat up carefully. There was a dull throb that traveled from his spine to the tips of his toes. He was exhausted. Right now, the idea of being back in the hospital in London seemed like a better idea. The relaxed spell he was under just moments earlier was broken, and he gritted his teeth to stop himself crying out from the pain.

But Cameron was right there, propping him up on the couch into a sitting position and even feeling his forehead to check he didn't have a temperature. Dax knew why he did this. Even though his recovery was going well, even the slightest infection could take hold so much faster when his body wasn't moving and he'd been in the sterile conditions of the hospital for the last eight weeks.

"You need to stay here for a few minutes and rest," Cameron said, and he stood up from the sofa. "I'm going to take everything upstairs, and I'll make the bed up."

"I have to climb stairs?" Dax asked, weakly.

"I'm afraid so," Cameron replied. "I promise you'll be fine. Now hang on and don't worry. I won't be long."

Dax was so incredibly tired that the idea of

climbing stairs was excruciating. He hadn't gone up a single flight since his accident, and he wasn't sure his brain would remember the cognitive function needed to lift one leg and then the other. He and Cameron had practiced it a little in the treatment room, stepping up just once, then going back down, but his legs never seemed to go the way he wanted them to. He tried not to panic simply at the thought of the task, and he closed his eyes and took some deep breaths.

Back in LA, he'd been a regular at a local yoga class. For one, it was a great place to sit and look at hot guys in all kinds of positions, and it also bore some excellent relaxation techniques. He liked to get up early on a Sunday morning after a heavy night of booze and sex, sitting in a swelteringly hot steam room, where he took deep breaths and moved his body as the instructor commanded, sweating out the alcohol and loosening his muscles.

As he sat on the couch, every muscle in his body aching, he tried to recall the breathing exercises he'd done many times, and he took in breaths through his nose, letting them out slowly through his mouth. Concentrating on the rise and fall of his chest and stomach meant that he wasn't looking at his watch, wondering what was taking Cameron so long. He heard the creak of wooden floorboards above his head, and heard several strange-sounding clunks, as though Cameron was shifting an elephant up there.

Finally, he heard footsteps on the stairs and Cameron appeared in the lounge, a little breathless. "I've put your cases and everything in my room," he said. "I was going to put you in the spare room but there's only a single bed in there, so I'll take that. I've made up the double, so whenever you're ready, we'll move."

Dax rolled his shoulders and moved his neck from side to side, and then he pushed himself up from the sofa. Cameron was there in a flash, his strong arms under Dax's armpits. Dax moved to the side and Cameron was right there behind him, and between them they limped gingerly out of the lounge and into the hallway. At the foot of the stairs, Dax held onto the banister and took a few deep breaths.

"You're doing great," Cameron said. "Think of this as the exercise program we didn't go through this morning."

With gritted teeth, Dax lifted his left foot onto the bottom step, followed by his right, so that they were together. He'd take one step up. Only twelve more to go, he realized, as he looked ahead of him into the dim light of the ascending staircase, counting each wooden step as he went.

There was a thin, threadbare carpet running up the center, with a pattern of white, faded flowers. He chose to concentrate on one of those flowers at a time, aiming his big toe on the largest of the flowers, so that he didn't have to think about how his body was screaming at him to give up and flop down. On the fifth step, he paused, breathing heavily. "Can we take a break?" he asked.

Cameron stood on the steps with him, holding him up. "You're nearly halfway there," he said. "If you sit down now, I'm worried you won't get back up. I promise that if you can just get to the top of the stairs now, then we'll skip tomorrow's exercises and you can sleep in as long as you like."

It seemed like a good deal, but Dax wasn't sure he had the energy simply to climb seven stairs. He lifted his leg up, but he didn't lift it high enough, and he stumbled on the lip of the next step. Cameron was there in a flash, steadying him. "I won't let you fall," he said firmly. "Let me take your weight. Slowly does it."

"This is ridiculous," Dax said. He wanted to cry, and he was frustrated by his own limitations for what must have been the millionth time since the accident. But Cameron was as good as his word, and the therapist practically lifted him up the steps until, mercifully, they cleared the last one. Dax saw that the wheelchair was already there, and with relief he turned around and sat in it. Cameron wheeled him across the wooden floorboards to the bedroom.

There was a slight, musty smell in the room, thanks to it having been closed up for so long. It was too late and too cold to air the place that night, so for now, Dax would have to put up with it. The room was large, without much furniture. There was a large bed made of iron, and on it lay a thick mattress covered with a heavy blue duvet and several pillows. Dax had never been happier to see a bed in his life, and Cameron helped to lift him out of the chair so that he perched on the edge of the bed and Cameron lifted his feet up so he could turn around and lean against the pillows.

The relief was immediate, and he let out a loud groan. Cameron grinned. "Worth it, right?" he asked.

"I'm never doing that again," Dax said. "Leave me up here. I'll be fine."

"Well, I don't have any catheters on hand, so I'm afraid you'll have to get up at some point to use the bathroom," Cameron said cheerfully. "But don't worry. You won't have to go downstairs. There's a bathroom at the end of the hall."

"What time is it?" Dax asked. Cameron looked at his watch.

"It's nearly two," he said, raising his eyebrows in surprise. "No wonder you're tired. Now, let's get you undressed."

Dax blushed, and swallowed. "Oh, don't worry," he said quickly. "I'm fine. I'll just sleep like this tonight. I'm too tired to get undressed right now."

Cameron nodded. "No problem," he said. "I know you've had a long day."

"I'm sorry I've had to kick you out of your room," Dax said. "It's really good of you to let me have this one."

He looked around, taking in the wardrobes, the antique chest of drawers, the huge mirror, and the opulent light fitting over his head. The light wasn't switched on; instead there was a warm glow in the room that came from the small lamp beside his bed. He strained his ear, but could hear nothing at all. Everywhere was so quiet and peaceful. He looked up at Cameron. "Thank you," he said.

"Oh, it's fine, I often sleep in the spare room if I have guests," Cameron said, checking Dax had enough support from the pillows behind his head.

"I don't just mean for the room," Dax said. "I mean for letting me come here at all. It must be really inconvenient for you."

Cameron grinned. "I just can't wait to tell everyone at the pub that I've got Dax Monroe in my bed," he said. Then he turned around quickly, and walked to the door. He looked back at Dax. "Sweet dreams."

He walked out and closed the door behind him,

and Dax was alone for the first time all day. The last few words rung in Dax's head. Had Cameron really made a joke about having him in his bed? He'd seemed awkward about making the comment and had left the room pretty quickly. Maybe that was the reaction of a straight guy who'd just realized that he'd made a joke that could have been interpreted awkwardly.

Or maybe he'd slipped up and let out something he hadn't yet revealed to Dax at all. Dax didn't have any time to think about it, though, because as his whole body relaxed for the first time that day, he closed his eyes and was asleep in seconds.

Chapter Twenty-Two

He was sure that Doctor Pravenda was over his bed, torch in her hand, shining it into his eyes, but he soon remembered that he was no longer in the hospital and instead he was lying on a very comfortable bed in an old farmhouse in Scotland. The light in his eyes came from the sun shining through the curtainless windows, and he had to lift his arm in front of his eyes to adjust to the glare.

Judging by how high the sun was in the sky he knew that he must have slept for many hours. He sat up carefully, his muscles still tight and sore from the previous day's travel. His bladder was full to bursting, so with as much haste as he could manage he pulled himself into the wheelchair and wheeled himself out of the door. It wasn't easy; the doorways were rather narrow and it was a tight squeeze. Cameron had made it seem much easier when he guided the chair through earlier that morning.

The bathroom was down the hall, exactly as Cameron had described, and Dax pushed the door open. He sat on the toilet and relieved himself, then pulled the lever and transferred back to the wheelchair. He looked at the bathtub. There was no shower and he prayed that somewhere in the house there was a third bathroom where he could wheel his chair in under jets of water and clean himself, otherwise he was going to struggle.

He washed his face and saw that Cameron had left him a toothbrush in a packet by the sink. It felt good to freshen up after such an exhausting day and he wheeled himself back into his bedroom and in front of the window. The stone walls of the farmhouse were so thick he could have lifted himself up onto the sill and sat on it with ease, but he settled for staying in the chair and looking out.

When they'd arrived the previous evening it was already too dark for him to see anything other than the occasional white blob of a sheep in the blackness, but now the sun was shining brightly and he was treated to his first view of the scenery. He was amazed to see how beautiful it was; as far as he could see in the distance everything was green; rolling hills that seemed to stretch right to the horizon, some of them scattered with sheep, and others with cows, lazily moving through the grass, chomping as they went.

Once again, the sheer silence of the place settled around him, and he sat there quietly for several minutes, simply looking out over the lush green carpet ahead of him. He wanted to get out of the chair and walk all over the hills, but he could feel the dead weight of his legs, the weakness of his back, and he was brought back to reality.

He was broken from his thoughts by the sound of footsteps on the stairs. Then there was a knock on the door. "Yeah?" called Dax, still looking out of the window.

Cameron entered the room carefully, balancing a tray on one hand. He wore a t-shirt and jeans, and it was the first time that Dax had seen the therapist out of uniform. His red hair was tousled and messy, as though he'd just woken up. He grinned his usual bright grin as he entered. "I hope you're hungry," he said.

"I hadn't thought about it until now," Dax replied. "I was just checking out the view."

"Aye, it's something special, all right," Cameron said, and he put down the tray in front of Dax on the windowsill. Cameron had clearly gone out to find some items in the hours that Dax had been sleeping. There was fresh toast, now spread liberally with butter, and there was a plate of scrambled eggs and even a few slices of bacon. Dax smiled and looked up at Cameron.

"You're a pretty good host," he said, and it pleased him to see Cameron beam with pleasure.

"I went into town first thing this morning," he said. "I can't sleep when it starts to get light but I've never got round to adding curtains in the place. So, I've been up since the crack of dawn. On the way back, I stopped at Ged's and got the eggs and butter, so they're fresh from the farm."

"It all looks great," Dax said. "And is this tea?"

He pointed to the squat pot and Cameron nodded. "I'm afraid I don't have a coffee maker," he said. "I'll pick one up later on today. I know you Americans like your coffee in the morning but I won't offend you by giving you the instant stuff they have in the supermarket."

"It's okay," Dax said. "The tea I had last night was pretty good."

He was lying. He hadn't liked it at all. It was strong and bitter and he couldn't get used to drinking it hot. He was used to iced tea on a hot day, sweet and refreshing, and with lemon instead of milk. But he was thirsty this morning, so he lifted the heavy teapot carefully as his hands continued to shake a little, and poured the hot, dark liquid into a cup. Cameron watched him, but didn't take it from him. Dax appreciated that his therapist knew there were some activities he wanted to do himself.

It made him think about the shower, and as he made a sandwich with some bacon and eggs, he asked Cameron about it.

"Hmmm," Cameron replied, nodding. "About that. No, we don't have a shower here. But the water gets really hot so there's always plenty for a good bath."

"I'm just not sure I'll be able to get in and out of the tub..." Dax trailed off, before taking a bite of his breakfast. It was delicious. He realized how much he'd missed having good food, even though the hospital didn't serve him terrible meals. The food was so fresh, as though the cow that produced the butter had been milked only that morning, and the hen had laid the eggs barely an hour earlier.

"You don't need to worry about anything like that," Cameron assured him, one hand on his shoulder. "That's why you're here, remember? So we can work on your rehabilitation without the stress of people looking at you and you feeling embarrassed."

"I know," Dax replied. "But I didn't think you were going to have to help me get in and out of the bathtub."

"Well, there's a hose outside the back," Cameron replied, grinning again. "It's supposed to be for the garden, so we've never had it hooked up to the heater. It means you'll only get freezing cold water coming out of there, but maybe that's better than me helping you have a hot bath?"

"Maybe I'll just keep my shorts on," Dax replied. He blushed and nodded at this sandwich. "This is great."

"I'm glad you like it. How's the tea?"

Dax dropped a little milk into the cup and stirred it with a teaspoon. This time he added some sugar, too, and when he sipped he was pleasantly surprised to find it much tastier than the last cup he'd drunk. "It's really good."

"Good," said Cameron. "I didn't put sugar in it last night because when I went to open the jar the whole thing had solidified into a huge white rock. I got some fresh this morning from the supermarket. You might have noticed the place can get a little damp."

He reached forward to the window fastening and gave the pane a push. It wouldn't budge, so he pushed it again, this time harder, and it opened with a creak. A cool spring breeze came through the window and then Dax caught a smell that made him wrinkle his nose and put down his sandwich.

"Sorry!" Cameron said, laughing. "You're living in the middle of farmland now. That's good old fashioned manure on those fields."

"Great," Dax said, going a little green. He picked up his tea and settled with drinking it as he got used to the smell. It wasn't too bad, really, and he knew that in the countryside he should expect strange sounds and smells. He'd soon get used to it, he thought. Besides, it was worth the odd strange whiff when the rest of the place seemed so perfect. In the distance, he heard a bleat. Cameron heard it too.

"Ged's got his hands full right now," he said. "It's lambing season, so every day he has new lambs being born. Maybe one time we'll drive over to the farm and you can see them?"

"Sure," said Dax, although he wasn't sure it was something he'd want to do. He hadn't grown up with so much as a hamster in the house, and had never considered himself to be a lover of animals.

"I'm going to jump in the bath," Cameron said.

"When I'm done, do you want to take a bath?"

"Uh, I'm not sure," Dax replied, still thinking about someone having to help him. "Maybe later?"

"Sure," Cameron replied. "We'll do it after your exercises."

"What?" Dax exclaimed. "I thought you said that after last night I could take the day off!"

"Did I say that?" Cameron asked. "I must have been so tired I was talking nonsense."

He left the room before Dax could protest, and Dax frowned as he looked out. It was difficult to be angry for too long, though, as the sight before him made him smile. In the distance, he saw two tiny lambs jumping around each other as their mother stoically chewed grass and walked around slowly. To see the lambs gambol and hear the birds singing on such a beautiful day, Dax wasn't sure he could get too annoyed about anything.

Chapter Twenty-Three

One of Cameron's bedrooms had been converted into a gym, and when he was wheeled into it along the hallway of the old house, he was impressed by what he saw. There was a rowing machine, a bike, and several different weight machines. There was a bar along one wall, and even a sink with water. "This is pretty cool," Dax said. "Did you put this in yourself?"

"When I worked as a personal trainer for the navy, a lot of the time the rehabilitation element was highly confidential," Cameron said. "A bit like now, really. Nobody ever stayed here, but we're talking some of the highest ranking members of the force. Sometimes even after they'd recovered from their injuries they still came over for a training session and it seemed to work well."

"Why did you leave it behind?" Dax asked, but Cameron was already setting up a machine and didn't seem to hear him.

"We'll do some light exercises today," he said. "Nothing too strenuous. Do you think you can come over to the bench here and sit on it?"

Dax wheeled himself over and transferred his weight on to the bench, facing toward the heavy weights rather than having them at his back as he usually would in his gym at home. He looked down at the increasing numbers embossed on the iron slabs. Ten pounds, twenty, fifty, a hundred and even two hundred. *I used to bench one twenty without breaking a sweat,* he thought. *Now, it'll kill me.*

"First, let's warm up," Cameron said, and as they always did before their workout, they worked through a series of short exercises. Dax lifted his hands above his head, holding first one wrist and then the other, stretching out his triceps. Then he worked his biceps a little, and rolled his shoulders along with Cameron. When it came to his legs, Cameron had to help him, crouching down in front of him and taking one leg and then the other on his knee, warming up his calves. Then, they were ready to begin.

"Okay, so take hold of the handles," Cameron said. "I'll start you off on ten pounds. It seems like nothing, but I just want to start at the very bottom and work our way up, okay?"

In the therapy room of the hospital, Dax had sat on a bench and lifted dumbbells, but it was the first time he'd been at a machine in months. Cameron slotted the pin in just after the very first weight. "Okay," he said. "Give me ten reps and we'll go from there."

Dax found the ten pounds easy, and while he was careful not to go too quickly, he didn't struggle at all. Years of fitness regimes with his own personal trainer meant that at the time of his accident, he'd been in the best shape of his life. While Marcus, who put him through his paces every day, advised him to stay off the beer as much as he could, he was still able to keep up with him. Cameron had mentioned several times that it was his peak physical condition before the accident that gave him the best chance of recovery afterwards.

"Ah, that's far too easy," Cameron said after the tenth rep. "You're making me look like a fool. Okay, we'll double it, and this time, I want just five reps to begin with. Nice and easy now, please."

So Dax pushed the handles forward once again, bringing them back to his chest and pushing them out once more. This time the weights gave him more resistance, but still he found them easy, and so Cameron pulled the pin out again and this time he benched thirty pounds, then forty. The pain kicked in on the second rep of the forty weights, and he grimaced and paused. "Too much?" Cameron asked.

"It's like my shoulders don't want to budge," Dax replied through gritted teeth.

"What about your spine?"

"No pain there," Dax admitted.

"Then I think it's safe to continue, he said. "Your shoulders are stiff. All it takes is a couple of days without working out and they can seize up, especially because you're spending so much time on your back. Try again."

This time, Dax concentrated on the feeling in his back, and once he knew there was no pain there, save for the dull ache that always seemed to be present, he carried on with the reps. Once he finished, he asked Cameron to take him up to fifty.

"I'm not sure," Cameron said. "Maybe that's pushing it a little."

"It's what I want," Dax said. "Let me try."

Cameron pulled the pin out and placed it under the fifty pound weight, and Dax gripped the handles and pushed with grim meaning. He made it to two before stopping, beads of sweat breaking out on his forehead. "Why the fuck can't I do it?" he asked. "My arms aren't the problem. The break's healed. I used to bench double this."

Seeing the frustration etched on his face, Cameron pulled the pin out and put it back to forty. Then he crouched beside Dax. "You've been here barely twelve hours," he said. "We've got all the time in the world. I hate to say it, but why are you trying to run before you can walk?"

Dax took a deep breath and looked at Cameron's green eyes. "All anybody's ever told me is what I *should* be doing," he said quietly. "You know, go here, go there. Sing this. Dance this. Lift these weights. Run faster. I've never had anyone tell me I can't do something."

"And who's telling you that now?" Cameron asked. "Not me. It's your body just asking you to have a little patience. Give it some time. That's the one thing we've got here, right now, so take advantage of it. Right. Give me ten more."

Dax steeled himself and pushed the handles away from him ten more times before Cameron was satisfied. He could feel the burning in his arms and shoulders, but his back was no longer warning him to stop. Instead, he felt warm, his heart was beating a little faster, and he was beginning to feel the familiar buzz that came from a good workout.

Next, Cameron had him stand up, and asked him to walk forward. Dax shook his head. "I don't think I can," he said.

"You climbed a full flight of stairs last night," Cameron reminded him. "Surely you can manage a few paces on a flat surface."

"I was desperate to get to bed," Dax joked. "I'd have done anything to get off that old sofa."

Cameron stepped back a little. "For that, you have to walk further," he said.

"But last night you were holding me up on the stairs," Dax protested. "Now I don't have any support."

"Do you really think I'll let you fall?" Cameron asked, and he held out his hands. Dax grabbed his fingers and moved his left foot forward slowly. Then he moved his right, and his left again, and as he did so, Cameron moved back slightly, so that before he knew it, Dax was walking around the room. He made it to the chair before sinking into it with relief.

"See?" Cameron said. "Day one and you're already a pro! What did I tell you?"

Dax nodded. He couldn't help but feel proud of himself. He was sure he'd never walk again, but here he was, making steps all by himself, save for holding onto Cameron's hands. "Must have been those magic eggs I ate," he said.

"Aye, Ged's magic eggs are famous," Cameron replied. "They could make a penguin fly."

Dax wanted to continue the workout, but Cameron was happy for them to stop for the day. "I was thinking we could have a drive out to the village," he said. "It's actually forecast to be sunny for the rest of the afternoon. What do you say?"

"I think I need a bath first," Dax replied. "I can't put it off forever, right?"

"Of course not," said Cameron. "I think you've earned it, anyway."

He walked ahead of Dax, deliberately leaving him behind so that the singer would have to wheel himself in the chair. Dax grabbed the rims of the large wheels and pushed them so that he slowly started to move across the floor of the gym and out into the hall. He went into the bedroom while Cameron began to run the bath. There was a large case standing on the floor and Dax grabbed it, and moved it across to the bed on its wheels while he pushed himself in the chair with one hand. It wasn't easy, but eventually he managed to get both himself and the case to the foot of the bed.

Applying that logic that as he'd just benched fifty pounds and the case could weigh no more than forty, he reached for it. It was flawed logic, though, as the case proved to be nearer seventy pounds than forty, and Dax realized in just one attempt that he wasn't going to manage it. The frustration at failing at the simplest of tasks once more hit him on top of the weariness of yesterday's long journey and then the workout he'd just completed. With an angry grunt, he pushed the case and it flopped down onto its side.

Cameron heard the bang and came running. "What's up?" he asked. "I thought you'd fallen off the bed."

"I was trying to get that fucking thing up here," Dax said, pointing to the case. "I can't even do that."

"Well of course you couldn't," Cameron said, walking over and righting the case. "Do you have any idea how heavy this thing is? I nearly gave myself an injury bringing it up last night. What the hell do you have in there, anyway? Is this your case of gold jewelry?"

Dax saw how Cameron needed to exert plenty of effort of his own to get the case on the bed, and he felt a little better to see it. He tugged at the zip and opened the case, lifting the lid to reveal piles of neatly-packed clothes and plenty of pairs of shoes. There were even bags of makeup and hats in there, and Dax shook his head. "I asked for a couple of things to be sent over about a month ago," he said. "I haven't even opened this up before now."

"You've got a whole wardrobe in there," said

Cameron. "Jesus, do you own anything that doesn't have a label on it?"

He picked up a pair of shoes that Dax had been gifted by his favorite designer. If he'd bought them, he'd have paid two thousand dollars. They were his favorite pair of sneakers, but here in the house, they seemed out of place.

In fact, most things in the case seemed gaudy and incongruent with antique furniture and stone walls. Dax was suddenly ashamed of his things, and he grabbed a shirt and some underwear and a pair of loose pants. Then he closed the lid of the case. "I think I need to go shopping for some more things," he said. "I don't suppose a lot of this would look right on me. And I don't think I could even get into some of those pairs of jeans."

"Fingers crossed we're the same size," Cameron said. "I think I spied some Reef stonewash in there."

Dax grinned. "You may have," he said. He shrugged. "Try them on. If they fit, you can have them."

"Later," Cameron said. "For now, you're having a bath, Mister Monroe."

He left Dax to undress down to his underwear, and then came back to get him. In the bathroom, he had Dax transfer from the chair to the edge of the bath, and then swing his legs into the water. It wasn't too hot. As Cameron had explained, he needed to sit down first, and add hotter water, rather than trying to sit in scalding temperatures with no way of getting out.

"Look, if it makes you feel more comfortable, then by all means sit in the bath in your undies," Cameron said. "But we're all guys here, and you don't have anything I don't, so pretend it's the high school locker room and live freely."

It made sense. After all, Cameron was a professional therapist, and Dax was his patient, and over the last few weeks of catheter insertions and bed baths by nurses, he was used to being naked in front of strangers. So he pulled down his pants and tossed them into a wicker laundry basket. He felt a little self-conscious about being naked and wished that there was a thick pile of fluffy bubbles that he could descend into, but he got the impression that Cameron Wilson wasn't really a bubble-bath kind of guy.

Cameron left him to it, and Dax leaned forward enough to turn on the faucet. He'd never understood why British faucets came in Scalding Hot or Freezing Cold mode. Why on earth couldn't they have a central tap like everywhere else in the world, so they could mix the water as they went, getting the perfect temperature? Instead, he had to shift his body as he turned on the hot, as the steaming water poured just inches from his feet. He gripped the sides of the tub and tried to move around a little so that water could circulate, performing a strange kind of underwater dance until the temperature was just right.

Then he sank down as far as was comfortable, and the hot water eased his tired muscles and helped him relax. There was only a small bottle of generic shower gel, nothing like the array of assorted bath and shower products in his huge apartments back home, and it was only as this thought crossed his mind that he realized he didn't miss it at all. He had peace and quiet for the first time in fifteen years, and he wanted to hold on to it for as long as he could.

Chapter Twenty-Four

They didn't go into town that day after all. The heavens became filled with gray clouds a little before three, and the weatherman had clearly made a mistake in saying that they weren't going to have rain that day, because within a few minutes of the clouds' arrival they emptied all over the countryside, and didn't stop all night.

After his bath, Dax felt a thousand times better and with Cameron's help, came back down the stairs and into the lounge. The fire was already lit, and the place was cozy. Dax wheeled himself into the kitchen and he and Cameron talked as the therapist rustled up a steak and fries later that evening. They ate in the lounge on mismatched plates, sipping water from plastic cups.

"It's only now that I've got a superstar in the house that I've realized how this place just isn't set up for guests," Cameron said. "You'd think I'd have made sure we had everything but look, I don't even have any glasses."

"It reminds me of going camping as a kid," Dax said. "My buddies and I would take our bikes and a tent and go hang out in the woods until we got bored. My mom didn't really like the idea but we never lasted more than a couple of days before the bugs got us. And one year, my cousin Nathan fell into a patch of poison ivy and he couldn't even ride home so we had to leave him in the tent and go get help."

Cameron laughed. "I can't imagine his parents were too thrilled about that."

Dax shook his head. "I was grounded for a week but it wasn't long before my mom was kicking me out of the house again and begging me to do something other than stay in and drive her crazy."

"She seems like a nice lady, your mum."

"Yeah, she is." He was hit by a sudden pang of homesickness, but it wasn't for his star-studded life back home in LA. Instead it was for his childhood home in Connecticut, a modest place in a town called Windham, situated between Providence and Manchester. It was only small, but growing up Dax had always thought it to be huge, one big back yard for him and his friends to play in. Sometimes he liked to go on the internet and look at the street, seeing where the basketball hoop his mom put up for him one summer was still hanging from her garage.

"Are you okay?" Cameron asked, and Dax realized that he'd been daydreaming, and he smiled.

"Just thinking about old times, I guess," he said.

"Do you get to go home often?"

Dax shook his head. "Never. I can't remember the last time. It sounds like I don't want to go, though I do, I really do, but the security would have to be so tight, and once the media get wind of it, they never leave the place. When my first album went to number one they camped outside my mom's place for weeks. She didn't want anything to change but in the end she agreed to get gates outside the house. Now she regrets it because it's the only place on the street with ten-feet-high steel gates as though she's some crazy drug godmother and she has to keep the other cartels out."

"How does she feel about you being famous?"

"I think she liked the idea at first. She's always been proud of me. But she's read too many magazines at the store and in the doctor's waiting room. She worries about the way the media makes shit up and sells it as fact because people lap it up. I can't blame them. When I was a kid I'd look at sports heroes and think they were the center of my world. I was the kid who hounded the batter outside the stadium because I was desperate to get my ball signed. I can't be mad about it. But it's too much for my mom."

"And what about the accident?" Cameron asked, and his voice was soft.

But Dax couldn't bring himself to talk about that night, or how Andy, the guy he'd had sex with just moments before in a grubby hotel room, had sold his story to anyone who came asking for it. He wasn't ready to say the words, and he wasn't sure that if he ever did, he'd want to say them to a guy who was looking after him in the middle of nowhere. It wasn't that he didn't trust Cameron, he just wasn't sure how much he wanted to reveal of himself just yet. After all, being naked in front of him when getting in and then later out of the bath was quite enough for one day.

He had his own questions for Cameron, because he knew nothing about his host, either. Both men seemed to be holding back, but Dax knew that this was the idea; they were employer and employee, simply in a slightly less than conventional living arrangement.

While he wasn't ready to talk about the night of the crash, though, he'd enjoyed talking a little about his childhood to Cameron. It meant that he was taken back to a time before all the nonsense, before everyone had a camera in their hands, wanting a piece of him. Before he had to worry about developing feelings that the rest of the world seemed to think he shouldn't have. Before his life was controlled by a guy in LA.

"I wonder what everyone's doing right now," he said aloud, staring at the crackling fire. "Whether Grant's waiting for my call."

"Did you want to call him?" Cameron asked. "What about Kelly? Or your mum?"

"I will," Dax said. "For now, I guess I'm just liking the quiet, you know?"

Cameron nodded and smiled, but it was a more serious smile, not the playful grin usually found on his handsome face. "I do know," he said. "I mean, if I were totally honest with you, I think I'd say that being here reminds me of camping out, too. That's why I'm not too fussed about pretty plates and glasses. I like the idea of having nothing in my hands but a good book, or going out fishing in a loch and bringing it home for supper."

"I didn't know you were so outdoorsy," Dax teased. "Do you wear a kilt while you do this?"

"Oh aye," said Cameron, his accent becoming broader and his voice deeper. He closed one eye and widened the other in a glare. "I doon't be wearin' a thing other than ma woolen kilt an' ma hair shirt."

Dax had to avert his eyes and look back toward the fire, hoping that Cameron didn't notice the flush in his cheeks that came from thinking about Cameron walking over hills in a kilt with no underwear. He needed to focus on getting well, not on lusting after the guy he was holed up with in the middle of nowhere.

"I forgot to ask, do you fancy going to a pub quiz with me tomorrow?" Cameron asked.

"What's that?"

"You've never heard of a pub quiz before?"

"Oh, I guess it's pretty self-explanatory. A quiz in a bar, right?"

"That's right." Cameron put the last of his steak into his mouth and chewed. "It's only a small place. Off the beaten track. But every time I come up, I go and see my old friends and have a few drinks. They know I'm here, and they've asked me to join their team tomorrow night."

"The only thing is that I'm a little worried about being seen," Dax said. "You know, with everyone thinking I'm in New York, and everything."

"Oh, somehow I don't think you'll need to worry about that," said Cameron. "Out here in the sticks, we're very ignorant about all things celebrity. Half of the village never even got a phone line, let alone internet, and most of them don't even own televisions."

"I can't imagine it's a very diverse quiz, then," Dax remarked, and Cameron laughed.

"You'd be right, there," he said.

"Okay," said Dax. "It'll be good to get out and take a look around the village. Will I be able to get in with my chair?"

"Thankfully, after old Michael McDowd sliced his leg off with a chainsaw a few years back, he got the pub to put in a wheelchair ramp," Cameron said. He got up off the couch and held his hand out for Dax's empty plate. "Was the food okay?"

"Sure," Dax said. "Great. Are you serious, though? About a guy chopping his leg off with a chainsaw?"

"Well, that's what he tells us," Cameron said, his voice disappearing as he went into the kitchen. He came back with a plate of biscuits and a mug of brewed tea. "His wife swears he had it amputated because of his diabetes, but I quite like the chainsaw story a little bit more. He swears that's what happened, and it's definitely more interesting, don't you think?"

"Yes," said Dax, taking a mug of tea. Cameron made a pot so many times a day that he was getting used to drinking it, and was even starting to enjoy it. "He sounds like quite the character."

"Oh, that's an understatement," Cameron replied. "You'll see tomorrow."

Chapter Twenty-Five

The next day began with a new set of exercises. Dax was resting well, sleeping like a baby at night, and eating delicious food that Cameron prepared him. The eggs were freshly-laid, the bacon and butter came straight from the farm, and the freezer was even stocked with tender lamb steaks and chops. Dax didn't like to think too much about the relation between the cute, bouncing babies in the fields outside his bedroom window and the meat in the freezer, especially when it tasted so good.

Cameron was a firm believer in the right diet aiding in recovery. He didn't care for expensive vitamin shakes or even pills, except for the ones Dax took when the pain became too intense. Instead, he cooked three times a day, and in between meals he often handed Dax a handful of nuts or a glass of fresh juice. It wasn't just the exercises that constituted therapy; every day that went by, Dax was looking after his mental health, as well as his physical body. Away from the noise and chaos of his life as an international superstar, he was rediscovering the things that were important to him.

The new exercises had him standing at the bars in the gym, one hand holding on like a ballerina. He was to walk ten paces, then lift one leg up off the floor for five seconds. Then he was to walk backward ten paces, and do the same. When Cameron explained what he wanted him to do, Dax pulled a face. "Walking backward and forward? What is this, a sobriety test?"

"Think of it as your brain and your spinal cord have had a massive argument," said Cameron. "They don't want to talk to each other right now, but they have to. They're stubborn, and they don't want to communicate. But we know that getting them talking is a good thing. It benefits the whole body. So, we're reminding them how to work together, the way they used to. So, your spine has to be coaxed by your brain to remember how to walk, and how to balance. We've put one foot in front of the other, but we haven't gone backward yet."

Dax shouldn't have been surprised by Cameron's tendency to be right in everything when it came to his therapy. But while he walked the ten paces with relative ease, when it came to lifting his leg, his whole body seemed to collapse in confusion. He knew he could balance on one foot perfectly before the accident. He'd done it plenty of times, whether it was when he learned a new dance routine, or played with his friends as a kid, or reached for something on a high shelf. So, when he tried it now and felt himself fall, his first reaction was to be baffled.

Cameron was there in a shot, holding him up before he ended up on the floor. "You're okay," he said. "I won't let you fall."

Trusting him once more, Dax allowed Cameron to take his weight and get him back up on both feet. This time, when he lifted his leg, he was better prepared, and managed to balance well enough to stand for several seconds on just one leg. Then he repeated the action on the other foot. The muscle memory kicked in, and he felt the fog between head and legs beginning to clear, just a little.

Walking backward was difficult, too, but this also became easier the more he practiced. He found that with every new challenge, an older one he'd previously thought difficult now came easy. Standing on one leg had been impossible at first, but once walking backward was introduced, then the balancing seemed simple. Dax found that previously challenging tasks, like putting on shoes, was getting easier.

He took a bath before they went out that evening to the pub quiz. Dax had never been to one before, and he worried about how little he'd know and how much he'd be able to contribute, but he didn't mention anything to Cameron. "This'll be the first time I've been in a bar in ages," Dax said, as they ate dinner that evening. "I don't even remember the last time. Every time we go to a club, we hire the space out, so it never feels like we're really part of anything."

"Do you miss it?"

"What, clubbing?"

"No, not just clubbing. The lifestyle. You know, partying all night, being recognized everywhere you go, having servants at your beck and call all day long."

Dax laughed. "It's not exactly like that," he said. "Sure, there's plenty of partying, but more often than not you're there to promote something or someone. If a DJ has a new set and they want to advertise it, they get me to come be the face of it for the evening, whether I like the music or not. So much of the life is about trading favors between managers. There are some things I miss, I guess."

"Like?"

Dax thought about it. "Pizza," he said, at last. "Really *good* pizza. Proper New York stuff. Nothing gourmet, nothing fancy. Just an original cheese and pepperoni. Damn, they're good."

"What else?"

"Beer."

Now it was Cameron's time to laugh. "We have beer."

"Yeah, I know, but I've been off it for so long, being on the pills."

"If you wanted a drink tonight, it won't do you any harm. You're not on the medication in the afternoon or evenings, so I can't see how one or two beers is going to be a bad thing. Unless you don't feel you can stop there."

"No, I can," Dax said. "I used to drink to just get a buzz, to distract myself from the stress, but now I don't feel stressed anymore. Not at the moment, anyway. I know it won't last forever."

"You've got a choice in your life every single day," Cameron said, and he took their empty plates from the dining table into the kitchen. Dax stood up carefully and walked slowly in to join him. Cameron often did this; he left the room and continued to talk so that Dax would have to physically rise and move with him. It was all exercise, only in a less formal arrangement, so that it felt less like work to Dax.

"If you never want to go back to singing, and selling out stadiums, then you don't have to. But if it's something you want to do, then do it. Just do the things that are right for you, and don't worry so much about what other people want from you."

"Grant must be pulling his hair out right about now," Dax mused. "I still haven't called him."

"Well, Doctor Pravenda's been checking in with me every few days, so I'm sure word's been getting back to him," Cameron said. "I wouldn't worry too much about him, though. If he's ever going to get his little moneymaker back, then he needs him back in one piece, raring to go again."

Dax leaned against the counter for support while Cameron washed the dishes in the sink. "That's all I am to him, isn't it?" he mused. "Just a moneymaker. He hasn't got a single clue about anything I care about. Anything that matters to me."

"Well, I guess it's a pretty pessimistic way to look at things, but yeah, people like that are out for everything they can get from a person. I hated him the second I looked at his bloated red face."

"I've known him for so long that I thought he must know me, too. But really, neither of us knows anything about the other. It's all so cold and... *necessary.*"

"Necessary?"

"Ah, you know what? Forget it." Dax forced a smile. "I'm killing the mood, here."

"No, you're not," Cameron said. "Keep talking. What's necessary."

"All the relationships I have with everyone. You know, family aside, everything in my life's a business. Or it's part of the whole business. My name, my colleagues, even my friends. They wouldn't be there if I weren't part of this huge brand. And I guess that along the way the two worlds have merged so completely that now I don't even know what I am anymore. That's what I mean by necessary. Every new contact I make, they're there to serve a purpose for the brand. They're not there for me."

Cameron wiped his hands on a dishtowel and took a deep breath. "You know, that might be true about everyone else. But it's not true about me. You know that, don't you?"

"What do you mean?"

"Well, if I were only interested in getting you well and packing you off to your next concert, then I'd have said that flying back to New York would have been a perfectly good option. They'd help you walk again. They'd certainly have better facilities than I have here. At least you wouldn't have to wait two hours every morning for a hot bath."

Dax grinned. "Getting used to baths in this place hasn't been easy, I'll admit."

"But none of the physical side would matter at all unless it's all good up here." Cameron tapped his temple. "I want to see you do well mentally, as well as physically. It's not just your back that's been broken."

They were words that made sense, but they brought up something in Dax he didn't want to deal with. A feeling that he needed to push down, because he didn't like where it was going. He shrugged and laughed off Cameron's words. "Ah, you didn't have to go to all this trouble," he said. "I hope Grant's sorted out paying you."

Cameron said nothing for a second, and he seemed to be choosing every word carefully. "To a lot of people, you're more than just a face that sells records," he said. "And once that sinks in, you'll be amazed at how much better you feel about yourself."

He walked toward Dax slowly, and put his hands in his pockets. The evening sun was coming through the window, hitting his red hair, so that it looked golden in the light. Dax could only stare at him. "You've no idea how much people love you," he said. "People who aren't just trying to get something out of you. But you don't love yourself, so you can't see it."

Dax looked at him suspiciously. "Have you been talking to Pravenda about this?" he asked.

"No, not at all," Cameron replied. "But I'm guessing that she's said the same to you, right? I can't blame her. So much of your recovery is wrapped up in feeling positive about yourself, and your future. If you think you're just going to go back to the life you had before, and it's not a life you want, then your recovery will take longer. But if you have something to strive for, a goal to achieve, something to be proud of, then it'll give you even more of a push."

"Am I not progressing as well as I should?"

"You're doing great," Cameron said softly. "But I don't want you to get well, just for you to be thrown back into the lion's den. Having everyone scrutinizing every little thing about your life. The night of your accident, it could all have ended so differently. You've been given another chance, so make sure that you're only doing things you *want* to do. Making yourself happy. Surrounding yourself with people who care."

Dax was beginning to feel the conversation was too heavy. He knew that what Cameron was saying made sense, only he wasn't sure he could bear to take it all in at that moment. "Got it," he said. "Anyway, shouldn't we be leaving for the bar by now?"

"It's a pub," Cameron corrected.

"Is there a difference?"

"Definitely," said Cameron. "In New York, you drink in a bar. In Invergordon, you sup ale in a pub."

"I what?"

But Cameron only laughed and shook his head.

Chapter Twenty-Six

It certainly couldn't be described as a bar; or at least, one that Dax had ever been to before. As Cameron pulled the car up outside the old stone building, Dax was sure that they'd stopped to pick someone up before going to the pub.

But this was it. Dax leaned forward and opened the door and Cameron came around to help him. "Hold on, let me get the chair," Cameron said.

"No," Dax replied. "I need to start walking more. Let me try it. Can I take your arm?"

"Of course," said Cameron. He helped Dax to his feet from the height of the large car. They began to walk slowly toward the door of the pub, where a few other people were walking in. Others were milling outside, smoking cigarettes. There was nobody on the door, no bouncer vetting the clientele and deciding who could come in and who wasn't welcome.

"Who are we meeting, again?" Dax asked.

"Caroline and Austin are friends from when I was at university. Then there's Will. He works in a hair salon in town. And sometimes he brings an old customer of his with him. That's Angus."

"Right. And do they know I'm here?"

"They know I have a new patient, yes. But they don't know who you are. Don't worry if they stare a little bit. Even in this remote place, they all know who Dax Monroe is."

Both men had to duck their heads to walk inside, as the ceiling was so low. The old stonework was ancient, similar to that of Cameron's house. It was held together with old mortar, still going strong against the cruel Scottish weather. Even on this spring night, there was a chill in the air, and Dax was glad to be inside, where it was warm.

"I've asked for Caroline to save us a seat near the fire," Cameron said. "Let's just get you set down and I'll get us some drinks."

As they shuffled past the bar to a small room to the left, Dax knew that people had begun to stare and whisper. He instinctively looked around for Rocky, but remembered very quickly that his trusty bodyguard was nowhere around, and that he was on his own. Well, not exactly. Cameron kept a firm grip on his arm and made sure that a clear path cut through the room to the small wooden table at the far side.

There was a woman with mousy hair and glasses talking with a man with a short beard and the largest Adam's apple Dax had ever seen. They both looked up as Cameron approached, and smiled until they recognized Dax, and their mouths dropped. Cameron helped Dax to sit down as a hush descended around the room. "All right, let's get this out of the way," he said to everyone, not just Austin and Caroline. "This is Dax, he's staying with me for a little while after an accident, and I'd appreciate it if everyone could respect his privacy. We're a close-knit town, and we'd really like it to stay that way."

Everyone was listening, hanging onto Cameron's words. Dax smiled uneasily and raised a hand. He felt underdressed in jeans and a shirt, and unlike most of his public appearances, now he wasn't wearing the slightest amount of make-up.

"So, if you want to talk to Mr. Monroe, then I'm sure he won't mind too much but please, no autographs, no selfies, and no videos. Nothing goes up on the internet. Okay?"

There was a murmur of consent throughout the room until a loud, high voice cut through the crowd. A tiny, birdlike woman with bony elbows and messy white hair came in, carrying a stack of beer glasses. "If ah see a single phone tekkin' any wee sneaky videos, yer'll be banned immediately, never ter return!"

Dax was terrified of her, and could barely make out the words from her clipped Scottish accent. She rolled her R's on every word, but he caught the gist of her message. Cameron leaned in and whispered into his ear. "That's Ginny Mallon," he said. "She used to own this place, and her parents before her. She had to sell it ten years ago after her husband died but she still lives in the flat upstairs and collects glasses every night. She must be hitting ninety. But she's sharp as a tack, and she rules the roost around here."

"I can see that," Dax replied. "I wouldn't cross her."

"Neither will anyone here," Cameron said. "She's a tough old bird. What she says, goes. You won't get any trouble here tonight."

"Great." Dax was still nervous, and he gave small smiles to Caroline and Austin.

"Shit, I'm sorry," Cameron said, taking off his jacket and putting it on an old iron radiator, where the others had put theirs. "I haven't done the introductions. Dax, these are my friends Caroline and Austin. Guys, this is Dax."

They shook hands and Caroline grinned at him. "He's had some pretty cool people stay with him over the years, but I've got to say that you're the coolest yet."

"Thanks," said Dax, and he meant it. He knew

immediately that there didn't have to be any fake, plastic grins or empty words of joy at meeting them. He could be himself. Caroline was warm and friendly, with slightly buck teeth and a crinkle in her nose as she pushed up her spectacles every few seconds. Her husband, Austin, was very quiet and serious, but he'd taken Dax's hand warmly in his large grip.

"What about Will?" Cameron asked.

"He's on his way," Caroline said. "Asked if we'd get him a drink and he'll get a round in later."

"I've heard that before," Cameron said wryly. "But I could murder a pint. What's everyone having?"

Caroline and Austin both ordered bitter. Dax didn't like the sound of that, whatever it was, and he looked over at the bar through the tiny gap in the door, wondering what to have. But Cameron told him not to worry.

"I'll get you something you'll like," he said. "Don't worry. What does Will want?"

"He'll have a pint, and get Angus a brandy."

"No way," Cameron said. "I'm not having the old man start on the shots this early. I want him nice and sharp for the quiz. He can have a beer, too."

He left, and Dax suddenly felt very exposed. He could feel eyes staring at him, but he noticed that they were simply curious, rather than unfriendly. From a quick scan of the room, he couldn't see anyone pointing a cell phone in his direction. It seemed Ginny Mallon was a force to be reckoned with in these parts, just as Cameron had described. Dax could do with someone like her when he was on tour. Most of the time, his management's calls for privacy were laughed at, rather than heeded.

"So, it must seem very strange, being here after the kind of thing you're used to," said Caroline. She seemed nervous to be talking to him, and Dax wanted to tell her that he was the one who was terrified.

"It's weird, I've got to admit," he smiled, "but Cameron's looking after me, and I'm getting there. Day by day."

"I saw about your accident on the news," Caroline said. "It looked so nasty. I'm glad you're okay, though."

"Yeah, it could have been a lot worse."

"Weren't you on tour at the time?"

"Just finished. About to head back to the States when I... when I went out for a drink with a friend, and he lost control of the car when we were escaping the paparazzi."

She nodded, listening. She had a kind face, and didn't seem to want to drag out any information that Dax didn't want to give. Instead, she was sympathetic, and warm. "It must be so awful, to have everyone in your business all the time. Wanting something from you. And they could have killed you out there, and for what? Just a picture."

She shook her head. Dax nodded. "Yeah, when you look at it like that, it seems dumb," he said. "But as I said, Cameron's looking after me."

As if on cue, Cameron returned with a handful of beers he carefully held onto as he crossed the room before setting them on the table. "Bitters for you two," he said, passing drinks to the couple. "Dax, I got you an ale I think you might like. It's brewed up here, but it's light. I can always go and get you something else if you don't like it."

"I'm sure it'll be fine," said Dax. He reached for his drink and took a sip. He was used to drinking his beers cold but this one was at room temperature, but he noticed that under the malty flavor was a fruity, orange tang. He raised his eyebrows and looked at the glass. "That's actually better than I thought it would be."

Cameron grinned and nodded, taking a long sip of his own drink. "Damn, that's just what I needed," he said. "I've been thinking about that beer all day."

He looked at Austin. "How's the lambing?"

Austin now spoke for the first time. He had a rich, deep voice, and he seemed to choose every word carefully, as though he had a quota assigned to him at birth, one that he wasn't allowed to go over, at any cost.

"Busy," he said. "Good weather makes for bigger lambs."

"Are you a farmer?" Dax asked. Caroline spluttered in her drink and even Cameron laughed.

"He's a vet," Cameron said. "And by that, I mean a veterinary doctor, not a veteran."

"Right," said Dax, and he blushed, wanting to kick himself for his foolishness. He felt so out of place. He could sit in a room of thousands of partygoers, with his arms around a whole number of strangers who took picture after picture, making him smile in every single one. He could belt out a ballad in front of a hundred thousand spectators at a stadium like it was nothing more than a walk in a park. But here, in this tiny room in a tiny Scottish pub, he felt more out of his depth than he had in a long time.

He was coming to grips with the accent, but

Cameron and Austin began to talk so quickly that he lost track of the conversation. He wanted the ground to open silently so he could slip into it without being seen, but there was little chance of that occurring. Cameron tried to include him, Dax knew, but he simply couldn't keep up. He wanted to escape, but at that moment, he heard a slapping sound, and he looked up.

There stood in front of him a young guy, slim and cute, and the slapping noise had been his hands on his own cheeks. His mouth was wide open in shock, and his eyes looked as though they were about to pop out and roll across the floor.

"You have *got* to be fucking kidding me," the guy said.

"All right, Will, close your mouth," said Cameron. "This is Da—"

"I know who it is!" he squealed. "Oh my God, I'm shaking. Oh Jesus, I'm shaking so much. I'm the biggest fan. I swear to God. I can't breathe. I can't breathe."

Cameron frowned and stood up. "Take a seat, Will," he said. "Let Dax have a little breathing space. Dax, in case you hadn't already guessed, this is Will."

Dax reached over and shook his hand. "I'm sorry for not standing up."

"Oh, it's fine, I know all about your accident." Will turned to Cameron. "I can't believe you didn't tell me he was going to be here! Jesus, Cam, I nearly canceled tonight to go see a band!"

"But you didn't," Cameron said. "And now you're here, and Dax has joined us, and you're going to be calm, and you're not going to go crazy, am I right?"

"Right," said Will. He turned to Dax. "That last album, oh God, I've had it on repeat in my car for about three months now. I never drive anywhere without listening to it."

"Will, I got you a drink but I think you and I need a little talk at the bar."

"It's okay," said Dax. "Really. It's fine."

Cameron took a deep breath. "I'm really sorry. I should have pre-warned him. He's only twenty-two. He gets a little excited."

Will turned around and scowled at Cameron. "Don't talk about me like I'm not here," he pouted. "You know the night wouldn't be anywhere near as fabulous if I weren't."

"Where's Angus?"

"He's talking with Graham about some cow feed outside. But stop interrupting me. I was talking to Dax."

Thankfully, a tap on the microphone from somewhere else in the pub meant the quiz was about to start, so everyone had to be quiet. An old man limped up to the table, sat down without a word, and picked up a pen. Dax could only assume that this was Angus, and that their party of six was complete.

Chapter Twenty-Seven

A hush descended on the room as quiz teams sat poised with their pens over their papers. Dax had no idea where the guy in charge was; he was speaking as if from heaven, his voice filling each of the small nooks and crannies of the pub.

"Question one," he boomed. "Which famous goalkeeper performed a one-handed save with a broken wrist at last year's World Cup?"

Furiously, Angus and the rest of the team started in low whispers. Dax leaned in to join them but didn't have a clue what the question was about. What goalkeeper? What sport? The question didn't even specify. Was it ice hockey? Soccer? He had no idea.

He looked up and saw that Will was staring at him, and he smiled. Will grinned back, but said nothing. Dax was used to the attention, but he'd never been in such a strange position before. Half of the room couldn't tear their eyes away. The rest of the room couldn't care less whether he was there or not.

"Question two!" came the voice. "Which famous king was said to have sat in a pile of nettles in his kilt on the way to Bannockburn Castle?"

Again, Dax was clueless. Thus went the first ten questions of the quiz, where he began to wonder why he was there at all. His beer was finished, having been constantly sipped merely as something for his hands to do while everyone else in the team was bent over their paper, asking questions. He wished that he was able to just get up and walk; he could go to the bar to get in a round of drinks, or he could even slip outside and get a cigarette from someone. Anything to stop the feeling that he was utterly useless.

Then, a miracle happened. "Question eleven. Which is the most populated city in the world?"

"It has to be Beijing," answered Austin, confidently.

Angus nodded. "Sounds right to me," he said, and started to write it down.

Dax nearly kept his lips tightly shut, but at the last second, made a noise. "Uh, no," he said. Everyone looked up at him, blinking.

"It's not?" Cameron asked.

"No, it's Shanghai," said Dax.

Angus frowned. "Are you sure about that, Son?"

"Positive," whispered Dax. "Last year I toured there. It was one of the facts about the place that I was told to learn for the crowd. You know, act like you know a little bit about the place."

"That's good enough for us," said Cameron, and he grinned as Angus crossed out the first answer and inserted Dax's.

"I'm still not sure," he grumbled, but he went ahead with it all the same.

From then on, Dax tried to feel a little more included. He answered a question about Mexico, and even contributed to guessing a famous actor, along with help from Cameron. He began to feel more included, and he noticed that he was actually having a good time. It was such a world away from a night out back home, and before his accident, he'd have laughed at the idea of sitting in a pub with a bunch of misfits. But they were so friendly, and warm, and most of all, they were like this while wanting nothing at all from him.

He liked Will. He knew the kid wanted to ask him so many questions, and quote lines of his music, but Cameron kept the young man's feet firmly on the ground with a threat and a growl. Dax knew he meant well, ensuring that Will didn't get too carried away, but he wasn't offended at all.

"When you recorded *"Out of the Red,"* did you choose the backing vocalists or was that the studio?"

"That was all the production team, I'm afraid," Dax said. "It wasn't one of my records. They recorded everything separately."

Will looked a little downcast. "I thought you'd record it all together. I wanted to know the name of the woman who takes the single line near the end. You know, when she's like, "*out of the red, you left me for dead!"*

His voice became a little loud as he got carried away, and Angus looked up and rolled his eyes and Cameron frowned. "Come on, we're supposed to be trying to keep *out* of the spotlight," he said.

"It's okay," said Dax. For Will, he tore off a strip of paper from the answer sheet and took Angus's pen while the old man was at the bar during the break. "This is the singer. Her name's Stacey Galvan. Have a listen to the rest of her stuff, her solo. Especially an album called "*Sweet Shakes the Night."* Beautiful lyrics, and she wrote the whole thing herself."

"Wow, thanks," Will said, beaming. "Oh my God, this is the best day of my life, without a doubt. I still can't even believe it."

"My pleasure," Dax said.

"How did you cope with the press and everyone, being in your face about being gay?" Will asked, suddenly, and Cameron coughed as Dax shifted a little uneasily in his seat. He could feel himself flushing, and he was lost for words. Caught off guard, he desperately wanted Kelly, or even Grant, to be there to step in, but they were nowhere to be seen.

"That's, uh, not what happened," Dax said. "I'm not—"

"Will, go get everyone a round," Cameron said. "It's your round."

"But Angus has gone to the bar…"

"I said *go*," Cameron said, and Will scurried off. Cameron looked at Dax. "I'm so sorry."

"It's okay," Dax said. But it wasn't. He'd been completely floored by the question. He hadn't been prepared for it at all. Angry with himself, with the situation, and so utterly lonely in this strange country, he was suddenly homesick. He wanted to go back to a place where everything was managed for him, where he wouldn't have to deal with questions like that without someone loud and authoritative shutting them down in a heartbeat.

Cameron whirled around on his chair and went looking for Will. Caroline and Austin were the only two left at the table, and Caroline smiled awkwardly. "Will's just a bit excited," she said. "You're his hero. You must get a lot of that."

"A lot of what?"

"You know, young gay guys having crushes on you."

"I guess," Dax said. "It's usually teenage girls who get a bit crazy. Maybe we should have warned him that I'd be here."

Or maybe I should have just stayed at the house, and nobody would have been any the wiser, he thought to himself. The mood seemed to have changed and Dax wanted to leave. He wanted to get right on a plane and go back the States, where people knew him, and he knew the rules. Where he could walk out of interviews or have other people answer for him. Where he didn't feel so helplessly *crippled.*

"He's had a really difficult time lately," Caroline continued. "This sort of place isn't the most diverse. He's had some terrible homophobic abuse. He used to come in here and just drink at the bar and we asked if he wanted to join us. Since then he's been part of our team. He's a bit of a giddy kipper at times, but he means well. And I think he looks up to Cameron, you know, as a mentor."

"Right," Dax said. "I can understand that. Cameron's looked after me so well since I arrived. I can't thank him enough, really."

"It's what he does best," Caroline said. "He's got a heart of gold. The last time he left, we were all sure he wouldn't be back again. I think he needed time to get over it."

"Get over what?"

"The break-up."

"Oh, that."

"Yeah. So, when John went back to the navy, Cameron disappeared back to London. I thought we'd seen the last of him. Thought the big smoke had swallowed him up for good. But here he is."

Dax could barely hear what she was saying. All he could process was that Cameron's heartbreak was what drove him to London. And the heartbreak came at the hands of another man. Called John. He wanted more details, but didn't want to seem too pushy, so he tried to be as nonchalant as possible.

"How long ago was that?" he asked. "He seemed on great terms with the team in the hospital I was in."

"Um, two years, I think it was?" Caroline turned to her husband, who was sitting like a large, bearded statue, his arms folded as he stared off into the distance. Caroline prodded him. "Austin? When did Cameron and John break up? Was it two years ago?"

"It'll be three years in August," said Austin. "It was the same year I broke my foot. I was in pain but Cameron wasn't around because he'd just gone to London."

"Aye, that's it. Three years, nearly. Goodness. Doesn't time fly?"

"Yeah," Dax said. "It must have hurt a lot for him to stay away so long."

But they didn't have time to talk anymore, because the rest of the team returned, this time carrying fresh beers. Dax could hardly stop himself from looking at Cameron. All this time, his handsome therapist, the only person he knew in the world in the whole country, was gay. Cameron had never breathed a single word. Dax wasn't sure what to make of everything. On the one hand, it was a huge revelation.

On the other, though, it wasn't a big deal at all. So what if Cameron was gay? Plenty of people were. It seemed that he wasn't even the only gay person in this village, either. Will, at only twenty-two appeared to be out to everyone. And yet Dax, global superstar and thirty-three years of age, couldn't bear to admit it to anyone, even another gay guy in a friendly pub.

It appeared the shackles of his sexuality were always going to hold him fast. He couldn't imagine a time when he would no longer hide behind a mask that Grant and the rest of his team had created. The night had been a strange one, full of frustrations and embarrassments, but also fun, and warmth, and even some very interesting information.

Their team, *The Pinkie Fingers,* came joint first in the quiz, with their old rivals, *Mutton Dressed as Lamb.* Angus groaned when he heard the result. Cameron leaned over to Dax. "If it wasn't for your correct answer about Shanghai, we'd be in second place," he said. "Good shout, that one."

"So, it's a tie-break question," came the phantom voice that had presided over them all for the last hour. "Write your answers on your papers, and then they'll be collected. Closest answer wins. Are you ready?"

"Heads together, lads," said Angus. They all huddled into the tiny table, waiting to hear the question.

"How many vertebrae make up the human spine?"

Cameron threw back his head and laughed. Then he grinned at Dax. "Do you know the answer?" he asked.

"Doctor Pravenda told me after the accident," Dax said. He rubbed his temples. "Oh my God, I can't remember. Shit! What did she say? Hang on."

He thought back to the conversation where his warm, soft-spoken doctor had drawn a picture of his back. What had she said? Made up of five parts... altogether there were...

Looking at Cameron, he grinned. *Thirty-three,* he mouthed.

"Bingo," said Cameron. That night, *The Pinkie Fingers* won a round of drinks and five packets of chips. For all the cheering and celebrating they did, anyone would think they'd each have won a thousand dollars. Or pounds.

As Dax carefully got into the car at the end of the night after saying goodbye to the rest of the team he thought about how well his night had gone. Cameron opened the driver's side door and hopped in, turning on the engine. Then he rubbed his hands together and blew them to keep them warm. "Chilly tonight," he said. "I could murder a brew."

Dax was beginning to learn the vernacular, and knew that Cameron meant that he wanted a cup of tea. Dax tried not to stare at Cameron's floppy curls falling over his eyes on the drive home. He tried to think about tea instead. It was much safer, though nowhere near as intriguing. He promised himself not to let his mind wander too much. After all, the last thing he needed was the complication of something other than therapy taking his concentration. It was going to be tough, though. He'd always thought Cameron Wilson to be gorgeous. Only now, he also knew he was gay, too.

Chapter Twenty-Eight

The rehabilitation was working. The therapy was going well, and complimented with a diet of good, fresh food and a lack of stress, Dax found that he was beginning to recover with speed. Over the next two weeks, he walked forward and backward, ignoring the dull ache in his spine that had become synonymous with everyday life. He lifted his right leg, and balanced, and then repeated the action with his left. His core was getting stronger.

Walking up stairs was still difficult. It meant that with every step, he had to pull up his own body weight, and his weakened spinal muscles struggled. "I can't believe how much I used to take it for granted," he groaned, as he slowly ascended the stairs one evening before going to bed. Cameron was right behind him, as always.

"I think we all do it," he said. "When we're sick, we wonder why we didn't appreciate the times we had good health."

"God, that's exactly it," Dax said. "Damn, I didn't appreciate my limbs when they were all working perfectly."

"You're doing great, though," Cameron encouraged. "Your mobility's much better, and I'm not supporting you anywhere near as much as I was."

"Sometimes I feel like I'm not getting anywhere," Dax said, as they got to the top of the stairs and he walked slowly to the bedroom.

"Do you see the wheelchair anywhere?" Cameron asked. "You've not used it in nine days. You're crazy if you think you're not making progress."

"Nine days? Have you been counting?"

Cameron grinned. "Do you think I'm doing this out of the goodness of my heart? I track every bit of your progress. I write everything down. What you eat, what you drink, how many minutes a day we work."

"Really?"

"Of course. I'm a professional."

They said goodnight and went into their separate rooms, as they always did. Dax lay on his bed on his back, mulling over the words. This was why he was never allowed to see Cameron as anything other than his therapist. Because their arrangement *was* strictly professional.

But over the last few days, ever since Dax had learned that Cameron was gay, he'd begun to battle with feelings he knew he shouldn't have. He'd always found Cameron attractive, but he'd pushed the feelings aside because he was sure the guy was straight. Now that he knew he was gay, though, and his attraction seemed to be validated, he felt he had the permission to think about him more. It was crazy, though. Just because Cameron was gay didn't mean he was attracted to Dax. Despite having lived together for several weeks, and having worked together through some very intense therapy, Cameron had never once overstepped the line.

It's not like it was a secret that Dax was gay. While they never once spoke about the night of his accident, the silence said everything. Cameron had never questioned Dax in the same way his publicist, or his fans had. He seemed to accept Dax simply as a person, rather than an icon who was duty-bound to explain the deepest of thoughts inside his head.

Once a week, he called his Mom, and then he called Kelly. It was an agreement he and Cameron had come to within two weeks of his arrival in Scotland. While his therapy was the most important thing, and while it wasn't in his interest to be burdened by anything to do with his career, he was still a commodity, still owned by a record label, and still duty-bound to report on his progress. Above all, he was still a son, and his mom was keen to check in with him whenever possible.

Now, he reached into his chest of drawers and pulled out his cell. As part of the agreement, he kept it off at all times, save for the nights he called home. Cameron had been clear about the rules from the start. "You're still your own man, of course," he said, "and I can't force you to stick to it. I just think you'll be better off without the distraction."

And he'd been right. Dax found that other than for the calls home, there was no need for him to have his phone switched on. He didn't miss the constant checks of social media or message boards. He didn't think about what the latest tabloids had to say. He was enjoying the solace, and the silence, and the chance to look after his mental health.

But, Kelly was expecting him to call, so he did. The phone rang for less than a second before his assistant picked it up. "Hey!" she cried. "How are you?"

"I'm good," Dax said. "Getting better every day, apparently."

"Great. I miss you."

Dax laughed. "You miss me?"

"Well, don't get me wrong, I don't miss going out for coffee at four in the morning, only for you to have fallen asleep by the time I get back," Kelly joked. "But yeah, I miss you. It's weird to be handling everything over here without hearing what you think of it."

"Without hearing me complain all the time, right?" He sighed. "Damn, I've been a real pain in the ass to you, haven't I?"

Kelly seemed a little taken aback. "Whoa, don't go getting all mushy on me, now," she said. "What's this guy been feeding you? Guilt pills?"

"No, he's been great," Dax said, his head on the pillow, one arm across his eyes. "He really looks after me. I'm eating well, and I'm feeling better than I have for as long as I can remember."

"That's amazing. And are you sleeping, okay?"

"I'm in bed before midnight every night, and I sleep until eight," Dax said, with a laugh. "I'm like a baby on a schedule. It's insane."

"I'm really happy that it's working," Kelly said. "It was always a big risk and I didn't like the idea of it at first, but it seems it was definitely the right choice for you."

"I owe it all to Cameron," Dax said. "There isn't a chance I could have done it without him. He has my meals ready, he has my workout planned, and even does my laundry. I couldn't ask for better treatment."

"Wow, it sounds like you really like him," Kelly said, and Dax wasn't sure whether there was a hint of teasing in her voice. He was about to ignore it, before she added, "is he single?"

"I guess, but I haven't even given it a second thought," Dax said, and he hurriedly changed the subject. "Anyway, hit me with the latest. I can take it."

She sighed. "The press are going crazy with the most recent rumors of your death. They're convinced that you didn't survive the crash, and that you're never coming back."

"And how's Grant managing it?"

"He's denying everything, of course, and the story is that you've now left the hospital, that you're back in LA, and you're recovering at home. Hang on, I've got a newspaper clipping here. It's online, too, but my laptop's just doing an update so I need to find the paper. Wait a second and I'll read it out loud to you."

She was silent for a few moments, and Dax imagined her rummaging through a pile of papers on her desk. Then she returned, and began to read. "*While the whole globe was in shock at the news of the world's most eligible bachelor's car accident, fans were cheered by the daily updates on his health. There's been barely a peep for weeks now, though, and Dax Monroe's representatives are declining to comment further, save for the usual 'no comment' comments. While we're all wondering whether we'll ever see him perform again, the most pressing concern is that he's alive and breathing. This reporter, for one, isn't too convinced.*"

Dax snorted. "That's from an actual newspaper?" he asked. "Jesus, and here I was thinking that the tabloids still had a shred of integrity. That reads like the shittiest online gossip column."

"Well, admittedly it's not from the most high-brow of papers, but it's basically encapsulating what everyone's thinking," Kelly said. "The phone never stops ringing. Grant never stops worrying. I've given up taking his calls because I don't have any news for him. He just gets mad at me and yells until I hang up."

"He's an asshole," Dax said. "Look, Kelly, I don't want you to have to keep dealing with this shit. Do you want to leave? Want me to fire you with severance pay?"

"I've thought about it," she said, honestly. "But I miss you. I miss working for you. I guess I'm like most people. I just want to see you back."

"I'll be back, I promise," Dax said. "In the meantime, I'll get a statement together and I'll stop being quite so distant. All right? I'll up my calls and I'll drop Grant a line."

"That's amazing," Kelly breathed. "There's a lot of publicity we can't handle without you, Dax. You know, about... about that night."

"Yep, got it," Dax said, quickly. He didn't want to go into it over the phone. Didn't want to think about that night, and what it meant when the paparazzi's photos of him sprawled across the bonnet of a stranger's car were still doing the rounds, complete with an interview with said stranger, an interview that revealed everything from the scent of Dax's cologne to the size of his dick and how many times they'd fucked.

He was going to have to reappear, to emerge from the shadows once more. He didn't want to tell Kelly that while he was physically able to come home and carry on his treatment in LA, he wasn't ready to leave yet. He wasn't ready to leave Scotland, and its wild beauty and comforting quiet.

He wasn't ready to leave Cameron just yet.

Speaking for a few more moments with Kelly, he

soon said goodbye and then called his mom. She'd been outside, mowing the lawn. She told him the reporters had slowly left, and were no longer camping outside. There was another celebrity crisis somewhere else, someone else's life collapsing in front of cameras and phones, another media circus documenting every second of their demise.

Dax Monroe was becoming old news, but this worried him, too. The conversation with his mom was short, and he ended the call, saying he was tired. Afterward, he lay looking at the ceiling, confused by his frustrations. In one call, Kelly was saying she needed him there. In the other, his mom was assuring him that people were moving on and forgetting about him.

He didn't know which troubled him more.

Chapter Twenty-Nine

It wasn't unusual for Dax to wake up and wonder what day it was. If it weren't for Cameron's strict plan of getting up, dressed, and down to the breakfast table for the same time every morning, he could easily allow his days to pass without ever knowing what time it was.

Before he knew it, he'd been living with Cameron for a whole month. He was getting better, the weather outside was getting warmer, and Dax was feeling more at peace with himself. Save for the pain in his back that reduced a little every day, he was feeling rather good about life.

For the first time since the accident, he realized how much he missed singing. One morning, while in the bath, he began to belt out one of his old tunes. *Stopping Time* was a lesser-known track from an early album, but he'd liked it as soon as it was played to him for the first time.

"*Minutes and hours mean nothing to a man like me,*" he sang while relaxing in the water. "*I can stop time with a turn of a key. Nothing locked down here, nothing set in stone. I've got the ability to transverse zones.*"

It was a dumb song, really, the lyrics forced together simply because they rhymed, but Dax had always liked the beat. It was never good enough to be played at any of his concerts; even the early ones that didn't have the luxury of a huge back catalog from which to draw still wouldn't feature it, but he'd always had a soft spot for the track. He had good memories of it, of sitting around the table and insisting he wanted it on the album. When everything in his career was still new, and exciting.

He was still a kid back then. Twenty, twenty-one, still loving the attention that came as he walked around shopping malls after closing, given personal time to himself while crazed fans and paparazzi took photographs of him. He loved walking out and waving to screams and cries and yells of affection, even marriage proposals. He didn't mind going out for dinner and being bundled into the back of a car by security when the crowd got too close. He loved that they wanted him so much.

Sitting in the bath now, twelve years older and somewhat wiser, he realized how naive he'd been. How he knew that the adoration from the crowds outside had been a substitute for the rest of the time he was holed up in hotels and mansions, alone in a room full of people he didn't know, or care about. People who told him what to wear, what to sing, what to think.

And, they always insisted, who to date. He'd been linked with models and singers, actresses and even gymnasts. His management team had made sure that he was never far away from a beautiful woman. Because they knew that coming out would spell the end of his career.

The reality of his situation now was hitting home a little deeper each day, and Dax knew that at some point, he was going to have to deal with it. He was going to have to reappear in public, and was going to have to address the rumors once and for all. And it was a huge choice to make: deny all and hope that people forgot about it, or come out to the world, and risk losing his entire career.

He thought back to how, a few years earlier, he'd been in the shower in his large New York apartment. He'd spent the night with a gorgeous backing dancer from the tour, and the dancer had, like most other partners, leaked details of his sexuality to the press. Grant had screamed at Dax, telling him to stop thinking with his cock and remember who he was.

Dax had slid down the walls of the shower that morning in New York and had sat on the cool tiles for a long time, while the water lashed his back. He hadn't grown up a religious kid, and his mom hadn't taken him to church, so he had no idea what he was supposed to say, but he'd only turned his head up to the ceiling, recalling from somewhere that God was always above him, in the heavens, and had pleaded out loud.

"Please, God, I don't want this," he'd begged. "I don't want to be gay. I don't want to like guys. Let me like girls, God. Please?"

But God either wasn't there, or didn't care. Dax never knew which was the right answer. But what he did know was that nothing changed. He didn't stop liking guys. And he settled into an unfulfilling routine of clandestine hook-ups and one night stands that he could never disclose to anyone. He ran the risk of being found out if he ever saw the same guy twice.

There were times he spoke to Grant about things. Now, as the hot water was becoming lukewarm, Dax found he couldn't pull himself away from the memory. He was sitting in Grant's office, and his red-faced manager was thrusting yet another pile of paparazzi photographs in front of him.

"This time you're leaving that seedy fucking hotel on West Nineteenth," he growled, his eyes bulging. "Nobody goes there unless they're sucking another guy's cock."

"Maybe if you just let me settle down with someone I wouldn't be forced into fucking guys in shitty places and getting papped," Dax fired back. He was so tired of explaining himself for yet another indiscretion. It was happening on a monthly basis.

"Yeah, settle down," Grant mocked. "That's gonna happen. Why don't you just fire a fucking shotgun at both of us and have done with it?"

"There are plenty of gay artists," Dax said. "Whether they're completely out, or whether it's just an open secret. It's not a big deal."

He took a deep breath and felt a rare surge of passion. "It's who I am."

But Grant had dismissed that passion in a heartbeat, waving his hand and casting it away. "Forget it. It's not who you are. You're a straight man who sells millions of records to lovestruck girls, and it's going to stay that way."

The memory dissolved suddenly as the lukewarm water chilled, jolting Dax out of his stupor. He stood up, reaching for a scratchy towel and stepping carefully onto the floor. It wasn't time for him to think about the past and the hurt it held, and yet he found that he was sad.

He slowly toweled his whole body and slipped into a pair of jeans and a t-shirt. Jeans had been difficult to wear at first, thanks to their rigid form leaving him unable to relax, but now his condition was improving, he was back to wearing some of his favorite designer clothes.

Walking down the stairs, he held onto the banister, planting each foot carefully on the steps so as not to slip in his socks. He heard whistling, as he always did when he came down from his room.

Cameron was banging about in the kitchen, making breakfast.

Since he learned how to make a good cup of tea, it had been Dax's job to look after that in the mornings. So, on entering the kitchen, the first thing he did was take two mugs from the cupboard.

"Good morning," said Cameron, cheerfully. "How did you sleep?"

"Good, thanks," Dax replied, and he walked to the sink with the kettle, filling it up. Back home, he'd put it on the stove, lighting a flame underneath, but here in the UK he plugged it in at the wall and switched on the power.

"That was some song you were belting out up there," Cameron said. He laid some pieces of bacon into the frying pan and immediately the delicious scent emerged from the crackles.

"I didn't know you could hear me," Dax said.

"That's a hell of a voice you've got on you. I wish I could sing like that."

"Thanks."

"Are you all right?"

Dax nodded, but the sadness that had started to fill him as he thought back to the memory of Grant humiliating him in the office wasn't shifting. Cameron was concerned.

"Let's sit down and eat, and we'll talk. Or not. It's up to you."

Dax didn't want to talk, that was for sure. He hadn't opened up to Cameron about anything other than the physical struggles of his treatment, and he certainly wasn't about to start now. He poured a little milk into the mugs, tossing in a teabag, and pouring over the boiling hot water from the kettle. With a metal spoon, he stirred the teabags until the tea was a rich orange color, and then he removed them and tossed them into the trash.

Before his accident, he would wake up and make himself coffee; either that, or Kelly would bring him some from a local place. He'd have a cigarette or two, skipping breakfast or having a piece of fruit if Kelly forced it down him. Now, he was having a large, filling breakfast that Cameron made him every day. Today, he was having toasted black bread with bacon and avocado, and a poached egg.

He moved his food around his plate, and Cameron probed, but Dax's mood had dipped. He couldn't exactly put his finger on what it was until, in a moment of silence, he looked up from his plate to see Cameron reading the paper, a mug of tea in his hand, and Dax realized why he'd been feeling so sad.

After having lived with Cameron for a month, they were now in a routine. And it was one in which Dax had never had before. He was waking up, bathing, coming down for breakfast and talking with a gorgeous guy. They were living together. It was as though he was in the life he'd always wanted. A normal life: him, with a guy.

But it wasn't a normal life. Because he and Cameron weren't partners. And this made Dax sad, too. Because he was once again attracted to a guy he couldn't have. A life that would never be his. A routine that was only temporary. And that's why his day had already taken a melancholy turn, when it was barely ten a.m.

"How about we get out of the house today?"

Cameron asked, his observant eyes noticing that perhaps another day indoors wasn't a good idea. "There's a place in town that has a hydrotherapy pool. I'll call them and see if we can use it. It's never busy."

"Pool?" Dax liked the idea. He missed swimming in any one of the three pools he'd had built in his homes. The thought of a change of scenery was welcome, too. He nodded. "Sounds great."

Cameron called and booked an hour's private appointment for one thirty. Until then, Dax had the morning off. He went upstairs and tidied his room, slowly changing the sheets on his bed. He made a pile of clothes, tossed them to the bottom of the stairs, and went down after them. Once at the bottom, he bent his legs slowly, picked the clothes up and carried them to the washing machine in the kitchen.

A simple task like laundry had taken him ten times longer than it would have done before, but the important thing was that he was doing it all himself. He was only going to get stronger, too. He just had to be patient.

Chapter Thirty

There was nobody at the pool. Dax had envisioned a bustling place with lots of people swimming up and down, some of them performing a leisurely breaststroke, others in goggles and swimming caps, bringing their arms over their heads in a perfect rhythm as they pushed forward to do length after length.

But not only was there nobody swimming, there wasn't even much of a pool to swim *in.* Cameron explained. "The guy who owns the place is Invergordon's elected MP. That's the member of parliament. I guess the closest you'd have is maybe a senator. His daughter was born with cerebral palsy, and she died a few years ago. He had the pool made for her, and now she's gone, he lets the public use it as they please. So, hospitals bring patients here from time to time."

"That's a sad story," Dax said.

"It is," Cameron agreed, "and it's a real shame for the family. She caught pneumonia after a really bad winter here, and she didn't recover. I think he likes knowing people carry on using the pool even though Cheryl's no longer with us."

There weren't even any staff working there. Cameron pushed open the door and Dax followed, pleased that he hadn't had to hide himself with a hat and shades, because there was nobody around. "It's a small place with very low crime," the therapist explained. "People respect their appointment times, and the doors are opened every morning by a caretaker, and then closed every evening. Until then, people come and go as per their time slot, so we won't be disturbed."

Even though the building was very small, there was the unmistakable smell of chlorine when they went inside. Dax and Cameron went into a changing area, and Dax slipped into a cubicle, taking off his clothes, under which he wore a pair of swim shorts. He had no idea what to expect from the session. Instead of slippery tiles underfoot there was a special waterproof carpet, so to Dax's relief he could walk steadily. He didn't even need to use the conveniently-placed handrail, either. He had just come out of the cubicle to ask where he should put his clothes when he was struck dumb.

Ahead of him, Cameron was putting his own clothes in a large locker, his back to Dax. He wore a small pair of red swim shorts, so they came up to the top of his thighs, and Dax could see the definition of his muscled legs. His broad back, dotted with the odd freckle, was strong and also muscly; and as he turned around to see where Dax was, Dax caught his beautiful body in full.

He was so hot that Dax had to pretend he'd forgotten something and turned back into his cubicle. "Just taking my watch off," he called, although it was waterproof and could have remained on his wrist. He had to close his eyes and count to twenty, in order to stop his cock from twitching. Just the sight of Cameron's incredible body was making him break out in a sweat, and he was already nervous about going into the pool.

Using calming techniques he employed before going on stage, he closed his eyes and took deep breaths. Then he scooped up his clothes and joined Cameron outside. They put their clothes in the locker and then passed under the showers for a quick spritz before walking to the pool.

It was, in effect, a small, kidney-shaped hole in the ground. The water lapped over the edges, and there were wide steps into the pool at one end. At the other, there was a hydraulic chair in which a patient could be seated and slowly immersed in the water. Cameron nodded to it. "Don't worry, we won't be needing that," he said. "Your recovery's coming on far too well."

He slipped into the water with ease. "It's lovely and warm," he said, ducking under the surface and coming up again, running a hand through his wet curls. Dax gingerly walked to the edge, too, but Cameron pointed to the steps. "Come in that way. Keep hold of the rail."

The steps were also covered in the same strange carpet that seemed to caress his toes like suede, as Dax moved down one step, then another, and another, until the warm water enveloped him. It was deliciously warm on this mild Scottish Spring day, but the water wasn't deep enough for him to be concerned. At the very deepest part it came only up to his chest.

He was still a little unsteady on his feet, thanks to a sensation that was new to his body since the accident, but as always, Cameron was there. The therapist took his hands. "Right now there's no current in here," he said. "But there's a panel just on the side, and I can change it so that we can cause a light current to flow through, which at some point I'll have you standing in, to help build your core strength."

Standing opposite Dax, he kept firm hold of his hands. "All we're going to do now is move from side to side. So keep your eyes on me, don't look down, and move your right foot one step, joining up again with your left."

The stepping was easy. Keeping his eyes on Cameron was not. Dax forced himself not to look below the therapist's chin, not to glance at his strong, defined pecs, or the stiff peak of his nipple in the center of each. He clenched his jaw and stared into Cameron's green eyes instead, but this didn't help much, it gave him a look of real fear, which Cameron immediately picked up on.

"Don't be scared," he laughed. "This is no different to the exercises we've done in the house. In fact, the water should be making them easier."

We weren't practically naked in the house, Dax thought, but he only nodded and said nothing. He could feel how the buoyancy of his body in the water meant he had to concentrate more, but that he was already feeling the heat of the pool relieving some of the ever-constant ache in his spine.

They walked up and down the pool in this way, before Cameron switched to Dax walking forward, and then backward. Dax moved his arms, pushing one out, and then another, slapping Cameron's open fist as though they were performing a very slow boxing spar. The hot water was loosening his muscles, so he was much less tense, and his range of movement was clear.

Cameron was impressed. "I can't believe I've waited so long to bring you here," he said. "I didn't realize it would have this effect. You're doing great."

Later, he turned on the current, and there was a whirring sound as the turbines in the pool's mechanism started to turn. Dax felt a wave coming toward him, and his instinct was to completely go floppy and let it take him, but Cameron urged him to stand firm. "Plant your feet," he instructed. "Hold the position as though you're stopping it from knocking you over."

Dax could feel the strength of the water against him; while before his accident he would have resisted it with ease, his body wasn't strong enough to withstand the force, and he moved backward, before feeling his legs slip from underneath him. His head was back, and his eyes opened in fear, but in an instant Cameron was there, holding his head so that he didn't once go under the surface.

"Maybe that's a bit strong for today," he said, leaning over to turn off the current. "We'll do that another time."

Dax nodded, getting to his feet, but Cameron got him on his back again. "While you're there, you might as well try a float," he said. "It uses core muscles, but without you even realizing it."

And Dax lifted his feet off the bottom of the pool again, feeling the water push him up naturally, so he lay on his back, staring at the ceiling, relishing the glorious feeling of being totally weightless. He breathed in deeply, Cameron's hands still on the back of his head.

"You like that don't you?" the therapist laughed.

"I could lie like this all day," Dax murmured. "Can't you have a pool built in your place? I'll pay for it."

"Nowhere to put it, I'm afraid," Cameron said. "I've thought about it before but it just isn't practical. It'd have to go outside, but the weather just isn't temperate enough."

On his back, Dax felt lighter than he had done in so long. He felt not just the weight of gravity lifting from him, but the weight of the last few weeks. Months. Years. Something as simple as lying on his back and floating gave him a feeling of deep calm.

But then he opened his eyes, and he was staring up into Cameron's face, and Dax couldn't relax any longer. He felt a pit of anxiety in his stomach, and when he was no longer relaxing, his muscles tensed, and he started to sink.

"Feet on the bottom," Cameron said, raising his head up clear of the water as Dax pushed down and felt his soles against the tiles. Cameron smiled. "You've done so much today. You must be exhausted."

"Yeah," Dax said. "I guess that's it."

There was a fluttering in his stomach, and the world around him seemed to sway, not just from the lapping of the water against the pool. His breath was quick, something close to panic setting in, but it was a feeling that made him act, made him do something he'd been desperate to do for so long.

He moved forward, closed his eyes, and pressed his lips against Cameron's.

Chapter Thirty-One

It was over in a flash, but it felt *right* for just that second. Cameron's lips were damp from the water that had dripped from his hair, and he tasted like someone who'd been in a pool. Dax pulled away, looking at him in panic.

"Erm, I think that's it for today," Cameron said, he moved backward, indicating the steps. He was telling Dax to climb up them, and out of the pool.

Dax was sure that if it weren't for the fact Cameron was looking after him, the therapist would get out, march to the changing rooms, pull on his clothes and screech away in the car. He couldn't, though. He had to make sure that each step up that Dax took, his feet were planted steadily, and that he wouldn't slip.

They were silent as they got out of the pool, as they walked to the changing room, as they collected their clothes, and as they dressed. Usually, Dax would shower after a swim, washing the chlorine from his body, but he wanted to get out of there as quickly as he could.

He pulled on his jeans with difficulty, gritting his teeth and wanting to scream with frustration. Not just because the denim was refusing to come up his thighs, but because he'd ruined everything. He'd been a fucking idiot to make a move on Cameron, and now everything was ruined. His therapy was going to come to an end. Cameron was going to ask him to leave. It was over.

If Cameron hadn't been in the next cubicle, Dax would have punched the wall in frustration. Finally, his jeans were on, and he pulled his t-shirt over his head. He put on his socks and shoes and stepped outside.

Cameron was waiting at the door for him, and they walked out in silence to the car. Cameron pressed the button to unlock it, and Dax climbed into the seat.

The ride home was made in silence, although Dax opened his mouth to speak at least once, before deciding against it. He was certain that more than once, Cameron did the same, but in the end, not a word was said.

When they got home, Cameron muttered something about checking the firewood in the barn behind the house, and he left Dax to get out of the car himself, something he'd been doing well for several weeks now. Dax walked morosely to the house, pushing open the front door, which Cameron didn't bother to lock. He walked up the stairs, thought about having a hot bath, before remembering that he'd used all the hot water already that morning.

He sat on his bed, pulling his legs up, resting his head on the pillow and then lying flat, looking up at the ceiling. "You fucking idiot," he said to himself. "You had to go and fuck everything up."

His heart was heavy, and he was suddenly very homesick. He'd have given anything to be back home in the sunshine of California, maybe sitting out on the deck or even by the sea. Somewhere where everything didn't feel so damn cold, even in the spring, and where he didn't feel so helpless.

The swimming had left him tired, and were it not for the anxiety of having made a colossal error of judgment, he might have been feeling very nicely relaxed. However, as it was, he couldn't sleep. He closed his eyes and focused on some breathing exercises, and was just allowing his mind to drift onto other things before the utter humiliation dragged him back to reality.

Gingerly, he sat up and kicked off his shoes and socks. He reached for his phone, although it wasn't the usual time for him to turn it on. He was just about to press the button when there was a tap on the door.

Before he could answer, Cameron walked in, hands in his pockets, looking a little sheepish. "I just came to see if you wanted a cup of tea and some toast," he said. "It's important for you to keep your energy levels up after swimming."

"I'm okay, thank you," Dax replied. "I'm not thirsty."

"Right," Cameron said, but he didn't move. He looked as though he wanted to say something, and the atmosphere was thick, the way it had been in the car. To Dax's surprise, Cameron came over and sat beside him on the bed.

"I don't want you to feel bad," he began, but then stopped.

"It was wrong, and I'm sorry," Dax said.

"No, it's not that it's *wrong*," Cameron insisted. "You've not done anything wrong. And I'm flattered, really. But you're a patient, and I'm treating you as a professional, and it wouldn't be, well..."

He looked at Dax, and Dax stared at him. The air in the room had changed. It was now electric.

"Well, I guess it would be, um," Cameron continued, before shaking his head. "Oh, fuck it."

And he was the one who made the first move this time, and he leaned into Dax and kissed him, hard, on his mouth. Dax was in shock for a millisecond, before returning the kiss with vigor.

Sparks practically flew between them as they hungrily explored each other's mouths for the first time.

Dax didn't want the kiss to end, but he was sitting on the bed with his feet on the floor and his back was twisted to the left in order to kiss Cameron, so he had to stop. He was scared that by stopping, Cameron would change his mind, so he shuffled back onto the bed and dragged Cameron with him, lying back and pulling the therapist on top of him. He yanked at his t-shirt, trying to pull it over Cameron's head.

Cameron pulled away breathlessly, staring down at him for a second, as though checking himself, before kissing Dax once more, and pulling his own t-shirt over his head. Now, Dax could finally touch the beautiful body he'd been fantasizing about for weeks, and that he saw for the first time that morning, and had longed to touch it then.

His pecs were as firm as they looked, and Dax's hands moved down his body, lower and lower. He was aiming for one place, and with haste he held Cameron's bulge in the palm of his hand. At this, Cameron took his own hand and moved Dax's away. Dax was confused. "Don't you want me to?" he asked.

"I'm not the sort of guy who's into quick fucks," Cameron said, and he rolled away so he lay on his side beside Dax. "I'm sorry, but if that's what you want, it's not for me."

Dax took a deep breath, running his tongue along his lower lip, still tasting Cameron there. "I'm so used to rushing everything," he said. "Usually when I'm with a guy we have to hurry up and just do it, and then I'm out of here. Now, I'm restricted in a lot of ways."

"Right."

Dax shook his head. "I don't mean it like that," he said. "I just mean that I'm no good at this at all."

Cameron smiled. "Oh, I don't know," he said. "You've certainly got me going."

He sat up, reaching for his t-shirt, but Dax touched his arm. "Don't leave," he said softly. "Show me."

"Show you what?"

"How to really make love to another man."

He blushed as he said the words, but it wasn't from embarrassment. Instead, the warm feeling that came from them surged up from his belly, and to his joy, Cameron tossed the t-shirt to one side again, and he lay back beside Dax, propping himself up on his elbow. "Kiss me," he said. "But properly. Not like you're just rushing to get from one place to the next."

So Dax reached up, cupped the back of his head, and pulled Cameron close. This time, when their lips touched, Dax didn't rush to plunge his tongue into Cameron's mouth. Instead, their lips moved together, over one another, and when it was time for him to taste him, Dax gently ran his tongue over Cameron's lips, searching for the other man's tongue with his own.

His fingers ran over Cameron's shoulders, his back and his chest, and he felt Cameron's fingers moving up his own, stroking his belly. "Oh God," Cameron breathed into his mouth. "When I saw you today it was so fucking hard to be professional."

"You're telling me," Dax replied. "Why do you think I said I needed to take my watch off?"

They laughed gently, but the nerves between them were still there. Dax could feel the blood pounding in his ears. He pulled Cameron close once more, and this time, their kisses were sure, certain. Cameron felt good. So good, that Dax was already hard. His cock pressed against his jeans and was almost painful, and yet at the same time it was so good to finally kiss this man that he didn't care. He embraced the pain as part of the thrill of kissing him for the first time.

Cameron was an incredible kisser. He was soft and gentle, but there was a surety in his lips, a firmness that showed Dax that he was serious. That he wanted this to happen, too. Dax wasn't about to question it, to overthink it. It was just too good.

He stroked Cameron's skin, smooth and pale, as though it had never been touched by the sun. His own skin was tanned from years of sitting by the pool, or at the beach, or under ultra-violet rods when there was a tour coming up and Grant said he looked too pasty. As he stroked, his fingers moved down Cameron's back, feeling the definition of the muscles in his back.

He felt Cameron explore him, too, fingers moving down his stomach, making him shiver with delight. Now, the fingers moved even lower, going below the belt of his jeans. Dax groaned as Cameron cupped his cock, and he felt a moan in his mouth.

"I'm pretty sure if I told anyone in the world that right now, I was holding Dax Monroe's cock, they'd say I was lying."

Dax laughed. "I'd say you were teasing."

Cameron took his hand away. "Is that better?"

But Dax gave a cry of frustration. "No!"

Now it was Cameron's turn to laugh, and they kissed again, and this time, Cameron's fingers didn't stop exploring Dax. He pulled down the zip of Dax's jeans, slid his hand into the gap, and brushed against Dax's cock, getting closer and closer; the only thing between them now was the thin cotton of Dax's very expensive underwear.

He was rock hard, straining against Cameron's hand, and he held his face with both hands, breathing heavily. "I want you so much," he said. "I've wanted you since the second you walked into my hospital room."

There was a slight hesitation from Cameron at this point, and Dax knew that he was having a crisis of conscience, panicking at the knowledge that as far as patient/therapist boundaries go, they definitely crossed it. But Dax shook his head. "Right now, you're not working for me. Don't think about it. Think about how good this feels, how much you and I want this."

To that, Cameron said nothing; instead, in response, he pulled down the front of Dax's underwear, and his cock sprang up against his stomach. Finally free, Dax groaned with joy, and his own fingers searched for Cameron's fly. He pulled open the buttons, as there was no zip, and he felt how rock hard Cameron was, too. "I need you in my mouth," he said, and Cameron groaned.

Dax tried to move, but he did so too quickly, and he felt a twinge in his back, telling him to stop and take it easy. He slammed his hand onto the mattress with frustration.

"What's wrong?" Cameron's voice was immediately full of concern.

"I'm so fucking tired of being unable to move,"

he said. "All I want to do is pin you down and suck you until you come in my mouth, and I can't."

Cameron licked his lips, his breathing heavy. "I don't mean to trivialize your pain right now, but hearing you say that, it's pretty fucking hot."

Dax stared at him. "Take off your underwear and get on top of me right now," he ordered. "Get that dick in my mouth."

Standing up on the floor, Cameron shucked off his jeans and boxers. Dax stared at him, naked for the first time in front of his eyes, and immediately he began to stroke his own cock. He couldn't help it. Cameron had him so horny that it was impossible for him to concentrate on anything else.

Cameron knelt on the bed slowly, starting from the end of the bed and moving upwards, crawling like a leopard stalking its prey. He began to tug on the waist of Dax's jeans, and Dax planted his elbows on the mattress and lifted his hips up for just a second, thanking God, or whoever was listening, for all the time he'd spent in the gym, working on his upper body strength, so that now he didn't feel any pain in his back as he lifted himself up.

In a second, Cameron had pulled his jeans off and now the two of them were naked, but Cameron didn't come up to Dax as Dax had instructed him; instead he stopped at Dax's cock, lowered his head, and licked his lips. "I can't resist," he whispered, and Dax couldn't scold him, because he watched as the hot Scot ran his hand up and down Dax's cock, then took him in his mouth.

Dax could have wept with joy. He'd never felt such relief. Cameron's mouth was hot and wet, and his cock basked in the depths as warm lips and tongue worked their magic. In his ecstasy, too, Dax was aware that there was no need to rush anything; there wasn't a human being around for miles. Nobody was going to walk in and catch them. Nobody was going to jump in and take his photograph to sell to a paper. For the first time in his adult life, Dax could actually enjoy sex.

And there was plenty to enjoy. Cameron was incredible with his mouth. It had been so long for Dax that he'd have taken even a *bad* blow job, but this was taking him to another world. Once again, he knew it was because there was no desperation involved, no frantic rushing to come just so he could zip himself back up and get the hell out of there.

Still, it had been so long that Dax knew if he weren't careful, then it would all be over far too soon. So he held onto a handful of Cameron's curls and lifted his head up. "My turn," he said. "Get up here."

Cameron seemed loath to leave, but he released Dax's cock from his mouth, now wet and slick with precum, and he moved up to his face again. He kissed Dax, plunging his tongue into the star's mouth, swirling it around and filling Dax with the glorious taste of his own dick.

He pulled Cameron up higher, and Cameron knelt with one knee either side of his waist, moving up his body. Dax cupped his bare ass in his large hands, feeling its smoothness, its strength. He resisted the urge to pull the cheeks of Cameron's ass apart and slip his finger in his hole. There was no need to be hasty. Besides, there was enough to keep him satisfied: Cameron's dick was inches from his face.

It was long and slim, the head pink and glistening with precum. Dax's mouth watered, and he moved his head up, but he wasn't close enough. He looked up at Cameron. "Higher," he said, and Cameron shuffled up. As he did so, Dax's mouth opened, and Cameron drove his cock into the cavern, Dax's flat tongue the perfect runway for the landing.

Dax's lips closed over his cock, and he groaned with the pleasure of having another man inside his mouth. Cameron's hips moved back and forth, doing most of the work, because Dax's neck couldn't move quickly enough. Chancing his arm, Dax paused, brought his finger to his mouth, and sucked it quickly. As he looked up at Cameron, he moved his hand around to Cameron's ass, searching for his hole.

Cameron stared down at him, open-mouthed, his red curls falling down in front of his face, and he groaned as Dax found his asshole, tight and puckered, and as Dax continued to suck him, he swirled his finger around the rosebud, before pushing inside gently. He groaned loudly as he watched Cameron hold his own ass in both hands and pull the cheeks apart, so that Dax's finger slid inside.

As Dax's tongue swirled around the throbbing cock, his finger pressed against Cameron's prostate, and Cameron cried out in ecstasy. Dax's cock stood straight up, stiff and desperate to do what it had craved for so long. He pulled his finger out of Cameron's ass and pushed him down his body. Cameron knew what was happening, and he worked up enough saliva in his mouth to drop a large glob on the tip of Dax's cock, working it up and down, getting it wet.

Then he knelt over it, spread his legs, and guided Dax to his hole. Dax's eyes were wide, and he watched in awe as Cameron slowly sat down on him, pushing his cock inside his ass. Cameron swallowed him slowly, and both men gave huge groans. Dax's was with pure euphoria, Cameron's edged with a certain amount of pain.

But the pain passed, and once Cameron had acclimatized himself to the invasion, he closed his eyes, threw back his head, and rocked on Dax's cock. He gave a loud laughing yell of delight. "Fuck!" he cried. "That's a fucking big cock!"

Dax moved his hips, and Cameron looked down at him, panting as he moved up and down. Dax could see his cock moving in and out of Cameron's ass, could feel it clenching him with its tight muscles, and he was in heaven.

Cameron fell forward, his fists on the pillow, lowering his head to kiss Dax. "I've wanted you inside me for so long," he whispered, and he began to pump his cock with one hand as Dax gripped his hips and fucked him. Both men knew they weren't going to last for long, and Cameron was the first to cry out, tense, and grunt as his cock twitched violently, his balls clenching as he fired his seed all over Dax's throat and chin.

He wriggled as the spasms of his climax almost seemed to take him by surprise, and Dax firmly held him down, burying his cock deep in Cameron's ass. The muscles of his hole gripped Dax inside, and within a few seconds he was following suit, only his seed shot out into the hot depths of Cameron's bowels. Both men groaned, the sweat between their skin holding them together, and Cameron lay on top of Dax, kissing him passionately, until their orgasms subsided.

Dax slid out from Cameron, feeling his own hot seed leaking out of the man kneeling above him, anointing him with the holiest of oils. He ran his hands up and down Cameron's back as they kissed slowly, neither man quite sure that what they'd done had really happened.

It was late afternoon, and they lay together for a while, until both men fell asleep, exhausted.

Chapter Thirty-Two

When he opened his eyes, it was dark. He could feel an aching in his limbs, but within a few seconds, he realized that it was a good kind of ache, the ache that came after having had sex for the first time in a very, very long time.

He could hear Cameron breathing steadily beside him. He was thirsty. Between the two men there lingered the sweet smell of sex, the musky odor of two men having finally given in to their lust. Dax could have happily fallen asleep once more but the craving for water was too strong. Besides, he needed to pee.

Carefully moving so as not to wake Cameron, he slipped into his boxers and padded out to the landing. He used the bathroom and then went downstairs. In the kitchen, he filled a glass of water and gulped it down. He heard the creaking of floorboards above his head and he knew that Cameron had stirred, too. In an old house like this, there was no getting away with sneaking around: the old place was bound to give you away at any second.

Now that Dax had drunk water, his belly rumbled with hunger, so he pulled some bread out of the packet and popped it into the four-slice toaster. As he did so, he felt two strong arms loop around his waist, bare skin pressing against his back, and two lips kissing his shoulder. He turned around and Cameron leaned in to kiss him deeply. For a few seconds the two men tasted each other's mouths, only this time with less frantic lust than before. More with gentle affection and tenderness.

That wasn't to say, of course, that the kisses had no effect on either of them. On the contrary, Dax felt his cock stirring within seconds, and he was hard, and as he moved his hips, he felt Cameron's erection rubbing against his hip, too. "Fuck," the therapist whispered. "What are you doing to me?"

Dax smiled. "It's all your fault," he said. "You can't blame me for any of this."

"There's something I need to ask you," Cameron said, his eyes serious. Dax pulled back and looked at him.

"What is it?"

"Please tell me that you've put some toast in for me, too?"

Dax laughed. "What would you do if I said all four pieces were for me?"

"I'd tell you that I'd never suck your dick again."

Dax groaned. "Don't say that," he said. "I'll give you all four pieces right now, I swear."

Cameron kissed him. "I wouldn't do that to you," he said. "Just two's fine."

"Butter and jelly?"

"Jelly?"

"Sorry. Jam."

"Yes, jam. Jelly's another thing entirely. It's a wobbly dessert you eat with ice cream at kids' birthday parties."

"Ah, yeah. You mean jello."

"No, *you* mean jello," Cameron teased. "You're in my country now, remember?"

He went to the fridge, and like Dax, was only wearing his boxer shorts. Dax took a second to appreciate the sight of his firm ass. His erection was subsiding for the moment, his empty belly a more pressing concern at present. He buttered the toast and slathered it with strawberry jam, and the two men munched on their snack. It was a little after ten, and Dax was disoriented, his body clock not knowing what on earth was going on.

He couldn't recall a time he'd slept so soundly, even long before the accident. So many of his nights were spent partying, and he would usually fall asleep in a drunken stupor in the early hours of the morning. His body was still working so hard to process all the alcohol in his system night after night that he never really felt rested. Now, though, whether because of the hours of slumber, or simply because of the endorphins rushing around his body thanks to sex with Cameron, he felt good. Healthy. *Well.*

Earlier in the day, he hadn't felt that way. The memory of his fight against himself had him looking down a very dark tunnel, and he'd been about to head down there, into the abyss, but he'd taken a chance, and it had paid off. A chance to declare his own feelings, and the response had been very favorable indeed.

That evening, Cameron came into his bed without either of them talking about it. They made love until the early hours, and Dax realized what it was like to have sex with someone who was still there the following morning. No sneaking out, no feelings of shame or embarrassment. And, most amazing of all, no photographer trying to land the snap of their career at Dax's expense.

Over the next few days, the two men saw each other in a whole new light. The sexual tension Dax hadn't even known was there had finally been addressed, and a weight had been lifted. Cameron was still keen to ensure Dax's recovery didn't slip, though, and they continued their time as therapist and patient.

Sitting at a weight machine in the gym upstairs, Dax reached up to a bar above his head, slowly pulling it down and releasing it back up again. He concentrated on lifting correctly, and although the weight still wasn't very large, he was careful not to tear any of the muscles in his back.

"So, did you know?" he asked Cameron, who was standing in front of him, his arms folded as he watched to make sure Dax's technique was safe.

"Know what?"

"That I like guys."

Cameron smiled, but it wasn't a cruel smile. It looked a little sad. He nodded. "Yeah, I guess I knew before we met," he said. "I mean, I've never been one to follow tabloids about celebrities, and I have to confess that I don't really know anything about your career, but it was pretty much seen as an open secret."

Dax nodded. "I know it must sound so dumb to you, but I had no idea it was that obvious. I didn't know that people knew. I thought that all this time, I was going out and meeting guys and getting away with it. Sure, there was the odd story in the media but my PR team cleared it up so fast that I didn't hear anything else about it. I didn't know that they were basically trying to protect my feelings but by doing that, they were keeping me from the truth."

He felt foolish. As though everyone else had known about him the whole time, but he'd been blind to it, thinking he'd been clever the whole time, thinking nobody had really noticed. But by confronting it, by saying it aloud, he knew that deep down, he'd always known that it wasn't a secret.

"What about you?" he asked. "Do people know?"

Cameron shrugged. "I've never denied it, and I've never withheld it from anyone who wanted to know. But I've never felt the need to tell anyone. I mean, I'm left handed. I never think about it. I just write with my left hand. But if you go back just a hundred years, or maybe less, people would think you were crazy for being left-handed. They'd accuse you of witchcraft."

Dax paused in his reps, releasing the bar above his head. "Maybe one day they won't think I'm crazy," he said, staring at the floor.

"Who thinks you're crazy?" Cameron asked.

"Everyone who tells me that it's wrong for me to have these feelings," Dax said.

"But who's telling you this? I'm confused. If the hatred for your feelings is coming from yourself, then you need to learn how to deal with it, and how to learn to love yourself."

Dax rolled his eyes. "Let me guess. You've been talking to Doctor Pravenda."

"I take it she's told you the same," Cameron replied. "And she's right. Because I can see it from a mile off, and so can she. You don't love yourself. You've got hordes of fans and millions of people around the world who adore you, but none of it means anything if you can't accept yourself for who you are."

Dax didn't say anything. He shook his head and looked at the floor. Cameron could never understand what it was like to be him, to have the weight on his shoulders that he'd had since he was eighteen.

"Look at me," Cameron said, and Dax lifted his head, staring into the green eyes that pierced deeply into his soul. "Anybody who tells you that being gay is crazy, isn't worth your time. They're not worth your love. They're not worth your attention. And I think you've been surrounding yourself with people like that for so long, that you've bought into their bullshit."

"I knew what I was signing up for when I wanted to be famous," Dax said. "It's my fault."

"What, what?" Cameron was incredulous. "You're holding yourself to a decision you made when you were barely an adult? Plenty of people have the skill and the dream to be a star. But the chances of making it are a million to one. So what, you have to spend the rest of your life selling out just to see your name in lights?"

"I don't expect you to understand."

"Good. Because I'm afraid I really don't."

"I have a duty to be true to the person they've created," Dax said. "I have responsibilities to my fans, to my team. If I fuck up and expose myself, then everyone loses."

"Wow," Cameron said, softly. "They've fed you this bullshit for so long that you've really started to believe it now. It's like you're in a cult. The kind of cult where you have to show loyalty to the supreme leader, because they're the one pulling the strings. But you can't see it's a cult until you're out of it."

He knelt down and stroked Dax's face. "They're wrong to tell you that you're anything other than perfect as you are," he said. "And I wish you could see what I see. Because once you do, your life is going to start properly."

Dax gazed at him. He could feel the touch of Cameron's fingers on his skin, and it was the most genuine thing he'd ever felt. He wanted so much to trust him, to believe that what he was saying was true, but each time he felt he might just be able to grasp at the chance, it melted away from him again, the reality of his life causing him to come crashing down once more.

"Work out who you really want to be," Cameron said. "If the fame and the stardom's enough for you, then keep at it. Go back to America and keep being the boy next door that all the girls go crazy for. But there's so much more to you than that. And it's really sad to see someone being forced to be someone they're not, just to line the pockets of assholes in suits, smoking cigars and counting their money."

In a flash, all Dax could see was Grant, sitting at his desk, doing just that. He thought about all the times his manager had barked at him, humiliated him, shouted him down. He recalled the way he'd pleaded with Grant, begging for just a little time off from the touring, or space to clear his head. Grant had always refused.

Now, in front of him, Dax had someone who seemed to have his best interests at heart, and yet this scared him too. Cameron's words made sense to him, and terrified him all at the same time. He sensed that in the distance, a new path was starting to become clearer, but he was far too scared to walk down it, for fear of what Grant had always threatened: the end of his career. Obscurity. Desolation.

Sooner or later, he was going to have to face things. For now, though, it wouldn't hurt to explore things with Cameron. He lifted his hand to Cameron's, which was still on the side of his face. He held it, leaned forward and kissed him on the lips, and Cameron's hands moved down his body. He kissed Dax's neck, murmuring with pleasure at the smell of fresh, clean sweat at the back of Dax's head.

Dax couldn't resist his touch, the sensation of his lips. He leaned back on the workbench and swallowed, groaning, as Cameron reached into his sweatpants and released his cock, placing it into his hot mouth and pleasuring him in the way for which he had a certain knack.

While the worry of tomorrow was never far away from his mind, for now Dax melted into ecstasy, the feeling of Cameron's mouth moving up and down his shaft enough to push his anxieties aside, at least for a little while.

Chapter Thirty-Three

Later in the week, they went to the pub once again. Dax and Cameron had been regular visitors and now the novelty had worn off a little for the young, excitable Will, Dax found that he looked forward to each week's outing.

In the beginning, people did turn and stare, and one week, Dax even posed for a couple of photographs after people came up and asked for them. Nobody pushed him, he didn't feel forced, and the smile on his face was genuine, rather than plastered on for the split second that the flash glared.

While he was no faster at answering the questions, he found he didn't care so much. His earlier victorious answer had not yet been eclipsed, but he lived in hope for a tie-breaker that might be about a certain star's record sales, or the number of people living in Connecticut. So far, though, his first week's moment of genius was yet to be bettered.

Angus was the star of the team. He pulled the answers to the most obscure questions seemingly out of nowhere, and was a bottomless pit of trivia. Many a time Dax stared at him, open-mouthed in wonder, when the quizmaster, a short man called Dennis who sported a terrible comb over and buck teeth, threw out a particularly tough question, only for Angus to dig into the recesses of his mind and stun everyone with the correct answer. Dax got the impression that each week Dennis created the quiz with the sole purpose of tripping up Angus.

Dax was becoming more and more fond of Caroline and Austin, too. The young couple often slipped into a brogue that Dax couldn't follow, but Cameron kept him up to speed with the conversation if ever he fell behind. They didn't do it on purpose; the colloquial language was simply alien to Dax, although he was becoming fond of the sing-song way the words spilled out of their mouths.

"So, how are you liking living here then, Dax?" Caroline asked.

Dax smiled, and couldn't stop himself from looking at Cameron as he answered. "Yeah, I like it," he said. "I like it a lot."

And Cameron blushed. Dax liked seeing it. He couldn't help but think back to earlier that day, when he'd stepped into a hot bath, only to find Cameron opening the door to the bathroom a few minutes later, joining him in the hot water. When he answered Caroline's question about being in Scotland, he told the truth. He did indeed like being there, and for one particular reason.

He couldn't recall ever having felt this way about another man. Sure, he'd been with plenty of guys he had lusted after, and who'd certainly had lust for him, but this was different. Each night when they went to sleep, Cameron was still there the following morning. Dax knew that whatever time he woke up, he wouldn't be alone. In the middle of the night, when he rolled over, he felt a strong arm slip around his waist and pull him close and even in his sleepy, half-conscious state, he felt safe.

The sound of the sheep in the morning waking him up was something he barely even noticed anymore. Having his favorite coffee places and food joints just around the corner was something he missed at first, but now he didn't care one iota about that. He was eating good, fresh food; food that tasted better than anything he'd been eating before.

The only thing he couldn't get used to was the beer. The lager he drank back in the States was light and fresh, and always chilled. The stuff they poured in glasses here, that they called *ale,* was always lukewarm and had a strange aftertaste. Dax had liked it well enough at first, but soon longed for the kind of stuff he got back home, where the beads of condensation running down the glass made his parched throat constrict and his mouth water in readiness.

"So, are you going to be staying here, now?" asked Will at the pub that night. His eager face peered over the table and Dax smiled at him.

"I don't think so," he said. "I'm getting a lot better, and my back's getting stronger every day, but I need to go home eventually and get back to music."

"Just think," said Will, dreamily, "you can make a whole new album when you get back, about coming back stronger, and beating the odds. That kind of thing."

"It's a good idea," Dax said. "I'll bear it in mind."

And as he looked up, he caught Cameron looking at him, and his stomach dropped a little. He knew what both men were thinking. Invergordon wasn't his home. Scotland wasn't where his life was. It was merely a place he had come to in order to recover, and it would soon be over, and he'd have to go back home. He already had an idea that Grant was nearing the end of his tether, and as much as Dax had tried to push the thought of his manager away, he couldn't escape him forever.

But for now, he could only enjoy being in this cozy little pub, around people he was getting to know and for whom he felt real affection. That night Angus was on a roll again, and the team walked away with more free pints. Cameron got a drink for Dax, but he shook his head. "Give it to Will," he said, patting his stomach. "I'm not sure I can take any more ale. I'm a little hungry, to be honest."

"That reminds me," Cameron said. "I thought we'd make a stop on the way home."

"Oh?"

"Aye. For a wee midnight snack."

"Oh God, you're not going to make me try haggis again, are you?" Dax groaned, recalling the time a couple of weeks ago when Cameron had sat him down and got him to try the classic Scottish dish of lamb offal, boiled in intestines. Dax had taken a forkful and hadn't been too put off by the meaty flavor, but once Cameron confessed exactly what ingredients went into making it, he'd clasped his hand over his mouth, retching. If it weren't for the fact that he simply couldn't move fast enough to the bathroom, then he would surely have barfed, but as he was pretty much stuck in his seat, he kept it down, settling for gulping down mouthfuls of water.

Cameron laughed at the memory, and shook his head. "No, I wouldn't do that to you again," he said. "I value my life too much. No, this is something I think you might like. Are you ready to go?"

"Sure." They picked up their coats and said goodnight to the rest of the group in the pub, and got into the car. Instead of driving back home, Cameron took a right turn and they went through the town. They stopped outside a shop that was lit up and full of people hanging around outside, and when Dax saw the sign above the door, he laughed. "I can't believe it!"

"Look, I know it's not going to be as good as the stuff you get back home in America," Cameron said, "but I hope that it might be a change from my cooking, at least."

He winked and went inside the shop and came back a few minutes later with two large boxes. They were piping hot, and blotches of grease marked the brown cardboard. Cameron handed the boxes to Dax, who closed his eyes and inhaled. "Oh my God, they smell so good!" he cried, and he couldn't resist lifting the lid of the top box.

The pizza was a welcome sight after so many weeks without his favorite fast food. It sat gleaming with hot, melted cheese, and nestled among the golden topping were pieces of ham. Cameron looked over. "Ah, that's mine," he said. "I got you the pepperoni underneath. You might not like the sort of thing I have on my pizza."

"Why? What did you choose?"

"I ordered the works, so there's ham and bacon and mushroom in there, but then there's also anchovy and pineapple."

"Yuck!" Dax closed the lid quickly, grimacing. "Who on earth puts pineapple on their pizza? It's a crime."

He opened the box underneath, his mouth watering at the sight of his pizza, scattered with pepperoni. "I know we should wait until we get back, but I can't resist," he said, and he lifted a piece of pizza out of the box. It was so hot he could only take a tentative bite, but he closed his eyes and murmured in appreciation.

"Good?" Cameron asked.

Dax could only nod, his eyes still closed, and Cameron laughed. "Go on, let me have a piece," he said.

"Of yours or mine?"

"Yours."

"Not a chance! I'm not letting your pineapple-loving mouth anywhere near my pizza."

"My mouth loves other things you don't mind me getting close to," Cameron teased, and Dax grinned. He picked a piece of Cameron's strange, eclectic pizza and handed it over, and Cameron took a large bite, making the same appreciative noises. "Damn, that's good. There's only one pizza place in the whole town, so I guess if they have the monopoly they don't have to make too much of an effort with the quality, but this is really good."

"It is," Dax said. "Thank you."

Cameron smiled at him. "No problem. I wanted you to have a little taste of home, even if it's not really authentic."

Dax shook his head, munching on his supper. The pizza was nowhere near as good as the kind he could order back home, but he wasn't about to say anything to Cameron. Knowing how much the other man had thought about him, and how he'd gone out of his way to try and give him the treat, touched him. He found himself staring at Cameron as they drove back to the farmhouse in the darkness. He was so beautifully handsome to look at, but it wasn't just that that made him so appealing. He was a kind man. A good man. The kind of man Dax could see himself wanting to spend even more time with.

When they got home, they sat in the lounge and ate the rest of their midnight meals. Before long there were two empty cardboard boxes on the coffee table, the only vestiges of their contents now a greasy sheen on the two men's chins. Dax yawned. "I think I'll get ready for bed," he said. "Are you coming?"

"Sure," Cameron replied. "I'll be up in a little while."

Dax lay in bed, staring up at the ceiling as his stomach gave a contented gurgle. He looked at his watch, the hands lit up in the darkness. It was nearly one. Back home, it was late afternoon. He wondered what Kelly was doing. She was probably at her desk, fielding call after call. She would have a large smoothie by her side, one that she'd have had with her since lunchtime, but that she slowly made her way through during the course of the afternoon, as she did every day. He wondered how many times Grant had barked at her, and he felt guilty for being the cause of the grief she was no doubt on the receiving end of.

When Cameron slipped into the bed beside him, Dax was already on his side. Cameron's arm came over his waist, and Dax was ready to fall asleep, but as he idly stroked Cameron's arm, he felt he was awake. He turned around to face Cameron, his face visible in the moonlight. "Do you think they know?" he whispered. "Will and the others, I mean."

Cameron put out his bottom lip, considering the question. "I don't know," he said. "Maybe. You've been here longer than they thought you would. They're not the sort of people to pry, though. They wouldn't really think it was any of their business to ask me, no matter what they might be thinking. I think Will thinks there's something going on, but I think that's more out of envy than anything else."

"How do you mean?"

With a soft laugh, Cameron reached out and stroked Dax's face. "I mean that he looks at me with envy," he said. "Because of the view I have every single night."

"Oh. And you wouldn't tell him anything?"

With a sigh, Cameron moved back a little. "Would you not want me to?"

"Well, I guess I mean that I don't know what you'd tell him," Dax said. "I mean, is there anything to tell anyone? Do we need to let anyone know what's going on between us?"

With that, Cameron moved his hand away. "You mean you want to keep this as a secret between us," he said.

"Well, yeah, I guess."

"I'm not someone who's going to ruin your life and run to the papers," Cameron said. "I get that you've had to live your life like that for as long as you can remember, but you have to understand that not everybody's out to fuck you over. Some people really care about you."

"I know. I've got my mom, and a couple of friends I trust, and—"

"Wow. None taken."

Dax gazed at Cameron. "You're my therapist," he said. "It's different."

With that, Cameron rolled onto his back. "Yeah," he said, quietly. "Sometimes I forget that. You know, because of all the sex we've been having. But you're right. I'm your therapist. Nothing more."

"Look, I don't mean it like that," Dax said.

"Yes, you do."

"It's not like I can put down roots here," Dax protested. "Will asked me tonight if I'm going to stay, and it sort of knocked me back a little. As if people think that's really possible."

"And it's not. I know that."

"Right."

"Right."

But Dax knew there was something in the air between them, a sense that all wasn't well. He got a strong feeling that he'd upset Cameron, and it made him feel terrible, but he wasn't sure what he'd done. It was frustrating, trying to navigate his way through an interaction between him and another guy that wasn't just based around who was going to fuck who, and who was going to sneak out of the place first.

He turned around, but Cameron placed a hand on his shoulder. "I know it's all new to you," he said. "You know, being so close to someone and having the connection we do. I imagine it's terrifying."

Dax shifted his weight so he was back facing Cameron. He nodded. "Yeah. I guess I just don't really know what's going on right now. I mean, I love being with you, and man, you're so hot, but what does it mean?"

"It doesn't have to mean anything you don't want it to," Cameron said. "It's me who's made the mistake, really."

"Mistake?"

"Yes. I swore I wasn't going to get involved with anyone else after my ex left, and certainly not with a patient. I'm the idiot who ends up falling so hard his heart breaks."

Dax gulped. He was hearing words he'd never expected to tumble out of Cameron's mouth.

Cameron moved onto his side, leaning on his elbow. "But have you ever thought that things could be different?" he asked. His green eyes were earnest. "Have you ever considered that maybe you could make a go of it with someone? That you could finally be happy, and settled, and, I don't know... *in love*?"

Dax's eyes were wide and his heart was racing. The words Cameron was saying sounded just as far-fetched as though he'd suggested they both took a trip to the moon. But in that split second, he had a vision. Of being back in his condo in California. Of waking up in the morning with the hot sun streaming through the windows, and Cameron beside him. Of getting up and making coffee for the two of them. Of going into the recording studio and singing every love song to Cameron. Of getting out of black limousines at premiers, as people screamed his name and he waved to them, but Cameron was by his side.

It felt wonderful. And the thought pushed him forward, and he planted his lips on Cameron's, and grabbed his face, hungrily kissing him, desperate to claim every inch of his mouth. *I want you,* he wanted to say aloud, but he couldn't find the way to say it. He tasted something hot and salty on his lips, and he realized that he was crying, but he didn't feel sad. He just wanted Cameron. Wanted all of him, forever, and he never wanted to let him go.

They were already naked, and they clung to one another desperately, and Dax held Cameron's face, millimeters from his own, staring into his eyes, pleading with him silently, to not give up on him, to understand how tough this was, but that if he were just patient, then amazing, wonderful things could happen.

Cameron moved on top of him, rubbing his cock against Dax's hip, but Dax carefully pushed him down, so Cameron was on his back, his legs apart. Dax fell between them, lying on top of him, their chests together, dark hair against red, and they moved together. Dax sucked on Cameron's lips, holding his arms above his head, and he no longer felt like a weak, injured bird but a strong, determined lion, powerful once more. He pressed his cock against Cameron's hole and plunged his tongue into his mouth at the same time he entered his ass, and Cameron gasped but clung to him, crying out.

With slow, sure movements, Dax made love to Cameron, feeling as he came that nothing could come between them. He knew that he was hoping for the impossible, but maybe, just maybe, they could stay here, in their own little bubble, and he could allow himself to feel things he'd only ever thought were reserved for other people.

Chapter Thirty-Four

The bubble burst five days later.

Dax and Cameron weren't at home. Since Dax's recovery was now progressing in leaps and bounds, or at the very least, in larger strides, they began to spend less and less time in the house. Dax was filled with a new kind of energy, and he found that as spring now slid into summer, there was plenty to see outside.

He and Cameron were taking a walk on the forest path on a hill above the house when Cameron whispered at Dax to stand still. "Don't move," he hissed.

Dax froze on the spot, sure that there was a sniper in among the trees, and he resisted the urge to turn and run as fast as he could in the opposite direction. He hadn't tried running just yet, having thus far managed only a lolling jog, but he was sure that if his life depended on it, he could flee.

But there was nothing to fear. From his side, Cameron pointed out a space in front of them, a little to the right, and Dax's mouth curled into a smile of wonder as he spotted a fawn, moving slowly between the trees. Its wide eyes blinked delicately, as it sniffed the air, aware that there was someone there, but until Dax or Cameron moved, they didn't scare it.

It stepped forward tentatively, lowering its head to munch on some grass on the ground that had grown in the space where light had filtered through the branches overhead.

"Where's its mom?" Dax whispered, barely allowing the words to slip out of his mouth in a single breath.

"She'll be around," Cameron replied. "That little guy's far too young to be out here on his own."

And then, as though on cue, out stepped a beautiful large deer, its stunning head moving left and right, concern etched on her face. Dax sucked in his breath, and he was so stunned by the view of the deer and her baby that he felt tears pricking his eyelids. He'd never seen anything so beautiful in all his life.

It was a reflex that made him raise his hand to his face to wipe his eyes, but it was enough to startle the deer. The mother bolted first, her fawn following behind her a split second later. "Shit," said Dax. "That's my fault. I'm sorry."

"Don't worry about it," laughed Cameron. "It's not like we could have stood like statues for the next hour. We'll see them again."

"That was amazing. I don't know how on earth you quit this place to live in London."

"Well, I kind of got my heart broken," Cameron said.

"Oh?" Dax was sure he knew what Cameron was talking about; he thought back to the man he'd heard mentioned in the bar the night he'd gone to the quiz.

"I used to do a lot of work for the navy," Cameron said, as they slowly walked along the path. "I think I mentioned it. I was a trainer, and so a lot of injured sailors would come to me. Not necessarily if they'd seen combat. Usually it was because of a daft injury they'd picked up on the boat. And one time I had a man called John referred to me. He was an officer, and he'd helped rescue a boat full of refugees off the coast of Malta, and one of them had panicked and kicked him in the shoulder so hard it shattered his scapula."

"Ouch. That sounds really bad."

"Well, he came to me for treatment. With an injury like that, if it doesn't heal properly it can mean the end of a career for a sailor, so it was important that he got the best care. He was flown to the base, not too far from here, and so I treated him at the house, and I suppose it went from there."

At the thought of Cameron being with another man in that house the way the two of them had been together in recent days, Dax felt a little nauseated. He swallowed, and his fists clenched in his pockets. He was jealous, but he'd never felt such a feeling before, at least not where another man was concerned. Cameron caught the look and stroked his back. "It was a long time ago," he said. "Nearly three years."

"What happened?"

"He was married, and I didn't know," Cameron said, simply. "I knew something wasn't right about the whole thing. And I was completely taken in by his lies. He hurt me really badly, and I just couldn't stand to be in the house anymore. It reminded me of being betrayed, and I was ready to sell, but I couldn't bring myself to do it. Instead, I moved down to London. The noise and chaos was a good distraction."

"Well, it sounds like he was a real prick," Dax said. He didn't know what else to say. Nothing seemed appropriate. He found himself wondering what this guy was like. Whether he was handsome, if he was tall and dark, or short and fair. He wondered whether Cameron had enjoyed sex with John more than with him. He found he didn't like to think about things like that. For the first time in his life, there was someone he really liked, and the idea that someone else would have touched him in *that* way made him feel things he didn't want to feel.

They walked back toward the house, but from the hill, Cameron pointed out and Dax thought there was another deer in front of them, but it was much worse than that.

Parked in front of the house was a huge black car, its tinted windows black and ominous. "I'm guessing that's for you," Cameron said. "I don't know many people who'd drive a beast like that."

Dax's heart sank. "Shit," he muttered. He didn't want to go back to the house, but there was no way to avoid whatever was there waiting for him.

Cameron never locked the front door, because people weren't generally so rude as to simply walk in and take a look around however they pleased. Grant Beaumont was not such a person. As Dax and Cameron walked into the house, they saw that the large, red-faced manager was already in the sitting room. He was peering at the bookshelf, and he looked up as the two men entered.

"Well, look who's all well again!" he cried, beaming, his hands outstretched as if to envelop Dax in a large hug.

"What the hell's going on?" Dax asked. "I didn't know you were coming. How did you even know I was here?"

But Grant ignored the question and instead held out his hand for Cameron to shake it. Dax could see he didn't want to, but he took the flabby hand out of courtesy and gave it a brief shake. "I'll go and put the kettle on, shall I?" he asked.

He left the room, and Dax sighed heavily. "You've got no right just busting in like this," he said, and Grant sat down on the sofa, still in his coat and leather gloves.

Grant ignored this, too. "Charming little place," he said, but Dax could hear the sarcasm dripping from his voice. "The English really *do* know how to build pretty houses, don't they?"

"We're in Scotland," Dax growled. "It's a completely different country."

At this, Grant matched Dax's stare with an icy glare of his own. "Don't you think for a fucking second I don't know where we are," he snapped. "I know exactly where we are. I know the fucking coordinates of this God-forsaken place. Don't imagine I haven't known where you've been all this time. And I've just spent the last thirty hours dragging my ass over here to see what the fuck you think you're playing at."

"I have no idea what you're talking about," Dax said. "I haven't spoken to you in days."

"Exactly!" Grant cried. "You haven't taken a single call, haven't answered a single text, and even Kelly hasn't been able to get a hold of you. Now I see you're up and about, looking better than ever, so I can only assume that you haven't been lying on your back the whole time."

"I've been recovering," Dax said. "I don't turn my phone on much these days."

I don't want to hear from anyone back home, he nearly added, but stopped himself. He knew that Grant had a right to be worried. Sure, he wasn't expecting to walk in and find him in the sitting room like this, but he should have been prepared for the fallout after not having made any contact with anyone back home ever since he and Cameron had first slept together.

"Your mom's worried sick," Grant said, changing tack in the hope that this would produce a more favorable response. His voice softened a little, but Dax could only hear the sickly sweet quality of the tone, as it dripped with faux concern. He'd never been so repulsed by the man as he was now. What was it Cameron had called him? The cult leader. The supreme ruler. The puppet master who dangled the strings, having Dax dance whenever he could.

"My mom knows where I am," he said, finally. "She doesn't have any reason to be worried, but I'll call her. Tonight."

"You don't need to call her," Grant replied. "You're not staying here another night. I've got a jet ready to leave from Edinburgh tonight. You're packing your things and I'm taking you with me. I should never have let you out of my sight the first time, and I'm not letting it happen again."

"I'm not going anywhere," Dax said, the words out of his mouth before he could stop them. "I'm happy here. I don't want to go back to that life."

Grant threw back his head and laughed. "It's almost like you and I don't have a multi-million dollar contract!" he cried. "It's as though we're not hemorrhaging money like a leaky faucet. As though I'm not fighting fires every single fucking second you're out here, having to explain to everyone that no, you're not dead, you're alive and well and you'll be back to your old self very fucking soon!"

Cameron appeared at this moment, stepping out of the kitchen. "Nobody talks like that in this house," he said, sternly.

"Fuck off," spat Grant. "Don't think I don't know what you've been up to here, Son. I've done my research."

"Oh?" Cameron folded his arms. "And what has that uncovered, exactly?"

"You've had him here as your little fucking pet," Grant said, his red face now a startling shade of purple. "You fucking faggot. The whole plan was to get a global superstar in your bed the whole time. And I bet you've managed it, too. Dax always was a bit stupid, and he's a sucker for a pretty face. You might have had him fooled, but don't insult my intelligence by thinking I don't know exactly what the two of you have been up to."

"Shut up," Dax said, pointing his finger toward Grant's face. He couldn't bear to see Cameron humiliated in this way. He'd been on the receiving end of Grant's poison so many times, but he wasn't about to let Cameron suffer in the same way.

He knew that Grant was lying. Not about having done his research, of course. He wouldn't have expected anything less. He knew that Grant was telling the truth when he said he'd known where Dax had been the whole time, too. But he knew that Cameron hadn't had any ulterior motive in bringing him to Scotland. He knew it with all his heart.

But he also knew that it was over. All of it. His time away had come to an end, and he had no choice but to go back. Because as much as he loathed Grant Beaumont, the man was very, very right about one thing. Their contract was binding, and he knew that they were losing millions every day he was gone.

It was time for Dax to leave Scotland, and return to the States. And with every fiber in his being, he wished that it weren't so.

Chapter Thirty-Five

"So that's that, then?"

Dax tried not to notice the sadness in Cameron's voice but it was impossible. He was throwing things into his case as Cameron stood in the doorway to his bedroom.

"It's not like I want to go," he said. "But you heard Grant. I've avoided it for long enough and I have to finally face up to reality."

"I get it," Cameron said. "Even though it might sound like I don't, I really do. But I don't know why you're so keen to face up to this reality, and not the other."

"Which is?"

"That you're gay, and it's killing you to have to hide it."

Dax paused his packing and leaned on the bed, digging his fists in the duvet. "I would have thought that of all people, you wouldn't be the one to throw that at me."

Cameron walked over angrily. "Are you fucking joking?" he asked. "I'm not using anything against you. I'm telling you what you already know. And the only reason you're leaving is because you're being sucked into that world once more. You've come so far. You've survived a crash that nearly killed you, for God's sake. And now you're just giving up."

"I'm not giving up," Dax said. He looked at Cameron, and he shook his head. "Please don't make this harder than it is. I've had an amazing time but I chose my life fifteen years ago, and I can't just walk away from it. I can't just drop everything I've worked for in my career because I'm having a nice time with you."

"A nice time," Cameron repeated, bitterly. "I'm so glad that's how you see it."

"No, wait, I didn't mean that," Dax said, but Cameron stood up and held out his hand.

"Take care. When you get settled, get your assistant to send for my notes. Your new therapist will need them."

And he turned and left the room. Dax heard him walk down the stairs and out of the front door without another word to Grant. Then there was the roar of the car engine, as Cameron drove away from the house. Dax looked out of the window at the back of the car, watching it leave.

He threw the last of his things into the one case he'd brought with him, and then he carried the case to the top of the stairs. Grant was at the bottom, and he jogged up to carry the case down for Dax. "So, he's not too happy about you leaving, right?" he asked. "I can't imagine he'll find another high-profile client in a hurry."

Dax said nothing. He knew that Cameron's reaction to his leaving was nothing to do with the money Dax had been paying him. In fact, since the first week when he'd called Kelly and set up the payment arrangement, he hadn't thought about the financial side of the deal at all. Cameron had driven away in a car that Dax had paid for, but he didn't care at all. Cameron could keep the car forever. It didn't matter.

Grant had given him two weeks, but Dax had taken two months. He had to respect that his manager had given him the time he needed, and more besides, and he had to go back home. He had commitments.

Contracts to uphold. Fans to keep happy. By leaving Scotland and heading back to the States, he was making the right decision.

Wasn't he?

He felt utterly out of his depth. For the past two months, even though his exercise regime was carefully planned, he hadn't felt forced to do anything he didn't want to do. For the first time since he first signed with the record company, he'd felt *free.* Now, Grant was back, and he was slipping back into doing whatever his manager said, without question.

Grant heaved the case into the trunk. He stood outside the car. "Get in," he said, looking at his watch. "I've got to get us to the airport in time for the flight."

It was only now that Dax saw that there was a man sitting in the front seat with his hands on the steering wheel. Of course Grant had a driver. He never did a single thing himself. There was always someone there in the background, doing his bidding. Dax wondered if he too were such a person. A minion, a slave making him all the money he could and being told exactly what to do with his life.

He felt a surge of anger rising, and he stood his ground. "I don't want to go back with you," he said.

Grant sighed and put his hand on his forehead. "Get in the car," he commanded.

"Things just can't go back to the way they were, Grant," Dax insisted. "It's not what I want. I've had time out here to think about things."

Slowly walking over the gravel, Grant stopped in front of Dax. "I get it," he said, his voice soft for a moment. "You've had a nice vacation out here, although not in the best of circumstances, originally.

It's pretty country out here. Too fucking cold for me, but I guess you two were keeping each other warm. No, don't look at me like that. I'm not an idiot. But you and I both know how this is going to end. You're coming home because you're Dax Monroe. You're a global superstar. And the world's been mourning your absence something terrible. It's time to go home and get back to what you do best."

"And what do I do best, Grant?" Dax asked, wearily.

Grant grinned, and Dax could see the flash of gold from his caps. "Sit on top of the world, my boy," he said.

The vacation, as Grant had put it, was over. He was well. His back had healed well enough for him to go home and continue his recuperation back at his house in California. Cameron had driven away, and was gone. Dax was sure the therapist would never want to see him again. He had nothing else to stay for. So, as Grant watched him, he stepped into the back of the huge black car. In case he changed his mind again, Grant leaped inside quickly, slamming the door shut after him.

"Let's get out of here, Carl," he ordered. Carl slammed the car into reverse and they squealed away from the farmhouse. Dax looked back, torn between wanting to jump out but knowing that the same time that there was nothing else for it. He had to go back. He hated to admit that Grant was right, but he'd been kidding himself to think that life could always be like this.

Grant reached into a bag and took out a bottle of vodka. He unscrewed the cap and handed it to Dax. Dax took a deep breath and shook his head. Grant was surprised, but shrugged and took a swig from the bottle himself. "In a couple of hours we'll be in the air and you can sleep it all off," he said.

"All what?"

Grant waved his hand at the window. "All of this. This grayness. This country with no climate. Jeez." And he shivered.

But Dax knew that the country wasn't gray at all. It was full of color, in its landscape and its people. And if he could, he would have stayed. He wondered where Cameron had gone. Sullenly, he lowered his head and pressed his thumb and index finger against his eyeballs. Just like it had when he'd been in the car that Andy was driving in the very beginning, his life had changed in the blink of an eye. Just a few minutes ago, he was happy. He was with a gorgeous guy who made him laugh.

And now he was back under the control of Grant Beaumont. And he'd gone willingly, too. Cameron was wrong about him. He wasn't brave, or strong. He was weak and pathetic and couldn't stand up for himself, or for what he wanted. And what he wanted was to demand that Grant stop the car and take him back. He was a grown man. He wasn't a prisoner.

He stayed silent in the back of the car while Grant swigged from the bottle until they were at the airport. "Stay here," Grant instructed. "I don't need any shit from girls right now. We need to be clever about this."

He left and came back in around twenty minutes, and instructed Carl to drive around the back of the airport. "Pulled a few strings to get us in the back way," he said. They drove round to where a security guard checked through their things and waved them through to a small airfield. Dax saw the plane sitting there waiting for them. It was the same plane that had brought him to the UK. His own private jet.

Wearily, he got out of the car while Carl took care of the case. Grant shoved a baseball cap in Dax's hands. "Put this on," he said. "I don't think we were followed but everyone's a fucking photographer these days."

Dax pulled the cap low over his eyes and slowly climbed the steps to the plane. Every movement of his legs was such that he felt someone else was doing it. He no longer had Cameron behind him, a voice telling him he was right there. That he'd catch him if he fell. He held onto the railing as he walked up to the door. Every fiber in his being screamed at him to stop and go back, but he knew he was powerless. Grant had him in the palm of his hand again. He could only keep walking.

"Welcome back, sir," smiled the pilot, whose name Dax couldn't even remember. He held his hand out and the pilot shook it in surprise. Dax understood the shock. He'd barely grunted at his staff before the accident. Now he felt guilty for the way he'd treated them in the past.

A flight attendant named Betsy smiled with full, red lips and Dax gave her a watery grin. "No champagne, thanks," he said, as she proffered the tray with a slim glass of fizzing golden liquid carefully balanced on top. "I don't want anything right now."

"Of course, sir."

"If you wouldn't mind taking your seat, Mister Monroe, then we can leave in just a few minutes," the captain said. "We've got an available slot."

"Right." Dax slid into his seat and fastened his belt. Grant came over and squeezed his shoulder.

"You look like you're in pain. Do you want some pills? I've got whatever you want back here. Saw the doctor before I came and he fixed me up with a whole bunch of things he said you're probably taking."

But Dax shook his head. "I'm not taking any pills," he said.

Grant looked worried, and lowered his head closer. "Don't tell me you started shooting up at that house of squalor," he said, and Dax was so disgusted he wanted to shove Grant back with both hands and make as fast a run as he could manage toward the exit.

"No!" he cried. "Jesus, nothing like that. I didn't need the meds, that's all. I was looked after."

He felt tears pricking his eyes and he wiped them away hastily. Grant got into his own seat and fastened his belt. Within a few minutes, they'd taxied onto the runway and then Dax felt the aircraft move into its familiar burst of speed before the sinking of his stomach told him they were in the air. Although he didn't want to, he turned his head to the right and looked out of the window, down on Edinburgh.

Then, just like that, Dax left the UK, and Cameron, and began the long flight back to the US.

Chapter Thirty-Six

He didn't want to stay in New York. Grant couldn't understand it. "I've booked you into the fucking presidential suite, for Christ's sake," he said.

"Thanks," Dax replied, in a monotone voice. "But I want to refuel and keep going."

He put his head into the cockpit. "Is that okay with you, sir?"

The pilot looked flustered, as Dax understood the expression on his face. It was the kind of expression that many people had when they knew they were upsetting Grant Beaumont. But Dax put his hand on the pilot's shoulder. "I'd like to go home to California and be in my house," he said. "If we can't do that, it's fine. But I'd like to try, and I'll make sure you're paid well for it."

"Well, it's not a problem," he said. "We'll need to refuel, of course, but—"

"Yes, that's right," Grant interjected. "The boy needs to rest. Needs to get himself together and get some proper rest. I have business to take care of here in New York, but take Dax to LA if you can, Captain."

"Of course."

"We don't have to if you're not up to it."

"No, sir, it's fine."

Dax nodded. "Thank you." Just a couple of months ago, if he wanted to go somewhere then whoever was flying the plane would make damn sure he got him there at whatever time he wanted. Dax thought back to his old self and was ashamed. He was a real asshole.

With relief, he watched as Grant disembarked.

He sighed and got back into his seat. The pilot came out. "I'm sorry, sir," he said, sheepishly, "but we need to be off the aircraft while it refuels."

"Oh. Right."

"We can sit in the lounge and wait to get the all-clear."

"Okay."

He stood up again and carefully stretched his back, the way Cameron had shown him. Cameron. At the thought of him, there was a sinking feeling in Dax's stomach. He hadn't wanted things to end the way they had. He left his case on board and walked slowly down the steps. His back ached. He wondered whether it had been a good idea to ask to keep going, but all he wanted was to be in his own house, where he could lock the doors and sleep for as long as he wanted.

In the lounge, he was asked if there was anything he'd like to eat or drink. He shook his head, then reconsidered. "Do you have any ale?" he asked.

"Ale? I don't know what that is, sir." The stewardess was apologetic, blushing and looking a little worried that he might flip.

"Don't worry," he said. "It's a British thing, I think. Just a beer's fine."

She nodded and went away to fetch it. Dax reached into his pocket and brought out his cell phone. He scrolled through his numbers, until he found what he was looking for. He grinned despite himself when he saw it. *Physical Terrorist.* He thought back to the day he'd taken Cameron's number and put it in his phone. It seemed like years ago.

Against his better judgment, he hit *call.*

He found he was shaking as he heard the phone ring halfway across the world. It seemed to drone on forever, until finally, he heard a click, and a soft, Scottish voice. "Hello?"

"Hey, it's me."

There was a pause, and Dax could see his shirt moving as his heart beat frantically. There was no response, but Cameron hadn't hung up either. Dax took a chance, and continued to speak. "So, uh, I'm in New York. I didn't want to stay here though. I want to get home to California, so we're just refueling and then we'll be on our way."

Still nothing. Dax pulled his phone away from his ear, thinking they'd been cut off. But they hadn't. Cameron was still there. Silent, but there. Dax carried on talking. "I just wanted to thank you for everything. For putting up with me, and looking after me. Uh, so... yeah."

"Is that everything?"

He sounded hurt. Dax lowered his head and sighed. "I don't know what else to say," he said. "It's just that— oh, shit, have I woken you up? What time is it?"

Quickly looking at his watch, he groaned. "Damn, it's nearly midnight there, right? Did I wake you up?"

"No."

"Oh." So he wasn't tired. He just didn't want to talk.

"Um, I don't know whether Kelly sorted out what you're owed, payment-wise, but please send me a bill."

"Okay."

"Did she sort it?"

"I don't know. I'll have to check my account."

Please talk to me, Dax wanted to say. But Cameron was clearly not in the mood. Dax sighed. "Well, I guess that's all I wanted to say, so I'm sorry for bothering you. All right. Bye, then."

"Wait," Cameron said, and Dax's heart leaped.

"Yes?"

"God dammit, Dax, you didn't have to leave like that." Dax wasn't sure, but he thought he heard Cameron's voice cracking on the other end of the line, and he felt sick.

"I didn't have a choice," he said. "It's so complicated. Grant—"

"Grant doesn't have a clue who you are, and he doesn't care," Cameron said. "He never sees what I saw. Remember what we talked about? About you being in a cult? He's the leader."

Dax sighed. He was exhausted. He wasn't sure why he'd called Cameron, but this wasn't the conversation he wanted to be having. And Cameron knew it, too, because his tone changed. "Look, I'm sorry," he said. "I'm guessing you're knackered and you don't need a lecture. I'm just... fuck, I don't know."

"Tell me," Dax blurted out.

"I'm sad," Cameron said, and he even gave an ironic laugh. "Sounds so stupid, but I'm sad. You were here one second, and then you weren't. And I thought you might at least give me a little bit of warning."

"I didn't know he was coming, either," Dax said.

"He has a habit of surprising people."

"I hate him."

Dax took a deep breath. "I know. I hate him, too."

It was the first time he'd ever realized the extent of his dislike for Grant. He thought that over the last few months, he'd become stronger. But all Grant had to do was turn up, and he was back to following meekly, like a sheep. Here he was, waiting for his private jet to be refueled so he could get his personal pilot to take him wherever he demanded. And yet all his manager had to do was appear, and Dax followed.

"Jesus, I'm so pathetic," he said.

"You're not," Cameron said. "You'll get there in your own time. Just don't stop believing in yourself. Listen to your gut. When Grant tells you something, trust your instinct to know whether what he's saying is good for you."

"I think you were my instinct for the last couple of months," Dax said.

"No, it's in there, all right," Cameron said. "You just need to find it. You need to see what I see. Saw."

The correction to the past tense stung.

"Dax?"

"Yeah?"

"Do me a favor?"

"Sure." *Anything.*

"Please don't call me anymore, okay?"

What was a sting now felt like a slap to the face. Not call Cameron? Why? Didn't he know how much he meant to him?

    But before he could ask, Cameron was gone.

Chapter Thirty-Seven

The water was fresh and warm. Thanks to the pool company, they'd completely emptied, cleaned and refilled the pool in two days. Dax slid into the water and pulled the goggles over his eyes. He began a smooth front crawl stroke, careful not to over-exert with his arms. They felt okay, though. The break had healed, and although there was still a little residual weakness in his right forearm, it was getting better every day.

His back didn't ache too much, but after the swim, he used the steps to get out of the pool, rather than hauling himself out via the side, as he usually would. He grabbed his towel and made his way back into the house. The same few words were buzzing around his head, as they had been doing for the past week, since his arrival back home.

"You said you'd catch me if I fell, but it was a lie," he hummed to himself. *"I fell so damn hard and well, you just watched from the side."*

There weren't just words; there was a melody now, too, and he didn't even bother getting dressed as he walked into the pool house and grabbed the guitar on the wall. It wasn't really for playing: it was the guitar his favorite singer from the sixties, Alton Coy, had played on his last tour. He was only twenty-seven when his plane crashed in Alaska. His guitar was being taken by truck. The guitar made it to its destination, but Alton did not. Dax bought the guitar a little after his first album went platinum.

It was a little out of tune after having been stuck on the wall for a couple of years since Dax had bought the house, but it didn't matter. He just needed to get the melody that was in his head down through his fingers, onto the strings. He was a great believer in muscle memory. Feeling the wire press into his fingertips made it seem more real.

He very rarely wrote his own music these days. The times that he was in the studio were when he was recording the kind of stuff that other people had written for him. Some of it was good, and catchy, and he liked singing it. But some of it was utter shit. Formulaic. Cliched. Sometimes he asked for a guitar to try out a chord he liked and a verse he penned, but he was usually cut off as Grant butted in on the mic and told him to "just stick to the script, okay?"

So he did. He stuck to the script. It was a script he'd stuck to for the past fifteen years and sure, it had worked. Grant knew what he was doing when it came to making records, especially the kind that made money. But every morning since arriving home, Dax had had words in his head that he couldn't shift. Words that went well to new melodies.

He took the guitar into the main house and into the studio in the basement. He had no idea what all the dials on the deck meant, but it didn't matter. All he wanted to do was to get the first few chords down onto a file that he could save and keep for another time. He wrote the words down on the computer. He set up a microphone and tuned the guitar properly. Then he recorded the first line of the song he'd been humming. He wrote down some more words, and plucked a little more at the guitar.

By the time he looked at the clock again, he saw he'd been making a new song for nearly two hours. And it was done. He emailed it all to himself and went back upstairs. He was still wearing his swimming shorts. "Where have you been?" Kelly asked. "I've been sitting here with coffees for twenty minutes."

"Sorry. I was in the studio doing something."

Kelly smiled at this, seemingly no longer annoyed about having been kept waiting. "Really? Have you been sent some new stuff?"

"No. It's something I wrote."

He didn't want to go any further. He was so used to being shot down whenever he talked about his own work that he didn't bother anymore. Instead he picked up his drink and changed the subject. "The coffee place still doing well?"

"Yep. They're thrilled you're back, of course. I think you kept it going. When you were out of town they probably had to let half the staff go."

"God, I missed good coffee when I was over there."

"Was it no good?"

Dax thought back to a memory of he and Cameron in the kitchen, long before anything had ever happened between them. Cameron was making instant coffee, with a spoonful of granules that looked as though they'd been cremated, not just roasted. Dax had pointed that out to him at the time, and he'd enjoyed seeing that way Cameron laughed. And he'd further enjoyed seeing the way Cameron brushed his auburn curls out of his eyes, as he always did.

"Hello? Earth to Dax?"

"Sorry." Dax blushed and sipped his coffee again. "Uh, it wasn't great, let's just leave it at that."

But I got to love it, he thought. *Because of the guy who made it for me.*

"What else did you miss when you were away?"

"Besides you?"

"Ah, you flatter me."

Dax sat up at the kitchen counter and stuck out his bottom lip as he thought about the question. "Let's see. What did I miss? Sushi. Definitely sushi."

"Want me to go get you some?"

"You've only just got back from getting coffee."

Kelly sat up at the counter with him and stared at him for a moment, her head titled to one side. Her gaze seemed to look right through his soul and Dax had to ask her what on earth she was looking at. She gave a slow smile. "I don't really know," she said. "It's just that you've changed. Not in a bad way. At all. You're just more... thoughtful."

"Huh?"

"Well, at one time, if you wanted sushi, you'd damn well make me go out and get it, no matter what time it was. Or if you wanted pizza or a burger or a seven hundred dollar bottle of champagne. And now... I don't know. You don't want to send me out because I've only just got back? It never would have mattered to you before now."

"I'm sorry for all the times I treated you like a slave," Dax said. He took a deep breath. "Damn, I really am a spoiled little brat, aren't I?"

Kelly shook her head. "Nah. You were, but not anymore." She grinned playfully, but her eyes were probing. "What was it like, being cooped up in a barn in a field with that guy?"

"It wasn't quite a barn. You'd be surprised to hear we had hot water and electricity and everything."

"And mega-fast Wi-Fi?"

"Ah, you've got me there. No. No mega-fast Wi-

Fi. No internet at all, actually."

"What? You never mentioned it as something you missed! How can you have put sushi over the internet?"

Dax thought about this. "You know, once I was there, and I didn't have phone calls every two seconds, and messages and more phone calls, I just liked the silence and I didn't miss it."

"And now?"

"What about now?"

"Do you miss England?"

"Scotland."

"Hang on. Where's London?"

Dax laughed. "London's England. But Ca— the place I stayed after the hospital, that was Scotland."

"Oh."

There was a silence and for just a second, Dax could smell the freshly-cut hay outside, and could even hear the *baa* of the sheep calling for their lambs.

"You really liked him, didn't you?" Kelly asked softly.

Dax froze for a second, but then swallowed, and nodded. "Yeah," he whispered.

"And why did you leave?"

"Why do you think? I've got shit to take care of here. Grant's already talking about getting on talk shows and being photographed in public again. Jesus, he's even mentioned calling Alicia and trying to get that started again. I couldn't stay in my barn in the field when I have too much going on over here. You know what it's like. Grant complaining about losing millions every day... all that shit."

"So why didn't he come with you? Cameron, I mean."

Chewing the inside of his cheek, Dax shrugged. "I don't know. He didn't want to."

"Did you even ask?"

"No. But he wouldn't anyway. He doesn't want anything to do with me anymore. He hates me."

"What?"

Without going into too much detail, Dax relayed the conversation he'd had on the phone with Cameron, when he was at the airport. "I asked if you'd paid him, and he just said he'd check. He was cold. Then he told me not to call him anymore."

"And you listened to him?" Kelly sounded incredulous, and Dax was confused.

"Of course. He doesn't want to hear from me. He's mad at me for leaving. Grant says he's sure Cameron's pissed that he isn't earning any more money from the deal. Which I was surprised at, really, because he never seemed to care about the cash side of things. I even offered for him to keep the car and he took it back and used his own, which was an old—"

"You've got no idea how this works, have you?" Kelly asked, cutting Dax off.

"How what works?"

"*Love.*"

The word hit Dax like a freight train, and in his confusion and embarrassment he tipped up the coffee cup to his mouth too fast and spilled it down his front. "Shit," he muttered. He leaped down to get a washcloth. He dabbed at the stain, not wanting to meet his assistant's eye, but Kelly wouldn't let it go. Instead she jumped down, too, and walked to him, putting her own cup on the counter.

"He doesn't want you calling him because he doesn't know how to deal with losing you," she said. "Jesus, Dax, I only met the guy a handful of times in the hospital but even I know what's going on here. He's hurt. He doesn't hate you. He pretty much the opposite of hates you."

Dax was quiet. Then he shook his head. "That's not what it feels like."

"Did you really just up and leave without saying goodbye?"

When she didn't get an answer, Kelly sighed. "I knew you liked him when you were in the hospital but I didn't know whether he was, you know..."

"Yeah."

"And he made you well and then you guys fell madly in love? God, it's so romantic."

"I hadn't even thought about that before," Dax said.

"Well, think about how you feel now. Do you think about him a lot?"

"All the time." The words were stuck in his throat for a second, and when they were released in a strained whine Dax was pretty sure he was about to cry.

"And do you dream about him?"

"I can't sleep most nights.

"Oh God, you're totally in love with this guy, Dax."

Dax didn't reply. Because he knew it was true. He was in love with Cameron, and it had taken his assistant, of all people, to finally spell it out for him. But he was five thousand and seventy-seven miles from Cameron. He knew because last night, on his phone, he'd been lying awake unable to sleep as had been the case for the last seven nights, and he searched the distance between them.

It was too late. He should have told Cameron how he felt when he had the chance, but he'd fucked everything up. Just like he'd almost fucked his career up by racing through the streets of London with Andy that night. Hell, he'd nearly fucked his whole existence up.

Maybe it was better that Dax had left. Because all he ever did was create chaos. That's how it felt. It made him sad. The whole thing made him want to cry. And as Kelly slipped her arms around her boss's waist and hugged him tight, he finally did. He began to sob, huge, racking sobs that echoed in the large kitchen. He slid to the floor and wept, tears running down his cheeks as he sat with his back against the kitchen counter.

"I lost him," Dax sobbed. Kelly sat beside him but Dax was barely aware she was there anymore. All he could feel was the hurt and pain, the hole of Cameron's absence now throbbing in his chest.

"I walked away from the only good thing that's ever happened to me. What the hell was I thinking?"

He looked up at Kelly and nodded.

"You're right. I love him."

Chapter Thirty-Eight

The microphone was pinned to his shirt and he smoothed back his hair. A short blonde girl with a pixie cut rushed into the room with a make-up brush and she quickly gave him a last-minute touch-up. Then she gave him a quick smile and scurried off again.

"On in thirty seconds," came the call from the green room, and Dax stood up and moved his neck to the right, and then to the left. Kelly smiled and gave him a nervous thumbs-up. Then Dax took a deep breath and stood in position.

He heard the voice introducing him. "So, ladies and gentlemen, we're so honored to have him here tonight. Please welcome Dax Monroe!"

The screen doors opened and Dax fixed a beaming smile on his face, although inside he felt sick to his stomach. The lights ahead of him were so bright that he couldn't see the audience behind the cameras, but he waved at them anyway. They screamed for so long that he could only stand and wave until finally, the host came to his rescue. It was probably less than ten seconds but to Dax it felt like a lifetime before she came up, held his hands, kissed him on both cheeks, and invited him to sit down.

The audience was still screaming, and Dax smiled and held up his hand again, before the hysteria finally died down. The host, Linzi MacDonald, crossed one leg over the other and shook her head slowly, grinning. "Dax Monroe, I thought we'd seen the last of you!" she cried.

The hysterical whoops and screams started up again but died down quickly as Dax chuckled. "Never," he said. "It'll take a lot more to get rid of me, Linzi."

"Well, we're honored to have you here tonight, Dax, and you've got a hell of a story to tell! Let's take a second to look back at some of the clips from your last tour. Check this out."

They both turned to the screen and Dax watched with a fixed smile on his face as frames and clips of him on stage in Tokyo, Moscow, Paris and London came up in a montage lasting around ninety seconds. Dax could hardly remember most of the footage; one night was like every other when he was on tour. Most nights he'd already had quite a bit of liquor before getting on stage, and even a line or two of coke if it was offered.

It was like watching someone else up there on the screen, an actor playing a role. And Dax was back to playing the role, too. Sitting in the chair in his designer suit and slick hair, a platinum watch on his wrist and smart, shining shoes, he was back in the saddle again. And if he could, he'd have run away in a heartbeat to escape to the middle of nowhere.

Grant was the one who insisted he did the Linzi MacDonald show. Once Grant had the thought in his head, there was no stopping him. "Thursday night, prime time television," he said, tapping his finger on the desk to drive home the point. "She's the best name we've got, and she knows where to draw the line. She'll make you look good without delving too much into things nobody wants her to talk about."

"Right," Dax said, agreeing. He always agreed. But things were changing inside him. Every time Grant suggested something, Dax went along with it, but a little part of him wanted to resist. And that part was growing stronger. In fact, Grant had given him an outfit to wear, and Dax had refused to put it on.

"Don't be a little fucking brat right now, I don't have the time," Grant said. "Put on the jeans and t-shirt."

"I'm going to wear a suit," Dax said. "I want to look smart."

"You've got a contract with the jeans company and it makes you look boyish. You know, cute. The kind of guys you usually like fucking because they look so much like you."

Usually a comment like that would have had him blushing and wincing but instead he simply shrugged at Grant, keeping his gaze steady. "I've got a smart suit lined up. Find me a sponsoring company that makes ties and I'll wear one with the shirt. I'm sick of looking like a kid. I'm not eighteen anymore."

There was a barb to the last sentence, and he knew that as he uttered it, Grant felt it. The message was clear. Dax wasn't a kid. He was a man, a man slowly beginning to take control of his own life. Slowly, of course. He wasn't ready to invoke Grant's full wrath just yet.

His manager's nostrils flared but even he knew which battles were worth fighting and which weren't. So Dax wore the suit he wanted to the show Grant wanted him to do. And now here he was, sitting in the chair, looking over at a screen full of heroic, Dax Monroe spectacular moments.

As it ended, the audience warm-up guy prompted everyone to applaud again. Not that they needed the prompting. Cue the wild screaming and appreciative hoots once more. Dax turned to Linzi with practiced charm. "Damn, you make me look good up there," he said.

"Oh, that's all you," Linzi gushed. "I have to say

it's such a relief more than anything, to have you on this stage again. I'm pretty sure we all thought you'd disappeared off the face of the earth. Isn't that right, gang?"

"Yes," the audience chorused, and Dax wanted to stand up and yell at them that they had no business knowing where he was at all times. That just buying a record or going to a concert didn't mean that he owed them an explanation for every single second of his day. If he wanted to get into a rocket and fire himself into space for a few years, that was his prerogative.

Of course, he only grinned, and pressed his palms together in a symbol of peace, bowing his head in silent apology. "You're right, I sort of slunk away for a little while, didn't I?" he said to Linzi.

"We heard all about your accident, saw the absolutely ghastly pictures." Linzi's voice was full of practiced sympathy, that came from years of hosting talk shows and grilling celebrities. Thankfully, she didn't put up pictures of his accident on screen. It was on the long list of things not to talk about that Grant had emailed over to her production team when he discussed the exorbitant fee for the Dax Monroe exclusive.

"Yeah, I was beaten up pretty badly," Dax said. "I broke my spine in three places and shattered my arm in three places, too. I guess bad luck comes in threes for me."

There was a smattering of laughter for something that wasn't even funny. Dax could have said black was white and they'd have hung onto his every word and agreed with him.

"But, uh, I took some time to recover and I

spent two months really working on myself. I couldn't walk for a few weeks, and I had to learn to do it all again. And slowly but surely I healed. And I had to heal myself in other ways, too."

"Oh?" Linzi leaned forward. "Tell me a little bit more about that."

His palms were sweating, but he tried to remain as casual as possible. "Well the tour took it out of me, you know, and I realized that I've been in the business for so long that I've never really had a break." He found his stride now, and began to talk with the confidence he'd learned to have in front of the camera over thousands of interviews. "So I would do a concert, move to another city the next night, and do another concert there. I was drinking far too much, and I needed to take stock of my life."

Remember who to thank.

"I mean, my manager, Grant, he was amazing. He made sure that I had the care I needed and told me that there was no rush to get back to work. I'm just relieved that the accident happened at the end of the tour so that I didn't let any of my fans down. Because they mean the absolute world to me, and their messages of love and strength are what got me through the weeks of rehabilitation."

More applause and a *"we love you, Dax!!"* from the crowd, at which Dax grinned and waved his thanks. He straightened his tie and cocked his head a little at Linzi, as though flirting with the host. "Being invited on here tonight has really helped me, too," he said, lying through his teeth as part of the deal. *Endorse the show, and we won't mention a guy called Andy and what the hell you were doing in his shitty car.* "To know my family and all my friends have been worried means that I've dug deep to find the strength to come back."

Linzi's lips quivered and she even wiped away an invisible tear from her dry eyes. "Oh God, that means so much, Dax," she said. "And I'm so lucky to count you as a friend, too. You look incredible, so am I right in thinking that you've completely healed now?"

"I'm getting there every day, thanks to my physical therapy regime and plenty of gentle exercise." He neglected to mention his new therapist, Darlene, a buxom, no-nonsense woman, had taken over. "I still have a slight limp when I run, but that'll get better in time. I'm fitter and stronger than I've ever been, my head's clearer, and I'm even getting back in the studio."

This was greeted by huge claps and cheers and Dax grinned at the audience while Linzi sat open-mouthed in faux shock. "Really?" she gasped as though she hadn't known about this already. "So soon?"

"It's the only way I can give back to the fans," Dax said. "And I have a little announcement to make, if you don't mind me hijacking your show for this?"

"Oh please, I can't think of anything better!"

"Well, as a huge thank-you to the fans and to everyone who kept me going after the accident, I'm announcing a one-night only special at Ledbrooke Park on December 22nd."

The screams were deafening and Linzi was pumping the air in over-exuberant joy. "Oh my God!" she yelled. "Oh my God! I'd better have a ticket!"

"Well, tickets go on sale on October 1st, so that's two weeks from now, and I hope as many people as possible can join me there."

Ledbrooke Park was the home of California's biggest soccer team, and their stadium was the largest in the USA, with a capacity of one hundred and ten thousand seats and even more for standing crowds. The announcement did the trick: the excitement in the studio was palpable and as they were going out live across the country, there would already be hundreds of thousands of eager fans chattering excitedly about it on social media and looking at ways they could get their hands on tickets.

"And, can I ask, will Alicia be there?" Linzi asked the rehearsed question and Dax gave a sheepish grin and tried to look as bashful as he could.

"Well, as you know, Alicia and I have been in love for many years and as much as we like to keep our private lives out of the gaze of the public eye, I have to thank her for being my rock through all of this, for putting up with all the terrible months of pain and hard work. She's the greatest woman I could ask for and I really hope she does join me at the concert because she's my ride home!"

More laughter from adoring fans, and with that, Dax had answered his critics, although with a lie. He'd barely said two words to Alicia on the phone after arriving back in LA, and she'd seemed disappointed that he was still alive, and that she'd once again be called upon to dress up and hang out with him in public. Her own career was going through the roof, and she was itching to leave him behind now that she'd made such a name for herself.

But for now, hers was the only name on his lips when it came to romance, and with that, the interview was pretty much over. Dax and Linzi wrapped up with polite chit-chat and a new singer came out to belt out her latest single. As the lights went down and the producer yelled "aaaand we're out!" Dax couldn't get out of there fast enough.

In the green room, he took off his tie and sipped a glass of soda water. Grant called. "Great job," he boomed. "Nice touch about Alicia. And the concert? Jesus, the ticket companies are ringing off the hook and they're not even out yet! Welcome back, kid! You did me proud."

"Thanks," Dax said, feeling as though something slick and slimy was oozing down his ear.

"You headed out the back to do a meet-and-greet?"

"No, I'm tired."

"Drinks with Linzi? Damn, I don't know why you like cock so much. Five minutes with that little filly and I'd be balls deep—"

Dax hung up. He'd pay for it later but he could always say the signal went. He was tired. It was late, and his back was aching. He was tired of being back on the hamster wheel. Tired of lying to make other people look good.

And it wasn't about to end, either. He had barely three months before the concert, and he wasn't about to get a single day off between now and then. Just the thought of it was exhausting. He left the studio before Linzi could come back and talk to him, and he and Kelly slipped out of the building and into the car Rocky had waiting for them.

He got home to his quiet house and didn't even bother turning on the television. Instead he went up to his bedroom and lay on the huge bed, staring up at the ceiling. All he wanted was a cup of tea and a slice of toast.

Chapter Thirty-Nine

"Okay, and one more just after the middle eight," came the voice through his earphones. Dax looked back at the words, nodded, and the music came in again. He closed his eyes and sang into the microphone, giving it everything he had. The mixer in the booth gave him the thumbs-up, and the final chords played out to the close.

"Great job," said Mixer Mike. His real name was Adnan, but for as long as Dax had been signed to TerrorCorp Records, he'd called him by the same nickname as the others had.

Dax pulled off his earphones and smiled at the woman next to him. She was tiny and waif-like, with long brown hair and huge brown eyes. She stared at him nervously and nodded. She looked like the slightest puff of wind would blow her over. But only a few minutes earlier, she'd belted out the song with the lungs of an opera singer. Dax had been the one to have been nearly blown over.

"Great job, Renee," he said. "I'm stunned."

Another voice came over the headphones. "She's a cracker, isn't she?"

Dax looked over to the booth and saw her manager, Terry. He nodded at him. "Never heard anything like it."

"Well, this track looks to be the big hit of the winter. I'm thinking we can get it on the lineup for Ledbrooke?"

"I'll run it by Grant, but I'm sure we'll figure something out," Dax replied, and he took off his earphones. He reached for his bottle of water and took a swig, then he and Renee left the recording room.

Outside Terry was beaming at his protégée.

"Tell him when your birthday is, kid," he said to Renee. She gave a nervous smile, and looked up at Dax.

"December twenty-second," she said.

"See? Ah?" Terry held out his hands to Dax. "Come on. She's going to be eighteen. Don't break her heart on her eighteenth birthday. You wouldn't do that, surely?"

Dax was used to being emotionally blackmailed in a lot of ways. Stopping to pose for photographs with kids who were in wheelchairs. Stopping to chat with a girl who told him her dog just died and could he give her a hug to cheer her up? Stopping to grin into the lenses of a million different smartphones simply because if he said no, fans burst into tears as though he'd just spit in their faces.

"Like I said, I'll speak to Grant," he said to Terry, who shook his head.

"That guy's got you by the gonads, hasn't he?" he asked. "What ever persuaded you to get in bed with that snake is beyond me."

It was a term used only in the business sense, but it pricked at Dax and he bristled. "Well, he's been good to me for the last fifteen years. I mean, look where I am."

Terry nodded, and held up his hands. "Hey, no offense meant. I think he's an asshole, but no offense meant. If anything, I'd say you deserved better. It's a compliment to you."

He put his hand into the inside pocket of his jacket and pulled out a card. He held it out to Dax. "Look. I'm pretty sure you know where I am, and how to get hold of me. If you ever change your mind and want to move on from being a teenager's crush forever."

Dax didn't reply. He took the card. Terry and Renee left and Dax looked at Mixer Mike. "Don't worry. I'm not going to call him."

But Mixer Mike simply shrugged. "It's nothing to do with me. Everyone knows Grant's an asshole. I just wish that Terry guy would hand me his card and ask me to call him."

Dax put the card into the rear pocket of his jeans. He could never give the real reason that he stuck with Grant. That Grant had too much dirt on him to ever walk away. He knew that as soon as he went with another manager, Grant would make sure that every shot of him kissing a guy, every check he'd written to men Dax had spent the night with, just to keep them quiet, would be suddenly and anonymously leaked to the press.

There was nothing he wanted more than to rid himself of the scourge of Grant Beaumont. But he was trapped.

The studio was quiet, and Dax jerked his head to the recording room. "Reckon I could lay out a couple of tracks of my own?" he asked. "I've been working on some new material."

"Sure," said Mike.

"And if you could keep this between you me…"

"What, Terry? You don't have anything to worry about—"

"Not just Terry. The music, too."

Mixer Mike grinned. "Discretion's my middle

name, dude. Just remember me when you're collecting your next award." And he winked.

Dax picked up his guitar from the recording room and sat up on the stool in front of the microphone. He tuned the guitar. "Let me just go through it a couple of times and tell me what you think," he said into the mic. "Let me know if you're getting the strings or not."

"Knock yourself out," said Mixer Mike.

Dax took a deep breath and began to strum the song that had been whirling around his head for weeks now. The words were there, the chords were ready, and he'd strummed the melody so many times that it was now imprinted in his brain.

"You said you'd catch me if I fell, but it was a lie I fell so damn hard and well, you just watched from the side.

Thought I'd recover, but then I discovered

I was watching myself from your eyes.

You couldn't fix me

No, you couldn't heal me

Broken bones mean nothin' if my heart's still sufferin'

No you couldn't fix me

You couldn't heal me..."

As he sang, he felt tears pricking his eyes. When he finished the song, he held onto the silence for a few more seconds until he heard Mixer Mike's voice in his ear. "Dude. Where the hell did that come from?"

Dax composed himself with a brief cough. "Is the sound okay?"

"Are you kidding me? That has to be on the next album!"

"It's not the kind of thing Grant wants."

Mixer Mike laughed. "Bet it's the kind of thing Terry would love."

They went through the song again, and Mike tweaked a few things here and there. Between the two of them, they had the track completed within the hour. Mike liked it without anything but Dax's voice and the guitar, and they both decided that it was better to have it clean and simple, without any extra instruments or effects.

Dax left the recording studio feeling strangely calm and rested. While singing the song he'd written for Cameron, he'd imagined he was singing it to him live, and it sent a shiver up his spine. He got in the car and Rocky drove him home. When he was there, he called Kelly.

"Are you busy?" he asked.

"Never too busy for you, boss, you know that," she quipped.

"Can you get hold of a VIP ticket for the show for me?"

"Sure. How many?"

"Just the one."

"And who am I making it out to?"

"If you can get it over to me in an envelope, that'd be great."

"When?"

"As soon as you can. And then if you could run to the post office and send it for me, I'll take you out for sushi later."

"You're paying me extra to do my job? Hell, I'm not complaining."

"See you in a bit."

He hung up and found that he was humming the song as he walked into his study. It was a room he rarely came into. When he bought the house he'd fitted the whole room out with the latest tech and expensive designer furniture but he barely turned the computer on these days. The tablet he bought hadn't even come out of the box, and as he turned on the lamp and found it didn't work, he peered over the shade and saw he'd never even taken the bulb out of the packet and put it in.

Opening one of the drawers of the desk, he pulled out a pad of paper and found a pen. He wasn't even sure what to write. He couldn't remember the last time he'd even written with a pen, save for the scrawl of an autograph he worked out he'd signed around a million times in his career.

He leaned over the paper for a while, and then he took a deep breath, and wrote a short note. He read over it several times, making sure that it didn't sound too dumb, and then he folded the paper up and put it in his pocket. When Kelly arrived a little later, he took the paper out, put it in the envelope with the VIP ticket, and sealed it. Then he carefully wrote the address on the front and gave it back to Kelly.

She looked at the address, raised an eyebrow, and smiled slowly. She looked up at him. "Really?" she asked. "For him?"

"I don't know if he's going to come or not," Dax

said. "But I've got to try one more time."

She grinned. "I'll go and post it now. I don't even know how much it costs to send something to Scotland."

Chapter Forty

"Do you want the lemon water, or the plain?"

Dax's head was still in the hole of the bed and he groaned and answered without looking up. "Plain."

He winced as the thick, strong thumbs of Darlene ran up his spine, deeply massaging his muscles. He gripped onto the bed and she slapped his hands away. "Stop tensing," she instructed.

Trying to relax, he closed his eyes and distracted himself by trying to remember the words to all the songs he was singing later that night. And, finally, Darlene was finished. She gave him a pat on the butt and he sat up carefully, making gentle stretches. "That's great," he said. "I think we're all set."

It was six-thirty, and he was already at Ledbrooke Stadium. He knew that outside, thousands of fans were queueing to try and get a floor space as close to the stage as they possibly could. Some of them had been queuing since the early hours of the morning.

Touring had never been a problem for Dax. Everything was managed so minutely, that all he had to do was show up. It had never mattered if the crowd was ten-thousand strong or a hundred-thousand strong. To him it was the same. Walk on, do the set, walk off. It had all been practiced so many times that he could do every set in his sleep.

The trick had always been, of course, to keep a screen within eyeshot with the name of the city he was in that night so he made every fan feel special. It was always the same. "Hey, Amsterdam! You've been the greatest!" or "Oh my God, Cape Town! We haven't had a vibe like this on the tour until tonight!"

Now, he was in his home town. He might not have been born in California, but he'd been here for fifteen years. He was a kid when he arrived. Now he was a man, and he had a man's responsibility on his mind.

Grant came into the dressing room while he was pulling on his pants. "Don't mind me," he said. "Just checking you've got the steps for the third track sorted."

The dance he'd always performed was now a little too tricky. His back was still healing, eight months after the accident, and while he was certainly almost back to full fitness, he wasn't about to risk his progress by spinning around and flipping over the way he had done before the crash.

"We're good," Dax said. "I'm switching up the final track, though."

His pulse raced a little as Grant frowned and checked the itinerary in his hand. "What? We always end with *Remembering the Future.* It's the moneymaker."

"The money's already been made," Dax said. "The tickets were being sold online for up to five grand each, and that was from the ticket company, not even scalps. I think the tour's more than recouped the cash you lost while I was away."

"Why have you switched the tracks? What are you finishing on now?"

"*Calling You Out.*" It was a lie, but there was a reason for it. On the lesser-known track of the third album, Dax had played the acoustic guitar and on some earlier sets, he'd chosen to play the track. Die-hard fans loved it as they loved everything else he'd ever sung, but it hadn't been too popular with the general public.

Grant wasn't amused. "No, no, no," he said. He took a pen and began to scrawl across the page but Dax stopped him.

"That's the deal," he said. "Or we can say goodbye to the whole night right now."

Grant sighed. He pointed the pen in Dax's face. "I don't know what happened to you in Scotland, but I'm sure as hell not liking the new Dax Monroe," he said. "Sort it out for the new year. Maybe that's something we can work in among your resolutions."

Dax gave a tight-lipped smile as a reply, but said nothing.

Kelly came in and gave Grant a wide smile. "Hello, Mister Beaumont," she said, and she fluttered her eyelashes at him. Grant grunted at her but took the time to stare down her cleavage. She was fully aware of his leering stare, and she'd normally cover herself instinctively but now, she pretended not to notice. "Do you mind if I steal Dax for a second?"

"Whatever," Grant said. "I'm going down to the bar. I'll be back in a little while."

Once he left the room, Kelly rushed over to Dax. "He's here," she said in a low voice, although there was nobody else around.

Dax's mouth fell open. "Are you serious?" he asked, wide-eyed. He sat down on the white couch, his head in his hands. "Fuck. I can't believe he came. I didn't think he would..."

"I was going to bring you down to him, but now that Grant's gone, shall I bring him up to you?"

"Sure. No. Wait. Yes. Bring him. No. Hang on. Let me think." He paced around the room, trembling. "Jesus, what do I say to him? It's been six months."

"I'm going to get him. You'd better sort yourself out before I get back." And with that, she was gone.

Dax paced the room, trying to recall everything he'd learned in yoga about his breathing. He'd never been so nervous in all his life. Finally there was a tap on the door, and he opened it. There, standing in front of him, for the first time in nearly half a year, was Cameron Wilson.

Cameron's auburn curls fell down in front of his eyes the way they always had. Dax had to resist the urge to lift his hand and brush them away. He swallowed. "Hey," he said.

"Hey," Cameron replied, his mouth curled into a lopsided smile.

"I'm going to leave you boys alone for twenty minutes, but after that I need to come and get Dax for the last rehearsal," Kelly said, and she gently prodded Cameron in the back so that he'd walk forward. When he was in the room, she took the door handle and closed the door.

They were alone for the first time in six months and Dax didn't know what to say. He dug his hands into his pockets and sucked air through his teeth. "So," he said. "Thanks for coming."

"It was a VIP ticket," Cameron said. "I'd be an idiot to turn it down."

"I was wondering if you might give it to Will."

Cameron gave a soft laugh, and Dax's heart swelled. "Yeah, well, I was going to but it turns out he couldn't make it."

"Right."

"We're still missing you at the quiz."

"I'm afraid my contribution was never that great."

"You'd be surprised. You were one of the team."

Their conversation was stilted. Awkward. There was so much to say, but neither of them had the words to say it. Eventually, Dax did the most British thing he possibly could, and he asked about the weather.

"Is it cold now, back home?"

"It'd freeze the balls off a brass monkey," Cameron said. "I've got to admit it was pretty appealing to come out for a couple of days to LA and get some sun. I'd forgotten what it was like to have to apply sun cream. But you know what us gingers are like. We burn in the shade."

"So you're not here for long?" Dax croaked.

"No. I fly back on Sunday."

"I was hoping you hadn't gone back down to London. When I sent the ticket to Invergordon I had no idea if you'd even be there to get it."

Cameron took a deep breath. "I thought about it. You know, I wanted to run away again but I've learned it doesn't work. Sometimes you need to face things head on."

"Can you stay a little longer, maybe? I can give you a tour of the place?"

But Cameron bit his lip, stared at Dax with his green eyes, and shook his head slowly. "I don't think so," he said. "I need to get back."

Again, the silence, but this time it was Cameron who broke it again. "Hey, I've kept you for long enough. I just wanted to come and say hello, and thanks for sending me the ticket. Break a leg out there, okay?"

He reached forward and put his arms around Dax in a hug. Dax fell into the embrace and the two men stood there, silently, for a few seconds, before Cameron broke away. "Take care," he said, gruffly.

"Thanks," said Dax. "I hope you enjoy the show."

He wanted to say so much more, but there wasn't any time. He had to get downstairs, to prepare himself for the biggest night of his life.

Chapter Forty-One

By the first costume change, he was breathless and sweating. He ran backstage and was given a bottle of cold water, which he gulped down while wardrobe tore off his clothes unceremoniously. They patted him down with a towel as the stage manager called out the instructions for the next set.

"We're going back in with *Until You Wake.* I need all fifteen dancers in front of me right now!"

Dax hurried to the make-up chair where the stylists and make-up artists reapplied the powder he needed to cope with the heavy lights. They highlighted his eyes, making them bright and alive, and they sprayed a little hairspray in to counteract the sweat. Then, in thirty seconds, he was ready to go again.

The show was going even better than planned. His voice was strong, his moves in time with the dancers, and he hadn't fluffed a single line. The lights on him were so bright that he couldn't see anyone in the crowd, and that made him feel better. He could hear the screams of all the fans, and in quiet moments between songs he remembered to thank them all for coming out and supporting him. He reiterated that he would never have recovered without them.

He went back out and did three more tracks before rushing backstage once more for his third and final costume change. He'd decided early on to go without an interval. In the past, intervals were for getting as much vodka down his throat and cocaine up his nose as possible before the second half. Now, nothing was stopping him. He was back, and he was better than ever.

Toward the end of the show, he started getting

nervous. Still, he didn't drop a beat or miss a step. When he went into his stellar song, *Remembering the Future,* he was pretty sure everyone was on their feet. He trailed off in the chorus and simply listened to everyone singing his song, grinning and nodding as they hit the crescendo together, over one hundred thousand voices, before he joined back in again and finished the track.

They thought it was over. The lights went down and, as arranged, everyone left the stage but his roadie, Theo, ran on and handed him the acoustic guitar. Alton Coy's guitar. Perfectly tuned, and ready to play, it sat in Dax's strong hand as he adjusted the microphone. His heart was racing, the blood in his head swishing in his ears.

The crowd fell silent, save for the occasional whoop, as Dax smiled out at them and wiped sweat from his forehead with his sleeve. "Damn," he said, looking out. "That's a hell of a view."

They screamed and called out, but then were silent as he talked.

"You know, this last six months have been insane. I nearly died, and when I woke up in a hospital bed in London, I thought it was all over. Not my life, but my career. The thing that kept me going all these years."

He paused. "And then I was given another chance. I was taught that it doesn't matter what's happened to you, you can always pick yourself up and try again. You can always find a way to make yourself a better person. And it's not always easy, especially when the world has you put into a box, a mold of the way they want you to be. Well, for me that ends today."

A hum went out among the crowd, but they were soon shushed by everyone else, who hung onto Dax's every word. They felt it in the air. Something big was coming.

"You see, since I was eighteen, I thought I had it all," Dax went on. "I had the money, the fame, the amazing, beautiful fans, and the life of a pop star. I thought it was what everyone wanted, and I was the luckiest guy in the world. But there were some things missing. I wasn't allowed to walk the street whenever I felt like it, because it wasn't safe. I wasn't able to just go sit on the beach without being mobbed. And it sounds like I'm ungrateful, but that was the way of it."

He took a deep breath and blew it out again. "I wasn't allowed to fall in love," he croaked. "The papers wrote what they wanted and I was seen with all kinds of beautiful women, but they weren't right for me. I wasn't right for them."

The hum in the crowd got louder. Dax was shaking as he closed his eyes and pressed his lips against the microphone. "I'm a gay man, and I've lied about myself to you, and to me. For that, I apologize."

He was cut off by a cacophony of noise. He was sure he caught one or two boos, but they were drowned out by screams and yells of support. The stadium erupted for five whole minutes with wild applause, and Dax felt the energy of tens of thousands of people giving him nothing but pure love.

With tears spilling down his cheeks, he thanked everyone. "I can't tell you what it means to me to share this with you. You're the people who got me here, and you don't deserve the bullshit any longer." He held the guitar up and licked his lips. "I want to tell the whole world that I'm sorry, and I want to apologize particularly to one person.

"Cameron, I love you."

Again, the stadium went wild and flashes of lights from phones and cameras coursed through the crowd as Dax told the whole world the truth. Emboldened, he continued.

"I walked away when I should have stayed, and you didn't deserve that. I'm sorrier than I could ever have been, and the last few months without you have nearly killed me all over again. This last song's for you."

And he was about to begin the first chord, when he paused for one last second. "Oh, and Grant? You're fired."

Most of the crowd didn't even know who Grant was, but they didn't care. They were swept up by the rapture of the moment and all its implications. The biggest pop star in the world had just outed himself live on stage. It was unprecedented.

Finally at peace, Dax began the song.

"You said you'd catch me if I fell, but it was a lie

I fell so damn hard and well, you just watched from the side.

Thought I'd recover, but then I discovered

I was watching myself from your eyes.

You couldn't fix me

No, you couldn't heal me

Broken bones mean nothin' if my heart's still sufferin'

No you couldn't fix me

You couldn't heal me..."

In the instrumental portion that followed, all Dax could hear was silence as everyone held their breath and absorbed the beautiful track. Then he launched into the chorus.

"Nothing could ever grow when the soil was stone cold

Nothing could ever live when the excuses all got old

Nothing could ever start when it felt life was at an end

Nothing could ever begin until I became my own best friend."

He thought of Doctor Pravenda, who told him he needed to love himself. He thought about how right she was. Because there was no denying the swell of love that burst out from his chest when he finally declared to the whole world that by loving another man so completely, it meant that he'd accepted himself.

He thought about Grant, who was probably clawing to get on stage and kill him, and he smiled to himself as he pictured Rocky and the others holding him back.

But mostly, he thought about Cameron. Because now the secret was out, and they didn't have to hide anymore, then maybe, just maybe, they had a chance. He could feel it in the way Cameron had hugged him. He could feel that there was a chance he dared to believe in.

As the song came to a close, and Dax bowed, the lights fell and he stayed on the stage for a few more seconds, soaking in every second, determined to remember this moment for as long as he lived. Then, he took a deep breath and ran off, to face a different kind of music.

Chapter Forty-Two

One of the many advantages of being a global superstar was that Dax didn't have to speak to a single person with whom he didn't feel the need. And while Grant was yelling his name and screaming so loudly Dax was sure he could actually hear it in the dressing room, there was no way that the detested manager would ever have to be in his presence again.

His lawyer, Susan, had carefully ensured the best way to end the contract. Dax had already been told what it would cost to get rid of Grant, and he'd paid it without a second thought. No more being beholden to the man who'd made his life a misery. Because now, the secret was out.

Kelly was stunned. Dax couldn't blame her. In the dressing room, where he was now back in jeans and a t-shirt, he too was sitting in frozen disbelief at what he'd just done. He wasn't sure whether it was really real. He sipped his water and wondered whether he might be better with something a little stronger.

"I can't believe it," his assistant gasped. "You knew you were going to do that all this time and you never said a word!"

"I didn't really know myself until the time came whether I'd have the guts," Dax said. "But seeing Cameron tonight, I just knew. I knew in my heart it was the right thing to do. I knew that if I didn't say the words, then I'd never get another chance."

"Grant nearly had a heart attack."

"He'll get over it. He'll find another innocent young kid to destroy. People like that always do."

"I saw Terry Cross back stage, earlier."

"Yeah, I know. He was here with Renee but

yeah, we're in talks. I don't know, though. I think I want a break from the whole thing."

"What about your mom? Do you think she'll have a problem?"

"She's always known. I don't worry about her at all. Diane's one of the good ones."

They were interrupted by a call on Kelly's cell. She swiped her thumb across the screen and answered. "Yeah?"

She looked at Dax and grinned. "Right," she said, into the phone. "Send him over."

Hanging up the call, she stood up. "Cameron wants to come and see you."

Dax nodded. "Good."

He wasn't nervous any more. This time, when Kelly left to fetch the man he loved and bring him back, he didn't pace the room or feel his heart racing so fast that he might pass out. Instead he sat, pensive and thoughtful, until the soft tap at the door came and he stood up and slowly walked across the dressing room floor.

Opening the door, this time when he saw Cameron's hair flopping in front of his eyes, he *did* reach up to brush it away. And Cameron held his wrist, walked inside, and put his hands either side of Dax's face.

They didn't need to speak. Their kiss was soft and gentle, speaking a thousand words, and it was a long time before Cameron pulled away and sighed. "Nothing will ever, ever be as cool as what you did tonight," he said.

Dax kissed him again, this time a light kiss, and

he looked into Cameron's green eyes. "I meant it," he said. "Every single word. I've been a dick. I couldn't see past the cult. But I'm awake. And I love you."

"I love you too," Cameron said. "Jesus, I'm in love with the world's biggest superstar."

"Maybe not anymore," Dax said, slipping his arms around Cameron's waist. "It's going to be a giant shit-show for a good few weeks. Are you sure that you want to stick around for that? I understand if this life's too crazy for you."

"Are you kidding?" Cameron murmured. "I'm here to catch you, remember?"

Manufactured by Amazon.ca
Bolton, ON

13094501R00162